BRAINEATER JONES

STEPHEN KOZENIEWSKI

Copyright © 2013, 2019 Stephen Kozeniewski.

Copyright © 2019 French Press

manuscriptsburn.blogspot.com

Cover and wraparound © Chris Enterline

This book or any portion thereof may not be reproduced or used in any manner whatsoever without the express written permission of the publisher and author, except where permitted by law. French Press books are legendary for their copyright pages. Just think of all the poor fools who bypassed this. Not you, though. You're a connoisseur. A wellspring of good taste. You deserve a joke. The punchline will be at the end of this page. What do you feed a dead zombie?

This novel is a work of fiction. Names, places, characters, and incidents are the product of the author's imagination, or are used fictitiously. Any resemblance to actual events, locales, or persons, living or dead, is purely coincidental. Nothing. He's already dead.

ISBN: 9781091588981

All rights reserved.

This book is dedicated to Neil Diamond, our nation's greatest treasure.

FOREWORD

Braineater Jones is not high art. In fact, it is meant to be nothing more than pulpy horror fun. Nevertheless, I feel obliged to warn and inform my readers that this book contains the sort of racist, sexist, and bigoted characters that were commonplace to the era in which it takes place.

In researching this novel, I was faced with a stark reality: the 1930s was a time of intolerance. Novels of that era jarred my modern sensibilities. Racism, homophobia, and sexism weren't just institutional; they were also casual and woven into the warp and woof of everyday life for every strata of society.

I had a choice: either whitewash the past and somehow attempt to ignore every issue of gender, race, and sexuality relevant to that time period, or address them and try to do so in a way that was true to life. You can probably guess from the fact that I have written this foreword that I chose the latter.

Readers who are familiar with the literature of the 1930s, and the noir genre in particular, will hopefully be more accustomed to this sort of language and behavior, though, I hope, will never be desensitized to it. For everyone else, please just bear in mind that these characters, including the narrator, are of a different era. If I nevertheless give offense, I sincerely apologize, and the responsibility is mine and mine alone.

Okay, with the heavy stuff out of the way, I hope you enjoy this book, my first, and I will leave you with the advice my father gave me on my wedding day. "Son, if you ever read a book about Nazi zombie robot detectives, try not to take it too seriously."

Stephen Kozeniewski

P.S. If you happen to come across a term you don't recognize—either 1930s slang or jargon specific to the world of Braineater Jones—please check the glossary at the end of the book prior to sending me irate letters.

OCTOBER 31, 1934

I woke up dead this morning.

Wait. What time is it? After midnight. Shit. It wasn't this morning. Better start over.

NOVEMBER 1, 1934

I woke up dead this morning. Yesterday morning. All Hallows' Eve. Whatever you want to consider it.

Not dead tired.

Not dead drunk.

Dead.

Dead dead.

As in no pulse, no breathing, dead as a doornail dead.

I mean, I've woken up a lot—I assume—and who really thinks about whether they're breathing or not? Who notices their heart's not beating? It's not something you're totally aware of. It took me a while to figure it out.

It took me less time to figure out I was stark, bare-ass naked.

I guess they did that to me—whoever killed me. They must've stripped me. I don't know if they wanted my clothes or my money. Or maybe they didn't want me to be identified. But if that was the case, then why didn't they smash in my teeth or burn off my fingerprints or cut off my face or something?

Who knows?

I was relatively whole—"relative" being an important part of that sentence. The first thing I remember is floating facedown. When I opened my eyes, I was staring at three beautiful women, and I thought they were angels and I was dead and floating on clouds. One was white, the second golden, and the third brown. They begged me with their eyes to come to them, and when I tried to reach them, I found water resisting me, pushing my arms back to the surface.

They were actually statues, carved from Titanic peat and painted in lifelike colors to stand out from the bottom of the swimming pool I was floating in. They craved the touch of someone other than the cabana boy who made eighty-five cents a day scrubbing the algae and grime from their crevices. They sparkled, clean, perfect, almost alive. They wanted to reach toward me—I could see it in their eyes—but instead, their hands were spread over their breasts, just barely covering up the naughty bits. I thought of the Greek Slave and wondered: How the hell do I know what that is?

I lay there for a long time, staring at the bottom of the pool and wondering how long it would take me to reach those sirens, before I realized what should have been obvious: I wasn't breathing. I hadn't been holding my breath; I simply wasn't breathing at all. The red hue tinting my gaze was my own blood leaking into the pool.

Here's the other thing: I have no idea who I am or how I got in this state. I'm keeping this journal so I can get my thoughts straight while I try to work this all out.

Here's what I know so far:

First of all, somebody killed me. Did I mention that already? I think I did. Anyway, after I stopped ogling those angels, I swam to the side of the pool and climbed out. One of the first things I noticed was the big gaping hole in my chest. I could stick my finger through it. I probably could've stuck my fist through it.

I don't remember much about guns. Of course, that's assuming I ever knew anything about them. But what kind of gun does something like that? I wouldn't think a handgun would. Maybe some big, brutal hand cannon. Or a shotgun. But don't shotgun pellets scatter? It was one solid hole.

I guess I could've sat there boo-hoo-hooing about it, but what good would that do me? Where would it get me other than still dead and sitting on the side of a pool with no memories? Dead is tough, but dead and still thinking means I've got a chance. I can reason my way back into the ball game.

So… somebody rubbed me out. Presumably for a reason. But they could've rolled me for my wallet then took my clothes, and none of it was planned. So what was the reason? Well, I aim to find that out. Let me put that in my list of questions.

1. Why did they bump me off?

I guess while I'm doing that, I'd better figure out who it was.

2. Who was the hatchet man?

Here's the rest of what I know:

The town where I woke up, where I guess I live now, is Ganesh City. Weird name? I don't know. Doesn't strike a chord with me. Maybe I'm a recent transplant? I haven't seen much of it besides the rich egg's pool where I woke up floating facedown and the flophouse where I'm shacked up now.

Oh, yeah, the rich guy. I guess I should talk about him for a minute.

After I finished fingering my hole, I went for the sliding glass doors. Standing there, naked and wet, I thought about praying that they were unlocked. The truth is, though, if there is a Heaven, I had just come from there, or I should have. I didn't remember anything like that: no trumpets, no babies in diapers with wings, and—sure as shit—no God to answer the prayers of a walking stiff like me. So I didn't pray.

It didn't matter. The doors were unlocked anyway.

As soon as I walked into the house, I knew his name: Ernst Rothering. I couldn't've missed it. It was engraved on everything he owned. European. Dutch? Still not sure. His name was etched into practically everything that could have a name etched into it. Golf clubs, plaques, a big "ER" on the fireplace, pictures of him with the president of the chamber of commerce or somebody signed "To Ernst."

Disgusting.

The rich guy wasn't there—thank… whoever—but I heard his dogs baying. They sounded as though they were in a kennel somewhere, not prowling around the mansion. In the hallway, old Ernst kept a trophy case full of sculling awards. In the kitchen, outside the cupboard, which would've been nice for a servant's nook, and to the left of the servant's nook, which would've been nice for a flat, he kept his collection of embossed wine glasses from different events, mayor's balls and the like. He had an indoor gym and a collection of tennis racquets that would've beggared a small country. It struck me that he owned all the stuff you figure rich weirdos with nothing better to do would have.

There wasn't a whole lot that indicated what he did other than schmoozing. I kept looking, but I wasn't seeing it. Was he a publishing magnate? Owner of the Ganesh *Tribune-Chronicle*? Old money? Nouveau riche?

Wait a minute. Do I speak French? *Je m'… Je t'…* no. I guess not. Just that one word. A few phrases here and there, maybe.

I went upstairs. Rothering was way into himself. Pictures of him with his fat alderman spilling out of his shirt and his damned hell hounds splayed around him plastered every spare surface. It was a good thing the dogs were penned. I didn't want any more holes in me than I already had.

A jarring thought hit me like a dame with a motorcar. What if I *was* this rich bastard? My hands jumped to my paunch, but no, right off the bat I could tell I wasn't fat enough. Besides, I had a divot where he kept his spare tire.

A looking glass big enough to choke a whale decorated one wall of the bedroom. I took a moment to acquaint myself with… myself. Short—too bad. My complexion was white, like bleached bone, with a green tinge from the chlorine. I musta been a real pretty drugstore cowboy before, but now I just looked like a drowned rat.

I wondered briefly whether Rothering was my brother, my father, my employer… my murderer? A galaxy of thoughts flew through my head at a breakneck pace, and I couldn't prove or disprove any one of 'em. I'd already figured out that I couldn't remember a damn thing from before waking up in the pool.

I knew enough to look for a wallet. It was a place to start. I didn't have a wallet. Stark naked. Things occurred to me. You know, common sense things, like a man has a wallet. But my first kiss, my last ice cream cone, even my name, my job, all that shit was gone like dust in the wind.

Damn, my brain is a jumble. Half the time, I have these facts and words, and I know what they mean, but I don't know how to arrange them. It's as if my brain is a string of Christmas tree lights: When the first one's out, none of them go on, even if they work.

The bed was big enough to catch Topsy the elephant when she fell. I lay down but then worried I might disappear into it like quicksand, so I got back up. The bedroom was more utilitarian than the rest of the house but still didn't lack all the beloved knickknacks with his name on them that seemed to litter every inch of the mansion.

I dove into the fat man's closet. I figured, hey, you wake up in a guy's pool, he probably at least owes you a new suit. So I took one. What would you have done? Less? More?

The closet was like a Italian piazza in the full bloom of spring. The floor was inlaid with an intricate design in tile, maybe a mosaic or maybe just patterns. He had more fur coats than a man should ever need, and the walls seemed to go up and up into the stratosphere. My neck got tired from me looking at them.

I sort of held out a faint hope that some of the clothes would be a smaller size, maybe from when he had been younger, but no dice. I had to tighten one of his belts to all but the last notch to keep his pants from hanging down below my ankles.

I probably look ridiculous right now. In fact, I'm sure I do. I'll probably have to find some new clothes once I get back on my feet.

Looking like a kid wearing his daddy's clothes, I looked around the bedroom, figuring that was where the good dirt would be. I checked his sock drawer and stumbled across a billfold with about eight clams in it. A nice cool payday for me. I didn't figure it was mine, but then again, better safe than sorry. I'd be kicking myself if I left my own wallet in some stranger's mansion. A pack of Luckies rested on his vanity, too. I racked my brain for a way to justify taking them, gave up, and just stole them.

Someone flung open a door downstairs, and I heard two mooks come in the house. I never did quite catch their names, but let's call them X and Y. Wait, why that? Why not A and B? Eh, well, X and Y will do.

"Come on," X, the one with the high-pitched voice, said.

"What if Rothering's here?" Y asked. He sounded a bit like Jimmy Durante.

That was the first time I heard the old guy's name, even though I'd read it a hundred times already in the shrine of St. Ernst. It sounded like "rote-hair-ing" not "ruther-ing" as I'd assumed. Odd. But then those Europeans are odd. Wait. Are they? I wouldn't know. At least, I think I wouldn't know. Or would I?

3. Who is X? Who is Y?

Not many leads. I didn't get a good look at them the whole time they were ransacking Rothering's place. But I was pretty sure I would recognize the voices if I ever heard them again. Isn't it true that a baby bird knows his mother because it's the first voice he hears? Wouldn't that be horrifying if I thought of Mr. X and Mr. Y as my mummy-poo and daddykins because they were the first mooks I heard after I pulled my little Jesus Christ parlor trick?

"He ain't here," X said.

"What if he's got dogs?" Y countered. "Or guards?"

Their footsteps stopped.

"He doesn't have any dogs," X said, sounding like the idea had gotten stuck up his nose.

A piercing howl broke the stillness of the night, and I heard the two terrified buffoons yelp. In my mind, I pictured them grabbing and hugging one another, like the Katzenjammer Kids in the funny papers. It probably didn't happen, but the idea made me laugh anyway.

"Lookit all these pictures!" Y shouted, his voice rising a full octave. "He's got hundreds of them mutts!"

"Yeah, I guess you're right," X said, audibly shaken. "You'd better go first."

"Why do I have to go first?"

They started bickering like a pair of dames fighting over a purse at Gimbels. I kind of tuned them out at that point. I didn't much want to get shot if they were packing heat. I had already been shot once, so it probably couldn't hurt me much more, but it never helps to press your luck.

I figured going out the window was the best option, with hiding in the rich guy's closet a close second. I could've fit a bull elephant in that closet. It was full of shoes.

How many shoes does a man need, fer Chrissakes? Maybe a pair for work and a pair for relaxing and a pair for putting on the Ritz. Who needs a rack of shoes?

Thing was, hiding in the closet would have all but boxed me in. Let's say those latter-end-of-the-alphabet morons woulda come bursting in with guns, and it turned out I was still vulnerable to guns. Well, it woulda been curtains for me. Lot of "what ifs." But hey, who's going to take their life into their hands over a case of not knowing?

Life. Funny word. Wrong choice. Dislife? Ex-life? Unlife? Whatever.

So that left the window. I thought of the old sheet-rope trick but panicked because there didn't seem to be enough time. And besides, all the sheets were silk or satin or something. Would they even hold my weight?

I flung myself at the pane. Turned out, there was a trellis, so that cut out the need for a middleman. Not only that, but the whole wall was practically full of ivy, so I could climb right to the trellis. It would probably be a tough climb, but it beat searching for enough sheets to tie together while praying they would hold.

Besides, by then, they were already at the bedroom door.

"What do you think?" X's muffled voice wafted through the crack under the door.

"If he's got it anywhere, he's got it in the safe," Y said.

"Yeah, you're probably right."

Do or die time. I grabbed two big handfuls of the ivy. With a little luck, I could just swing over to the trellis like Tarzan, Viscount Greystoke. Then a climb down, and boom, I'm done. Easy Street.

Well, it didn't hold. Rich bastard had brand-new ivy. Brand spanking new. It didn't even hardly stick to the wall.

I fell.

I fell like a sack of wet newspaper.

Then I was lying on my back with two clumps of cheap-ass ivy in my hands, my nose in the dirt, and my neck twisted all the way around like a bowtie pasta.

"Son of a bitch." I stood and found myself looking down at my own backside.

You ever have one of those days? One of those days where you wake up and you're already out of cigarettes, but it doesn't matter because it's raining and your umbrella has a hole in it? Then, by the end of the day, sometime between when your boss handed you the pink slip and your old lady left you for your brother, nothing fazes you anymore because you're so numb?

I may, and I may not have, but I must've at some point in my past life, because that's what jumped to mind at that point. So what if my face was on backward and I was still thinking about it and able to move? That was all after being naked, wet, dead, chased, and jamming myself into some fatbody's clothes.

I took a minute to twist my head back the right way. But then, it was twisted all the way around instead of just twisted back the way it came. I grabbed the sides of my head and got it all straight, and by that point, it had been too long.

They shot at me. Dumb bastards. They sat up there in that window and watched a man literally screw his head on straight and then took a potshot as if a bullet would do something.

I took off running.

"Hey, come back here!" X yelled.

I don't guess they got a good look at my face, but, heck, they might've with all the time I sat there rotating it in different directions.

Daddy Warbucks had a hedge maze. A hedge maze! Who really has a hedge maze? Nothing Rothering owned surprised me at that point. I was waiting to trip over King Tut's sarcoffa… sarcaca… coffin. From the wild gunshots, I figured X and Y were pursuing me even as I plunged into the bushes.

What can you say about a hedge maze? If I ever get to Vegas, I'll put down good money that it spelled out "Ernst Rothering" if read from an aeroplane. But from on the ground and in the weeds, I just saw an unnavigable mess. I almost wished I was back in the pool, staring at those three lovelies, but there wasn't much for it.

I would figure that with two guys, one would go in one entrance to the maze and the other would go to a different one, then they could cut off their quarry. But no. Those guys weren't exactly Rhodes Scholars. They both chased me, coming from the same direction.

I kept hitting dead ends. But, then, you know what I did? Just went straight through it. I mean, it was a shrubbery fer Chrissakes, not a brick wall. What good even is a hedge maze unless you're willing to go along with the illusion? I got all cut up from the briars, but compared to the scratch in my chest and the kink in my spinal column, that was small potatoes.

So after a spell, I gave them the slip. I discovered that I was in the suburbs, so to speak, of Ganesh City. I didn't see a whole lot of green, which was strange because the rich guy's mansion wasn't all that far from the part of Ganesh called the Welcome Mat.

In my ill-fitting clothes, all I needed was a bindle and a glove with no fingers, and I would've fit in perfectly.

The Welcome Mat is a slum. They don't call it that because it's welcoming. They call it that because it's where the city wipes the shit off its shoes.

Turning toward the Mat from Lionel Avenue, I was greeted by a decaying gothic archway, a relic of the last century when the Mat was a different kind of place, proclaiming it had once been called Matthew's Parish. I was reminded of the entrance to a carnival, partly by the archway and partly by the weird smell of carnies.

The graffito was good there. Some of it was glow-in-the-dark. I ran my finger across a tag, wondering what made it glow. I stopped almost as soon as I started. It occurred to me that whatever was making it glow was not something I wanted to get on my bare hand.

The entrance had a message in Bohunk or something. I grabbed a *Tribune-Chronicle* from the ground to write down the words. There, I saw the date—October 31, 1934.

Of course, it's after midnight now. I copied the note with a piece of charcoal I found on the pavement.

Now that I've got this notebook, I'm going to recopy it. I'll keep all my clues here, just in case. Never know when I might need to be reminded of something.

I don't know if it's important or not. The graffito was in a different language. Rothering was a foreigner. Coincidence? I think not. Here's what it said:

PER ME SI VA NE LA CITTÀ DOLENTE,
PER ME SI VA NE L'ETTERNO DOLORE,
PER ME SI VA TRA LA PERDUTA GENTE.
LASCIATE OGNE SPERANZA, VOI CH'INTRATE.

4. What does the cryptic entrance sign mean?

I read the paper to get my bearings. It took a whole lot of words to say not a whole lot of things. All the articles were about the rich part of town, the Altstadt, and the landscaping work in Kelly Park. No mention of Rothering. If he was as big of a bigwig as his house made him out to be, that was a little surprising, but maybe he was trying to keep a low profile for some reason. The paper never mentioned the Welcome Mat, so it seemed like a convenient place to disappear.

I felt like a troll when I settled under the footbridge. A couple of other derelicts were already there.

Christ, I've only been undead for a day and I'm already thinking of myself as a derelict.

Anyway, I was feeling tired. Bone tired.

That raises all sorts of questions.

5. Why does a—whatever I am—need sleep?

6. What am I?

I guess I'm a dead man. A living dead man. A nonbreathing, walking, jumping, tap-dancing living dead man. Or something. Damn it. Leave it to me to get philosophical now while I've already got six mysteries to solve. Where am I getting all of these big ideas from? Maybe I was a professor before I died, or a doctor.

7. Who or what was I before I died?

8. For that matter, why can't I remember anything from before I died? Is that artificial, or is it part of the resurrection process?

This list keeps getting longer and longer. I've got to get to the bottom of it all. I guess I'd better figure out how I'm going to tackle this. I need information, first and foremost. I'll have to find out if there's a library or a university where I can look up some of this egghead stuff. For the rest of it, I'll have to hit the streets and find some underground contacts. Do I have any underground contacts? Probably not. And if I did, I doubt they would talk to me now or even recognize me. Well, maybe I did. Maybe I have family.

For some of the more existential stuff, I'll have to find others like me. Unless I'm the only one, which is a depressing thought.

9. Are there others like me?

Anyway, I collapsed under the tunnel and threw the pages of newspaper that I hadn't written on over my face. I wasn't there for more than a few minutes before I started feeling a dull thump in my sides, like when you're watching a clock pendulum and you can sort of feel it moving back and forth. It wasn't until one of the bums snatched the blat off my head that I realized they were putting the boots to me.

You wouldn't think that bums would be so picky about their company. But then again, I guess you never know when somebody's a wolf in sheep's clothing.

There were two, one on either side of me, and they were kicking damn hard, too. One was even wearing steel-toed boots. And you know what? It didn't hurt. It was annoying. Degrading, even. But I felt no pain.

A third bum flitted in and out of my field of view, encouraging the other two.

"You're the king of the devil's army of fishermen Visigoths," the third said.

The crazed kingmaker started folding up my newspaper into a little hat.

I raised my hand. "Hey, I need that." I heard my voice for the first time.

Do I really sound like that? Is that what I always sounded like, or was it just my vocal cords rotting out? Well, it couldn't be worse than getting my neck twisted the wrong way around. My voice sounded as though, instead of just a frog in my throat, a whole swinging big band of amphibians had set up shop in my neck.

"Get out of here, braineater!" said one of the kickers, who was clearly more cogent than the one wearing the newsprint crown.

"Yeah, we know what you are, you bastard," Steel-toed Boots said.

They didn't really let up on the kicking enough for me get out of there. But hey, logic takes a holiday with these people, right? Their spiritual leader was spouting sweet nothings into the cold, empty universe. Unfortunately for me, I was thinking, "Hey, here are some answer men." Yeah. Right. Derelicts are always full of useful information.

"What do you know about me?" I croaked in that unfamiliar voice. "What am I?"

"You're not welcome!" the boss yelled, the first meaningful thing he had said since muttering to himself about "techno-vampires" and infested fruits and Sha and God alone knew what all else.

I tried to get up, but my muscles refused to respond. It was as though my whole body was revolting against my brain. I thought it was a symptom of the booting, but there was something deeper there, a sluggishness I hadn't felt before I went to sleep under the bridge. I probably muttered some nasty black curses.

"Wait, hold on. Stop, you pus-burning, flag-growing handy cats," the leader said.

Believe it or not, the two kickers took a break. I thought to myself that maybe those guys should go out for the all-bums international soccer team, if such a thing exists.

The leader didn't show pity. He grabbed his old bindle, which was sharpened up like a pencil, and jabbed it into my leg. I grunted, but honestly, it didn't hurt any more than the kicking. It seemed to help get my leg moving, in fact. At least enough for me to kick out.

I forced myself to sit up, and let me tell you, it was a hell of an effort. All my muscles and bones were tightening up like one big sprain. I clutched the sharpened bindle stick and wrenched it out of my leg. I stood, hoping against hope I would tower like a giant over those street people, but they dwarfed me.

"You can have this," I said, throwing the stick at the boss man, "but I want the paper." I snatched the little newspaper hat off his head.

His eyes grew so wide he looked like one of those kids in a velvet painting. "You're a leaf-drawn chariot. You're an unwanted little orphan of the radio tower universe. Avast! Avast!"

That didn't answer a whole lot. The two who hadn't seemed fit for the loony bin had called me "braineater," though.

It's a funny term for whatever I am, and I don't know if I like it, but it was the first real description I'd heard. What did they mean? I haven't felt hungry all day, or if I have, it's just been a dull ache like every other emotion and feeling in my body. If I was hungry, would I want a brain? And why would that be different than normal hunger when I feel like I want a pie or…

What do I like to eat?

No, that's not a numbered question. I don't need to get to the bottom of that. Just kind of an idle thing to wonder about.

Since they were so desperate to have me gone, I left the bums to gibber and bite one another's thumbs or whatever street loonies do. I regretted it though, because they really seemed to know more about what I was than I did. Then again, it could've all been crazy talk. I can't pretend they made a whole lot of sense even when they were talking to me instead of their invisible pink elephants.

Braineater. That's what the lucid ones called me.

Huh.

I elected at that point not to go to sleep again. Or at least, if I did, to do it somewhere nice and quiet and secluded so I could take as long as I needed getting up. I had kind of a tingling terror in the hairs on the back of my neck that no matter what kind of seclusion I went into, I'd never be able to get up if I went to sleep again. I'd be locked in, like a lobsterman in a diving bell.

Could you imagine? I went to sleep for a few minutes, and my body became numb and unresponsive. What would happen after a few hours? I might never move again. I might sit there, unalive, and who would be able to tell? Unless I left my eyes open, I'd be unable to see anything but still be aware. Terrifyingly aware.

Maybe that's what it's like for everybody once they're dead. Who knows? I probably never gave it much thought. Despite having been over to the other side, past the Pearly Gates or whatever they call it, I have disturbingly few answers. And even fewer impressions. I'm just another soul, lost and damned.

I guess the bums gave me a kick in the ass that I needed, along with all the kicks in the ribcage I sure as shit didn't. I got to thinking about all these questions swirling around in my head and how I needed to gather my thoughts, and how I probably needed more than a charcoal note on a newspaper to get anything done.

Then I remembered the billfold. Well, there was only eight bucks in there, and it was stolen, but I figured it was a start.

There was a five and dime not far from the bridge. The great thing—if you can call it that—about the Mat was that I wasn't even the weirdest looking one in there. I snagged a fountain pen and a notebook—this notebook, come to think of it—and somehow got fewer weird looks from the clerk than the shirtless, tattooed street prophet trying to buy a telephone slug.

So all that was left to find was a clean, well-lighted place. Why did that phrase stick out in my mind? It seemed important. Clean and well-lighted. Not a dank bridge to hang out under and get accosted by Herbert Hoover's bastard children.

The flophouse I found had a neon sign on the roof that was missing a couple of letters, and the word "VACANCY" ran vertically down the side of the building. It also boasted hourly rates. That made me scratch my head.

What's it even actually called? I don't know if I ever looked. Maybe it's just called "VACANCY."

The swarthy front desk clerk with the Greek accent looked at me as if I had a tree branch growing out of my forehead when I said I wanted a room for the night.

"How long?" he asked.

"The night."

"How much of the night?"

His English was fine. It was, you know, the idea of actually staying overnight that had him confused. Actually sleeping with all the bedbugs and cockroaches and maybe half-smoked cigars that other patrons had left there in place of pillow mints. It was just kind of baffling to him, I guess.

"All night."

The clerk looked me up and down. "This the Welcome Mat. Nobody stay all night. I stop even charging for that. You wanna stay all night, maybe you go find the Ritz-Carlton in the Altstadt, huh?"

I stuck my hands in my pockets and shook my head. "Fine." I turned toward the door.

"Hey, wait!"

I didn't turn back, but I halted mid-stride.

"You got money?" he asked, and his skeptical tone made it clear he wouldn't believe me no matter what I said.

I pulled out the billfold and showed it to him.

He shrugged. "Two dollars a night."

I knew he was trying to chizz me, but I didn't know if I could do any better anywhere else.

"What's your name?" he asked.

He had one of those guest books where all the names were the same. Smith, Smith, Smith, Smith. I guess I paused too long, because he prompted me.

"Smith?" he asked. "Is usually Smith. Or Johnson. Sometimes Jones." He didn't seem to care. I guess a guy in his position can't be made to care too much.

"Yeah," I said, "Jones." That struck a chord for some reason.

"Okay, Mr. 'Jones,'" he said. "You in Room 217."

He handed me the key. Something struck me as odd. The arithmetic just didn't add up.

"You got two hundred seventeen rooms in this joint?" I asked.

"You stupid? Forty rooms. Two floors, twenty each."

"Oh." The old stiffening I felt when the bums were kicking me was coming back like a prizefighter on the ropes. I stretched and felt as if my muscles were snapping apart. I knew one thing I would kill for. "Hey, you know where I can get a drink around here?"

It might've knocked my flophouse money down to two nights instead of three, but it would've been worth every penny.

"You a cop?" the clerk asked.

"No?" I guessed.

"You get out of here," the clerk said. "Nothing illegal go on here. No prostitute, no alcohol. You get out of here." I had a white flash like a migraine of me drinking a bottle of Yuengling, not that Mexican crap that had gotten us through Prohibition. Prohibition… but surely that was over if I was drinking American-made? Ganesh could just be a dry town. Or county. Either way amounted to the same thing for me: a dusty throat.

So here I am. That's about all I know so far. That, and I think I'll die—or double dog die—if I don't get a drink in me. Luckily, Luckies aren't outlawed, so I'm toasting through my bullet hole right now. Time to wrap this up. Time to get some sleep, although I'm terrified this journal entry may end up being my suicide note.

If you find me here, looking dead, don't bury me until you jerk my eyes open and check if they're still moving. I'm leaving this out so you can read it. Please read it. Please find it.

Here's hoping I see you tomorrow.

Knock came at the door late last night.

"Who is it?" I moaned. I wanted to leap out of bed, but I couldn't. I could barely move.

"I heard you talking at the front desk," a voice barked. "I think I can help. Can you let me in?"

I struggled. I felt as if I was covered by a mound of dirt. No, better not to think about that image. "I can't!"

"Oh, yes," the voice said. "I suspect you can barely move." He sounded smart. Too smart for his own good.

The door flew open, and the chain went flying in a hundred pieces. A shadowy figure stood in the doorway with a brown paper bag in his hand. He shuffled in and swiftly closed the door.

"Sorry about the damage," he said, kneeling next to me. "I had to kick it in."

I was splayed out. I could rock back and forth, but that was about it. I got my first good look at the Roman-nosed Valentino in vest and shirtsleeves. He looked as though he should've been in pictures instead of a lice trap like this. He stared at me like a hyena on the prowl.

"Who are you?" I grunted.

"No names," he warned. "According to the registry, you're Jones. Yeah, sure. Braineater Jones."

That was the second time somebody had called me that.

"What's that mean?" I asked.

"Don't worry about it," the stranger said. "You can call me Mr. Lazar. That's not my real name. I'm like you."

9. Are there others like me? Yes.

10. Who is Lazar? What is his real name?

"No kidding," I said into the mattress.

"Boy, you really are newly turned," he said. "I thought I might sell you a bottle for the night, but you might be an unlifelong customer. I don't normally take to childrearing, but a friend in need, you know."

"Get bent," I said.

"No, that's what we're going to do with you."

Lazar, or whatever his real name is, flipped me onto my back. He pulled a bottle of Old Crow out of the bag and poured a little into the ashtray.

I guess there wasn't a glass. I hope it wasn't full of ashes. I couldn't taste a drop.

"Here, have a little tipple of this." He poured the ashtrayful down my throat.

I should've choked, lying on my back like that, but of course, someone like me doesn't breathe. Rushing down my throat, it reminded me more of the liquid in my ear popping after a summer cold than taking a drink by choice.

I tried to keep an eye on him, but I wasn't entirely sure why he was ripping the lamp's power cord in half. Son of a bitch. If there were a deposit on my room, I would've lost every dime of it between the door and the lamp.

"Feel better?" he asked. "A little clearer?"

"Yeah," I said.

"Booze keeps the brain pickled," he said. "It keeps people like you and me alive. Unalive. Whatever you want to call it."

"What are we?" I moaned.

"Oh, that's a big question," Lazar said. "And not one for your unbirthday. You're just a baby. We'll get to all that, but hopefully after you've got a job and can start paying me for the sipping whiskey. The booze will keep your mind tip-top, but I'm sorry to say the body is another story. It's a good thing our kind doesn't feel pain, but, ah, this is still going to be a bit uncomfortable."

He carefully peeled back the rubber from the severed end of the cord to reveal an inch of naked copper. He stuck the plug back in the outlet and started zapping me with juice through the wire. In, out, in, out. "Electrical stimulation" he called it, same as they did down in old Sinclair's *Jungle*. It tickled. Anyway, old Lazar zapped the statue stiffness right out of me.

When he was done, he sat down on the edge of the bed. I offered him a Lucky, but he waved it away.

"Cigarettes will kill you."

"Too late now," I said.

"Filthy habit, anyway. Listen, the rigor—that's what it was, by the way, rigor mortis—won't come back as bad ever again. Keep drinking to keep your brain right. You may have to shock yourself now and then if it creeps back in, but I've shown you how to do it now. The important thing is, I'll be around whenever you need some bootleg."

I pointed at the open bottle. "How much for that?"

"That?" He scratched the back of his neck. "Consider that an unbirthday gift. But trust me, it'll be your last free lunch in the Welcome Mat." He stood and strode toward the door.

"How can I find you?" I asked.

"There's a fence on Keene Avenue. There's a little something extra in the back. You can find me there."

Well, thank Jesus, Murphy, and Joe Hooker for that fellow Lazar. He might've seen me as an easy mark, but I'd be dead if not for him. Double dog dead. You know what I mean.

NOVEMBER 2, 1934

With my morning cup of Crow in hand, I'm going to take a minute to write about yesterday. I'm going to try to stick with writing every morning from now on. I've got to inject some structure into my life, or I think I might go mad. As long as I'm distracted, as long as I've got something to do, I can avoid thinking about the hole in my chest and the shattered discs in my neck and the briar scratches festering instead of scabbing and…

Dammit, I've got myself thinking about it now. Let's move on.

With so many questions mounting up and not much in the way of leads, I figured I should head over to Lazar's pawnshop. Keene Avenue wasn't exactly in the nicest part of the Welcome Mat, but I sensed it wasn't the most degenerate place I'd ever set foot in. On the screen of the theater of my mind, I was struck by an image of a fecund bathhouse packed with hairy bodies.

Damn flashes of memory. It's as if I'm seeing somebody else's life in a nickelodeon.

Despite a few letters dangling from the sign, I identified the joint as Hallowed Grounds. What a ridiculous name for a pawnshop. But at least I wouldn't forget it anytime soon. Not that I'm legendary for my memory.

The old, bald fence, quivering slightly with age, hunched over the counter. A scraggly cat prowled the store, having his run of the place. I was surprised there weren't more scratches on the old guitars and milk bottles. Junk festooned the joint, and where there wasn't junk, there was garbage. The entire back of the store was caged off, but I didn't see a whole world of difference between the worthless items he kept under lock and key and the ones he left out as scratching posts for his pussy.

"I'm looking for Lazar," I said.

He looked at me. Looked through me, maybe. His eyes are coated with cataracts, totally white and pupil-less, like a buzzard's. Bald and blind. Mangy cat. Worthless store. Considering the way life gives with one hand and takes with the other, he probably goes home to Jean Harlow. "Never heard of him."

"Maybe I ain't clear." I laid down a few wadded-up bills on the counter from my ever-diminishing supply. "I'm looking for a guy who called himself Lazar. Don't know if it's his real name. Don't care. Probably not, actually. He said I could find him here."

He snatched the cabbage off the counter. Maybe he wasn't so blind after all. How could he see through all that chalky goo, though? Maybe he was so used to getting kickbacks for everything he just knew to take it.

"I know what you're here for, but I guess you don't know the password," Baldy said. "If your friend from Slumberland didn't tell it to you, I don't know that he wanted you to get in."

I kicked the counter. I didn't do it to bother the old bat and certainly not to threaten him. I did it out of frustration. But he took it the wrong way. Or maybe the right way, from my perspective. Guess I don't know my own strength.

He held up his arms to surrender as if he was president of a Banana Republic. "All right, all right! Come on back." He opened up the cage. How unintentionally clever of me.

I assume even the cops don't get past the cage much, unless they've got a warrant. Not that I've seen a single cop in the Mat yet. Doubt they come around much. But even if they did, Baldy could hide a speakeasy or an underground card game or what have you back there, and they'd be none the wiser.

As I walked back, I noticed a little silver flask in the cage underneath the glass. Must've been worth a little something. It had some Russki-Polski writing on it, though I couldn't talk it.

Guess I'm not Russian either.

I grabbed it, though. It had a picture of somebody on it. Lenin? "How much for this?"

"What is it?" he said, slipping into the blind old codger role again.

I stuck it in his hand and let him feel it a bit.

"Oh, that?" he said. "Not subtle, are you?"

"How do you mean, friend?" I said.

"Coppers catch you with paraphernalia, they take it almost the same as having booze. Almost the same. Hey, you take it, buddy. We'll call it even, so long as you don't tell anyone where you got it."

I must've really given him a case of knocking knees. "Thanks."

I poured myself down a metal spiral staircase into the speakeasy.

Or is it called a clip-joint now? No, I suppose it's still a speako, even if only the city is dry.

I didn't spot Lazar anywhere, although honestly the joint was dead. (Ha!) Clearly no one trifled with the bartender, a bear of a guy who could've doubled as the bouncer. They probably saved on payroll that way, muscle and drink jockey all rolled into one.

He stood there wiping down the bar, and from the looks of it, he had had been wiping that rag in the same circular divot since Christ was a corporal. When he spotted me, he gave me a stunned look as though he had seen me somewhere before. Then he settled into all-business mode.

"What'll it be?" Hercules asked.

Being low on funds and lower on patience, I opted to get right down to business. I plopped down in a stool right in front of him, real casual-like. "Looking for somebody."

"Beat it," he said. He turned around as though a couple of customers were hidden back with the bottles and jars.

"His name," I said, "or anyway, he called himself—"

"Hey!" The gorilla turned back around. "I told you to scram."

"I'm new to all this." Earnestness was the name of the game. I could've played a real Studs Lonigan tough guy, but the difference between snarling with the blind old fence and that big gorilla was that only one would make me put my money where my mouth was.

He looked me up and down. The towel never left his hand. Instead of rubbing the bar nervously, he wiped his hands nervously.

"You are, aren't you?" He sounded as though he could scarcely believe me.

I shrugged. I didn't even know what we were talking about anymore.

He pinched his nose. At first I thought maybe it was some funny way of saying "I'm right there with you." He started blowing, though, as if he was sneezing but holding it all in. Then his eye popped out.

It was a sign. He surreptitiously popped his eyeball back in, but judging from the clientele, he probably didn't need to. The few in there were either dead already or too swacked to care.

"Thank God," I said. I pulled open the shirt I was swimming in to show off my bullet hole. It was rotting a little and itching a lot. I'd have to look into purchasing some eau de cologne. The bartender stuck his finger in my hole.

Is that a violation? Wish he would've bought me dinner and flowers first. Maybe it's pretty normal in our world. What do I know?

"You'd better watch your booze intake," he said. "It keeps your brainwheel turning." He slapped some liquid bread onto the counter. "On the house. Welcome to the club, kid. What's your name, anyway?"

"Eh, they call me Jones."

"So what do you need again?"

"Looking for a guy calls himself Lazar." The mook's expression was blank. "Might be a pseudonym."

"A what?"

"You know, a fake name."

"Well, fake name or not, I never heard of him." The gorilla shrugged. "Sorry."

I took a pull from my oat soda. I pulled the old billfold out of my pocket to take a look at how bad I was doing. That was the first time I noticed it was engraved with a rigid eagle and the letters WH.

WH. Not ER. Hmm.

Who is "WH" and why was his billfold in Rothering's house?

The barman had turned around to show he was done talking to me. I tugged on his stained, white button-down.

"Hey, you know where I can get some work?" I showed him my all-but-empty billfold.

"Well," he said, "that rich lady's been crying over there in the corner all morning. She's always a big tipper. Maybe you can help her out."

I thanked him and dropped some change on the counter. The woman wasn't really crying. I guess we don't have tear ducts, or they're empty. She sat there sobbing and rocking and going through the motions of weeping without actually doing it. It was the most pathetic thing I'd ever seen in my solid day and a half of unlife.

I tapped her chin. It seemed like the thing to do. "Hey, chap up."

She snorted the nonexistent boogers into her nose and wiped the invisible tears from her eyes with a handkerchief.

Habits, huh? They're a bitch.

"Who are you?" she sniffled.

I bit into my forefinger to give myself a moment to think, but I stopped when I realized I was about to sever it. "Call me Jones."

"What's your Christian name?"

"Oh, I don't know. They call me Braineater."

"That's horrible!" she cried. That set off a whole new round of imaginary crying.

"Okay, okay, cheer up, pretty momma," I said. "It ain't that bad."

"It's a slur," she said. "You shouldn't let them call you that."

"I don't get it," I said.

"Would you call a wop Ginzo or a harp Mickey?"

Oh. Now I got it.

"It don't bother me," I said. "Everybody's gotta be called something."

"But don't you know your real name? Mine's Claudia. Claudia Winston."

"Nice to meet you, ma'am." I tipped my lid. "Listen, nobody here could help but miss the waterworks. It's like Niagara Falls's dog got shot, you know, if it was all dried up. But anyway, maybe I could help."

She gave me a face like a patient being told the doctor had made a mistake and it wasn't the clap after all—just a bad case of chafing. "Oh, no, I couldn't possibly impose, Mr. Jones. Not without compensation."

Well, yeah, that was the idea.

Hmm. Then again, it seems as though maybe I had played a skirt or two like a fiddle in my old life. I seemed to know exactly what to do.

I grabbed up her hands. "Shh, shh. We'll worry about all that later. Just tell me about it now."

"Very well then," she said. "I'm a reverse widow."

"Howzat?"

"My husband is still breathing."

Oh. Must be a big problem in our community.

"So you can't go back?"

She shook her head and started mock crying again. I could tell I would be there for the rest of the morning if she went on in that fashion.

"I'm certainly resigned to that," she said. "Really, I am. I understand that the children wouldn't want to have to look at some kind of monster and pretend it's their mother. And Howie, he wouldn't… Well, I mean, would you?"

Aside from dressing like some kind of Victorian damsel, she wasn't too hard on the eyes, death and dying and rot taken into account. I would've given her a jolly old humping. "You look fine," was what I said instead.

She blew her nose into her hanky and left it on the table. I waited for her to continue.

"It's not that I resent not seeing them again. I fully understand it. It's just that not seeing them—as in not *seeing* them seeing them—well, that's too much for my silent little heart to bear."

I tried to puzzle out what she meant. "You want… a photograph?"

"Oh, no, not at all," she said, "Or not entirely. I *had* a photograph. I want it back."

"Well, where is it?"

"Well, when I woke up as one of us—one of our kind—I was fortunate. Grave robbers had opened my mausoleum."

"Fortunate how?"

"Could you imagine being trapped like that? Dreadful, even the thought of it! But my memory was ailing, as yours no doubt was when you crossed over."

"Yeah," I said, not adding that I was still in that unenviable state. "How long does that usually last?"

"Oh, it varies from person to person," she said, waving off my concerns with her still-dry handkerchief. "It was only a few weeks for me. But when my memories finally came back, I realized those grave robbers had left a heart-shaped hole in my chest."

"It broke your heart to lose that photo?"

"No." She opened her corset to show me where the thieves had carved a heart out of her bosom. "They took my locket. I suppose it must've been a bit embedded, so they carved around it. I've got a ring-shaped hole in my finger, too." She tugged at her glove to show me the next gruesome bit of her body the thieves had violated.

"That's… that's all right. I believe you. Why didn't you go to the cops?"

That set off her phony-baloney boo-hoo-hooing, and finally I had to buy a round of firewater to turn off the "waterworks."

"I did go to the police," she said. "I went there to the 1-2-5. I sat in the waiting room all day. All day. They kept walking by me, waiting for me to leave. And I asked again and again to be seen. But they wouldn't see me. Finally a detective came out, and I thought, 'At last, someone will help.' But you know what he said?"

"What did he say?" I asked.

"He said, 'I think it's time you left.' They refused to see me. Like I was a pariah or something."

"They never help our kind," the bartender said. "Pretend we don't exist. Cops only help breathers." He wasn't really eavesdropping, but he wasn't really not either.

"It was just like that," Miss Claudia said. "Like I was invisible or something. Like I didn't count."

I said, "You count. We all count in our own little ways. Even if they can't count our heartbeats, we count. I'm going to get your locket back. I promise."

All my other questions have to take a back burner now. I've got a new number one question.

Who stole Miss Claudia's locket?

I'm also running dreadfully low on Crow. I'll have to do something about that.

NOVEMBER 3, 1934

Another night in the rundown dumpfest. Good old Room 217. By all measures, this should be my last. If the innkeeper gives me one more funny look, I'll clock him in his ugly mug. But even if he wasn't getting so damn wary, my stack of bills is down to a leaf and an IOU.

Oh, I finally got an answer to my question. Not one of my numbered questions, unfortunately. The flophouse does have a name. It's the Three Rivers, although you wouldn't know it to look at the place. Only place I've found the name actually written down was on a signed picture of Louis Armstrong, made out to the owner of the Three Rivers. They oughta put up a sign. "Satchmo slept here."

Went to the cemetery. Nice part of town. Nowhere near the Welcome Mat. Miss Claudia must've been a rich bitch, although I could've told that from her disposition.

I felt as out of place at Buffalora Cemetery as I did in my clothes. It was all fancy landscaping and $64,000 monuments. Not a wooden cross or even an inground plaque in that place. You would think a fellow in my position would feel more at home in any boneyard, but that place was just creepy. Rich and creepy.

The gate read "RESVRRECTVRIS." I guess *V*s must be fancier than *U*s. Only us vulgar underlings (or "vvlgar vnderlings," as they would spell it) use *U*.

I had to climb the fence. I spent a while searching for Miss Claudia's grave with no luck. Row upon row of tombstone after tombstone, but no Claudia Winston, nor anything close enough. I realized that grave was a dry well.

Well, not literally. I just realized that's a rather unapt metaphor. My grammar school teacher Mrs. Argento would've rapped my knuckles for that.

Wait a minute. Where did that come from? Did I really…? Crap, the memory's gone. If it was ever really there. Moving on.

I decided to take a different tack. There was a little shack in the boneyard, humbler by a power of ten than the humblest mausoleum. It was nothing but twisted boards and home-smelted nails. No doubt it was the gravekeeper's shack.

I kicked in the door. Kicking it in didn't seem entirely necessary, but then you never know. A poor old hunchback was sitting there, tuning a tombstone radio (appropriate, I guess). He nearly fell out of his rocking chair. It took me a second to take in the room, but only a second. Every nook and cranny was filled with little bells, like the kind you would find around the neck of a nanny goat, and each bell was marked in purple ink with a number and a letter.

I didn't waste much time taking in the sights because the hunchback was struggling to his feet and reaching for a gun by the radio. It turned out to be a lucky stroke that I kicked the door in after all because I managed to beat him to the bean-shooter.

I'll have to remember to kick all my doors in from now on.

After he stood, I waved him to sit down. "Grab some upholstery."

"Who are you?" he said. "What do you want?"

"That ain't important." I closed the door. "You run this place?"

He nodded. It was a little difficult for him, what with the hump and all.

"You try to ice all of your visitors, or just me?"

"It's just for protection," he insisted.

"From what?"

He was silent.

"Name," I demanded.

"Gnaghi," the hunchback said.

I could see his name perfectly fine on his nametag. I didn't care. "All right, Noggy. I'm looking for a grave. Claudia Winston. Where is it?"

He looked as panic-stricken as a rabbit moments before becoming hasenpfeffer. "No Claudia Winston."

"You got every name on every grave memorized?"

He tried to nod.

I leaned in real close and waved the gun for good measure. "You calling me a liar? Or just the broad who sent me?"

"She… came back? Like you?"

He fidgeted in his seat. He seemed unduly upset at the idea of not noticing somebody had been brought across.

"Yeah," I said.

"You mean Claudia Baumer!" he realized. He rubbed his hands together profusely. A little too profusely, if you ask me. Like he had something to hide. I shook my head. "Maiden name. Or married name. Or something. Happens sometimes. R51. These are all graves." He pointed at the little bells.

I grabbed the bell for R51. A wire led out of it. I ran my fingers along the wire. "Why?" I turned and pointed the gun at him.

He cringed. "It's to save you. In case you come back."

"What do you mean 'in case'? Can't you tell whether someone's going to come back?"

He shook his head.

"You can't predict it? There's no rhyme or reason to it? You have to leave a bell so the walking corpse can ring it?"

He nodded.

"That's all we are, isn't it? Walking corpses? There's nothing special about us, nothing deserving or damning. We just…" I made a raspberry with my lips.

He stared at me with a look of horror in his eyes as though I was about to do a lot worse than kick in his door and wave a gun in his face.

"What causes it?"

"I don't know," he said. "I don't think anybody knows. I'm just the gravedigger."

6. What am I? A dead man walking.

"So you dug up Claudia Winston… Baumer, whatever you're calling her. You stole her locket."

"No, no, I would never," Gnaghi said. "I respect the dead too much. Anyway, I wouldn't get away with it. My luck, the one I rob would be a corpsie like you. Miss Baumer, she was already gone. Never rang her bell. I just filled the empty grave with dirt."

Huh. It just occurred to me that she said she had been in a mausoleum. I wish I had asked the little twerp about *that.* Well, one more clue to wonder about.

"You know who dug her up?" I asked.

He looked like a caged rat. He knew. Getting him to spill might take some digging.

Digging, ha! Damn, I'm hilarious.

"Who was it?" I growled, baring my teeth.

He shrank into his hump like a turtle into its shell, terrified of me. I caught a glimpse of my reflection in one of the bells. My gums were black, making my teeth stand out like a monster's. That might come in handy in intimidating folks, but I'd have to look into whether I could brush my teeth without knocking them out of my head.

"They come around sometimes. The old one is Ed, and the young one is Joey."

"They got last names?"

"I don't know. I only hear them talking to each other."

I growled, hoping my lips were rippling like a dog's. That was sure to give him a fright.

"Okay, okay!" he said. "The only other thing I know is that the young one has a mark on his neck."

"A brand? A birthmark?"

Gnaghi shook his head. "A tattoo. Bright pink, and it glows in the dark like a neon sign."

Something barely registered in my subconscious. I had seen something like that before.

“A snake,” he clarified, “eating its own tail.”

I knelt down and tried to be less threatening since I knew what I wanted to know. My smile, though, was only making it worse. I clamped my jaws shut. “You don’t get out of here much, do you?”

“No,” he said. “I’m too busy taking care of your kind.”

Two Christian names wasn’t a lot to go on, but a tattoo like that had to stand out. I figured the best place to start was by canvassing all the inkaterias around the city. If I couldn’t find the artist who did it, maybe someone could at least tell me where it had been done.

I went to a drugstore to flip through the phone book, but I didn’t buy a slug, which pissed off the drugstore owner. Three inkslingers in the city actually hung up shingles and didn’t just work out of some guy’s basement. I was hoping one of them would be a winner because going from door to door looking for a faker might take me the rest of my unlife.

Two were on the docks, and one was in the seediest part of the Welcome Mat. Figuring I could use some fresh, salty air, I went to Sailor Jimmy’s. The place was packed to the gills with Navy pukes who all looked like they wanted to give me a pop in the eye. While Sailor Jimmy’s attention was torn between his cigarette and a coxswain’s neck, I snuck in the back room of his store.

The cockroaches scattered when I turned on the lights. He kept his inks in little mixing barrels on a shelf. I peeked through them, but none were glowing. I crossed his joint off the list, but maybe I'd stop by again when it was less swimming in seamen. Then it was on to Henk's.

Henk's at least was empty. It was tough to tell how he could see well enough in the dim, flickering lights to mark up anybody's skin. He didn't seem to care though. He was happy to have his shop empty so he could light his opium pipe and fiddle with the calibration of his electric tattooing needle. He didn't even get up when I came in. I guessed, by his name, that Henk was a Dutchman, or maybe a Swede.

On second thought, the guy I met may not have actually been Henk. You know how restaurants and hotels sometimes trade hands and keep the old name? Or for that matter, if the original Henk still owned it, that guy might've been a hired artist. Anyway, I'll call him Henk. And he was Danish or something.

"Looking to get a piece," I said. "Thing is, I know which needle monkey I want to do it, I just don't know where to find him. Think you can help?"

After a long pause, Henk (or whoever) said, "Name?"

"Mine or his?" I asked.

Nothing.

"I don't know his name," I said finally. "I saw a feller—younger feller—with a piece exactly like the one I want. Bright pink, if you can believe it. I might change the color, of course. A dragon eating its own tail or something. Any chance you did it?"

"No. Get out."

I may not know much, but I know people. He knew something. "Tell me who did the tat."

He pointed his tattoo gun at me, one of those shiny titanium electric machines. He made it buzz like a streetlamp, and the needles went haywire. If I wasn't already dead, it would've been threatening. I didn't much want a brand-new pirate flag or pinup girl done at punch-throwing speed, so I stepped back. But either way, I had the advantage. I felt no pain, and I had a real gun. I decided to flash Gnaghi's piece.

"Why don't you talk, you dumb Swede? I'm all out of bribe money, but I've still got a few bullets left."

"You the dumb one," Henk said. "You don't know who you messing with. Get out before you get hurt."

Who stares down a gun and doesn't get scared? I didn't even know if it was loaded. If it was, what would I do, shoot him in the leg? And how much metal could I squirt if he had friends?

A half-dozen longshoremen were loitering outside, and if more sailors and salt dogs weren't hanging all up and down the street, I'd eat Ernst Rothering's girdle. What if somebody heard the shot and called the coppers? We weren't in the Mat. They'd come, and I wouldn't make it real far. I didn't intend to find out how much damage I could take before I got double dead, either.

I got mad. Real mad. "I will jump over there and rip your throat out of your neck." I showed my teeth, and old Henky baby took real notice.

His pipe clattered to the floor as he jumped up. He tried to keep me at bay with the buzzing tattoo gun. I chomped the air a couple times like a dog.

"I'll rip you to shreds," I growled. "You know what I am?"

"Yeah!" he said. "I know what you are. I know how to put you down, too."

That gave me pause. Everyone I'd met so far had told me to make sure I drank enough booze or I'd regret it. No one had mentioned other ways to put down our kind.

He waved that fancy ink-throwing machine at me again. The needle shredded the air like an electric carpenter's drill. False bravado. I actually lunged and knocked it out of his hand. It skittered to a stop in the corner, still chattering away like one of those windup sets of fake choppers in a dentist's office.

"Tell me what I'm looking for," I said. "You don't got to die tonight."

"All right!" he said, holding up his arms to ward me off. "It's a gang sign. The Infected or the Infested, something like that. I don't do them. They do them themselves. I don't know how they get the ink to glow either."

"Where do I find these gangsters?"

"The Mat," Henk said. "Between 68th and Russo."

I spent the night walking the Infected's turf like a cheap whore. Only about every third street lamp was lit on those few blocks, and the jabby sidewalks were covered with a thin layer of broken glass. It didn't take me long to spot the biting serpent logo on a few walls. The same guy who did the long graffito motto I spotted my first day in the Mat must've did those, too. They glowed the same way.

That reminds me, I still have to figure out what all that gibberish on the archway meant. Something's going on in the Mat that gives me a queasy feeling. I know it's not my stomach because that doesn't work anymore.

I took a pull from my flask—the last of the Crow that Lazar had bequeathed to me. I glanced around, suddenly worried. I knew I probably had no reason to be. Everyone near enough to be looking at me wasn't, and not one of them looked less like a stewbum than me. Besides, the fuzz refused to come to the Mat. A woman's shouts in a not-too-far-off alley gave me the first proof that axiom wasn't just hearsay.

By the time I got there, she and her assailant were gone. I hoped it had been a mugging and not something more sinister. I spotted a couple of eggs who could have been trouble boys with the Infected, but they bolted as soon as I walked toward them.

Couldn't find Ed or Joey. With no place to stay and no money, I hunkered down in an alley. Way off in the nice part of Ganesh, where you could afford to pretend the dead didn't walk, a siren played me a lullaby. I slept in a box last night with only my flask to keep me company. Right where I wanted to be.

NOVEMBER 4, 1934

Success!

A wide-ranging orchestra of derelicts banging trash can lids and cats in heat screeching woke me up this morning. I had to take a few swigs of Crow to even roll out of the newspapers. I wish I'd had a shock stick, but there's no juice in the alley. All out of Crow now. I had to get back to Hallowed Grounds later that day, but I didn't have to go back empty-handed.

I knocked on a few doors, and eventually some scared folks pointed me in the right direction. Couldn't tell whether they were scareder of me or the gangsters. Some of them must've hoped I would clean up the block. *Sorry, folks. Narrower mission for me.*

Turned out Ed and Joey loved the whores. Everyone on the block who had seen 'em had seen 'em walking in or out of one particularly delightful joint. A cathouse, to hear the neighborhood Romeos and Roxettes tell it, but one that breathers didn't usually go to unless they were looking for a weird old time. And don't get me wrong, sometimes you meet some fat old bastards who like to dress up like mama and ask baby to suckle their man-tits. Whoa. That was an unpleasant flash of memory.

The hookers were supposed to be our kind, and the johns were either our kind or the weirdo breathers who love our kind.

The joint was all plush and purple, layers of velvet and silk. Expensive, if any of it was real. Could've been felt and cotton for all I knew. They were going for some exotic harem from faraway Araby or a

Manchurian opium den notched up to 106%. I wasn't surprised, honestly, to see a few johns sprawled out here and there, hitting the pipe. It was that kind of place. The scent of dope smoke mingled with the slight smell of decay.

"Hey, man," one of the johns said, choking on his puff of mootah then laughing like a goober on parade. "You work here?"

"Nah," I said.

"Hey, wait, chum. I'm almost out." He reached out with no real energy. "You tell the management I'm sucking on ashes here?"

I'd like to think my response was reasonable and well measured. I grabbed the little pipe-head by the short and hairies of his lapel and flung him against the wall. The other johns either buried their heads in their blats or laughed between puffs.

"Yeah, the management, sure," I said. "I'll let 'em know to come around and fluff up your pillow. Maybe comp you a handy while they're at it."

"Hey, ease off, man," the pipe-head said, sputtering. "I didn't mean nothin' by it."

"Sure," I said, "and the iceberg didn't mean nothing by crossing the path of the *Titanic* either."

"What do you want, man?" The pipe-head held up a fistful of cash. "I ain't got much. Just enough for a… you know." He gave a couple of hip thrusts that made me want to beat him even more.

I grabbed the cash and stuffed it back into his jacket pocket. "I don't want your cash, jackass. You know Eddie and Joey?"

He shook his head. "Never heard of 'em, man."

I believed him. Too high or too stupid to lie. Leastways to lie properly.

"All right," I said, letting him go. "So where's this management you're always on about?"

He slid down the wall and came to a rest, butt-first, on the floor. He looked up at me, smiling perversely, no doubt the effects of the tea. "You mean Mighty?"

That was just about confusing enough to rile me up again. I stopped a hair shy of decking the kid and figured, hey, what the hell, you catch more flies with honey than with cheese. "Sure. Why not?"

"He's over there, man." He pointed at a cotton-candy-colored counter straight out of a malt shop, with a lift-up leaf and everything. All it lacked was a soda jerk with a paper hat polishing the top and a list of prices in white letters on a black chalkboard.

Come to think of it, a price list might've done wonders for that place.

I turned my attention from the little twerp with the pipe and stepped toward the counter.

"Hey, man," Pipesy McGee said, pressing his luck. "While you're over there—"

"Watch it, you," I growled.

Actually, there was one nice touch once I got over there: a little bell like they have at fancy hotels and auto garages to ring the attendant. I rang. A colored fellow decked out in a bespoke purple suit strutted out of the back room. He seemed to slide across the floor and did a little twirl when he reached the counter.

"Hey, my man," he said. "Give me some skin." He held out his palm.

"What?" I said.

"Man, are you square," the man in the suit said. "Mighty Dull. What you want?"

"I'm sorry?"

"You are pretty damn sorry. I said my handle is Mighty Dull, and what kind of whore are you looking"—he made a little show of twirling his hands like a butler, clearly pleased with the rhyme he was about to make—"for?"

"Oh, I'm not looking to get screwed," I jawed. "Leastways I don't pay for it when I am. Or at least I think I don't." I chuckled.

Mighty probably had no idea what I was on about, but he clearly didn't like me running down his chosen profession of pimpology. He popped up his collar and shook his hands like he was casting me off of his dynamite suit. "Man, I don't even need this jive. If you ain't here to pay, you ain't here to play, so why don't you go take a long walk down a short pier?"

I thought about it for a second. "If I did that, I'd fall in the water."

"That's the point, joker!"

"All right, all right," I said, holding up my hands. "I'm here for a whore if that's what it takes to get some questions answered."

"It's five bucks."

"That's extortion."

"That's the going rate, my man."

I shrugged, figuring I could figure something out. Worst case scenario, what was he going to do, kill me? Well, he might. Or leastways he could try.

"All right," I said.

"Aight?" Mighty said, mushing the words together.

"All right," I repeated, carefully pronouncing each syllable in turn.

"Aight," Mighty said again, rubbing his hands together. "Well, come on back, son. Let's git you a look at the hos."

Mighty lifted up the counter's movable leaf and let me come inside. Good thing he didn't ask me for the money up front. Then again, maybe that sort of thing's not kosher in brothels. I wouldn't know. I don't spend much time in cathouses as a rule. I was surprisingly sure of that. Who the hell knows what my rules are? Or if I have any.

"Welcome to Hat Scratch Fever," Mighty said proudly. His hand was out with a wave as if he was showing off El Dorado to a beggar.

And it was, truth be told, pretty impressive. The room was good and wide. It looked as if it was a converted coat check. Up top, in the boxes where an average hat would go, sat row upon row of severed heads, each one giving her own distinct "come hither" wink.

"Hey, baby!" one of the heads, a pretty delightful-looking Abyssinian beauty, called out to me.

The cacophony of catcalls that followed might have made me flush red if I still had any blood in my veins. There were some cuties and, to be damn straight about it, a few real ginchy dames. What a surprise, I found myself thinking, how much you get out of a face. Was I a face man? Maybe everybody was, once a face was separated from the rest of a body.

In the next level down, where the coats should have been, hung a row of torsos. It would've been pretty gruesome had I seen it at a crime scene. I could imagine the headlines: SERIAL KILLER LEAVES COAT CHECK FULL OF CORPSES. As it was, the girls—if that was the proper term for it—were heaving their bosoms and wiggling their tum-tums like Lebanese belly dancers dying for it.

Down where the snowboots and galoshes would've been were, of course, the hips on down, including the gams. They kept those together.

I guessed exactly what was going on, but I figured I'd play dumb to buy a little time with Mighty Dull. I'll tell you, though, I was starting to think I wasn't so much a face man as a leg man. A couple of those pairs seemed to go on forever, or at least they would have if they hadn't been so crudely separated from their torsos.

I suppose they could've separated limb from limb, but maybe there's a certain amount of charm lost when you start switching out arms and legs. How did one control…? Do we still control our own bodies? Or do they act independently? What a funny question.

"Well, what do you think, my man?" Mighty asked.

"Huh?" I said.

"Come on, man, don't play dumb." Mighty said, giving one of the pairs of thighs a good stroke and setting a Japanese—or maybe Chinese—prosty's head twittering. "This is prime meat for your money. Well worth the fin, I tell you what."

"Come on, baby," one of the heads said. "Pick me."

"Don't pick that bitch," another one said. "You know you want my fine ass."

"And if you want her fine ass," Mighty Dull said, "but not her nagging face, hey, go for it."

I looked around at the "merchandise." Seemed a bit crass to call hookers that, but hey, when a spade's a spade, you don't call it a Sunday dinner, I suppose. "So how does this work? You just pick a head and a body and a cooch?"

"What?" Mighty exclaimed. "Don't tell me you've never been to the Fever before."

"I have not," I said.

"Well, damn, son, why didn't you say so?" Mighty put an arm around me paternalistically. "You put your money away. It's no good here."

I hope he didn't notice me heave a sigh of relief. Funny that I would even make such a gesture, being as I don't breathe. Some behaviors must be hardwired, I suppose. Either way, I didn't have the money he wanted me to hide.

"Aw, come on, Mighty!" one of the hookers shouted.

"Shut up, ho!" Mighty replied. "First taste is on the house." He turned to me and whispered, "Comes out of the girls' common fund, if you can call them girls."

"Fuck you, Mighty!" one of the girls called out.

"You know how it is, bitches!" Mighty replied. "Go on, son, you pick out exactly what you want. And I do mean 'exactly.' Mix and match as much as you want."

He shoved me forward so hard that I had to shake it off a bit. I had seen a lot of weird things since my untimely death, but that had to be by far the peculiarest. I cocked my head over my shoulder to look at the pimp. "Mix and match body parts? Isn't this kind of degrading?"

Mighty shook his head as though he was holding in a belly guffaw. "They hos, my man. How much more degraded can they git?"

Fair enough. I shrugged and took a few steps closer to the hat rack. And the rack of racks. "Hey, girls."

"Hey," they said back, almost like a gruesome, head-y chorus.

"They call me Braineater."

"Hey, Braineater," they repeated, and a few more catcalls and sweet nothings followed.

"Damn, man," Mighty said, "you don't gotta tell 'em your name, but don't use that kind of shit around here."

"Can't help what they call me," I said.

Mighty shook his head. "Whatever. It's your stupid-ass reputation. You think I let them call me Spooky Dull? Hell no!"

"Can you give me a minute with the…?" I waved my hand sort of like Harry Houdini in the general direction of the head shop.

"You want a minute alone in the meat market?" Mighty asked. "Sure, baby, sure. Just keep your sausage packed up." Mighty strutted off. He was a hell of a character.

I turned back to the row of heads. "Hey, girls. I'm looking for a pair of deadbeats called Ed and Joey. Supposedly, they frequent these premises. Anybody know who I'm talking about?"

"I do!"

I focused on the first head to answer. A couple were scowling. They probably didn't know the hoods at all. A couple more were huffing and puffing like maybe they knew but were too slow on the uptake to beat the first girl.

"What's your name?" I asked.

She seemed flattered and smiled. "Brigid."

"Damn, john," the Abyssinian-looking head said. "Names cost extra."

"Well, I ain't paying anything, so charge me double," I said, which elicited some laughs from the decapitees.

"I don't mind," Brigid said. "It's kind of sweet, a john giving a squirt about your name."

"So, Brigid, I'm looking for—"

"Why don't we head someplace more private?" she asked.

"Oh, sure." I gingerly grabbed her by her brunette locks. I started to head up to the suites, but almost everyone in the room, body-free or not, started laughing at me.

"Aren't you forgetting something?" Brigid, or Brigid's head at least, asked.

"Oh, right," I said, again afraid that if I hadn't been utterly exsanguinated by lying in a pool with a gunshot wound, I would've been blushing like a schoolboy. "Which body's yours?"

"Don't take hers!" one of the other girls shouted. "Grab mine."

"I want a third of it!" another girl shouted out. "Take my gams."

"Stupid bitches!" Mighty announced, catching wind of the kerfuffle. "I already told you this was *pro boner*. All the wear and tear, none of the cabbage."

That shut them up. Seemed a bit weird. I guess they divided up their fees along with their corpses. Hell of a way to run a business.

Hell of a country we live in, isn't it? Only in America.

I stood in what Mighty charitably referred to as the Honeymoon Suite, which wouldn't've passed muster for a broom closet in the Three Rivers. Then again, who knows?

Maybe I'm a natural snob. I have no idea if I was a caviar eater or a garlic eater in life. Either way, I wasn't even shacking up in the Three Rivers luxury estates anymore, so I hardly had call to complain.

Brigid stood at the mirror, which hada big chunk missing from the upper right side, and applied a thin line of caulk-like makeup around the seam between her head and neck. I took a zozzle from my flask while she was turned away. I wasn't sure whether it would brace my nerves, but I didn't know what else to do.

Finished, she sat on the edge of the bed, not quite naked. She was wearing some kind of slip draped over her ample bosom and fetching frame. I suppose the seam between her hips and torso either took too long to patch up or just didn't matter when a bit of fancy French lawnjeray—is that how you spell it?—could cover it up. Gotta say, the girl was built, even if she had to be built from scratch. I had grabbed all of the parts that were properly hers, and from the way she luxuriated in it, it had been a while since anyone had put her together with her own bits.

To be fair, though, she seemed a bit uncomfortable in her own skin. Kept readjusting her head. Hazard of the job, I suppose, being uncomfortable with your own body. I wanted to ask her what wearing someone else's body was like, how it even worked, but everyone else seemed so matter-of-fact about it. I didn't want to look like a rube.

"Why don't you sit down next to me?" she asked, patting the bed in a manner that only a woman had, making a dumpy, cockroach-infested flophouse mattress seem inviting, enticing even.

"Nah, better not," I said.

She cocked her head and looked at me funny. She had a bit of gum in her mouth.

I suppose the gum helped to pass the long hours in the hat rack. How old was she? Couldn't've been older than twenty-five before she died. Whores tended to show their age more quickly than others, too. Maybe I *was* a bit of a whoremonger in my old life after all.

"You funny or something?" she asked.

"Funny? Oh!" I realized what she meant. "No, I'm not. Leastways, I don't think I am. Hard to tell."

She laughed. A giggle, really. A schoolgirl's laugh. "You ain't been back long, have you?"

Was she even twenty-five? I didn't want to contemplate the alternative. If she was nothing but a kid… well, she was nothing but a kid no matter how old she was. Surely she wasn't growing any older.

I shook my head. "How can you tell?"

"You've got the worst case of brain drain I've ever seen," she said. "You should start hitting the bottle a little harder. It'll help."

I shrugged. I couldn't really imagine taking any more slugs a day than I already was. Well, I could imagine it, but I certainly couldn't afford it.

"So, you don't remember if you're funny or not," she said.

Something about the way she said it scared me. She definitely turned me on, but Lazar was a really pretty boy, too. Maybe I swang both ways. I didn't even want to think about that right then. I changed the subject. "That's not why I'm here."

She shrugged, or at least gave a credible attempt at a shrug, and left the divot in her neckline more exposed than before. I had a sudden unbidden image of the two of us having a roll in the hay, and me going at it so hard that her head rolled off her body and onto the floor. Didn't seem impossible, really. It made me shudder.

"Who cares?" she said. "Mighty is comping you, and he doesn't comp anybody. Any. Body. Might as well take advantage of it."

I grinned. "Lord knows I'd love to, Brigid, but who even knows if it even still works?"

She giggled again, and I had a sudden flash of Shirley Temple. Yet another memory I don't need or want returning instead of some of the more pertinent ones. Good old Shirley Temple singing and tap-dancing, that's what the prosty reminded me of. Did I have a little grade school–aged daughter somewhere wondering where her daddy had got to? Or did I have important, grown-up reasons for watching a little girl sing and dance on the silver screen?

"It still works," she said. "Heaven knows why. Here, I'll show you." She kneeled in front of me and undid my zipper for what it was worth.

I had to jump away. "Come on, now. I told you that's not why I'm here."

Frustrated, she threw herself back on the bed, and then my worst fear was realized. Her head flopped off and rolled onto the ground. I slapped my palm against my forehead. How much cosmetic goo did those hookers go through if their heads were flopping off and getting dented all the time?

"Could you grab that for me?" she asked sweetly.

Leaning off the bed, I grabbed the brunette by her hair and dangled her a bit like a paper bag full of day-old sturgeon. I dropped the head into her waiting hands, and she adjusted it back on like a dandy fitting a hat.

"What do you want to know about Eddie and Joey?" she asked with a resigned lack of edge to her voice.

"Where do they live?" I asked.

"Oh, that?" she asked. "That's easy."

Ed and Joey lived together. Couldn't tell if they were like that or not, but I didn't much care. Funny how little I cared about once I was dead. They liked Mighty's whores, but I've known a few who swung the pendulum in both directions, if you catch my drift. Maybe they went to Hat Scratch Fever for fun and then home for all the domestic stuff. How could anyone deny that joint was fun to be in, even if they were queerer than a squid on Tuesday?

The boys—and word on the street was, the whole Infected gang—occupied a dilapidated old house on Russo Avenue. The place was about as well maintained as the windmill in *Frankenstein*. Most of the windows were boarded up, and a strong wind could've blown away the whole damn attic.

I watched and waited until I was pretty sure that only Joey was home, pink ink and all, sleeping off the night before. I wanted to kick his shit in for sleeping in a bed while I had to sleep in an alley, but I restrained myself. I ripped Little Nemo out of his Zs and out of his bed in one swift action.

"Who—who are you, man?" he said, shivering in my grasp.

I slammed him against the wall. "You don't want to know."

"You don't know me, man," Joey whispered.

I let him away from the wall. He relaxed. Then I threw him against it again. "I don't care. I'm looking for something, and you've got it."

His eyes were burning. Burning… green. Weird. Something was shifting under his shirt, as if his stomach was churning all on its own. "You don't know me, man." That time, his voice held a little stainless steel. "I've got friends. You don't want to mess with us."

That wriggling… I decided the stomach was getting out of hand. It had to be punched, independent of what happened to the rest of the little delinquent. *Wham.*"I don't care about you. I don't care about your friends. For all I care, I can never see you again. All I care about is the locket."

"What locket, man?"

Wham. He didn't like that. He seemed to find it jarring, especially since I did it at odd times. Nice talk, mean talk, indifferent talk. As long as he couldn't tell when the hits were coming, I had the edge.

"All right." He coughed, and I noticed a little blood leaking out of the corner of his mouth. At least I knew he wasn't one of us.

I let him down. He took me up to the garret. I kept fingering the gun in my pocket. Not much else I could do. He might try to get the drop on me. As long as I had the gun, I had the advantage, even if he had one too.

Of course, I don't know my own limits. I need to ask someone. Lazar, maybe, if he ever comes out of hiding.

I made Joey walk up the steps ahead of me, which he didn't like one bit. He kept turning back to check me out. He'd see me fingering something in my pocket, and then he'd turn back as though he hadn't seen me doing it ten times already.

"Listen, man"—he was trying to lull me into a false sense of security, I guess—"I didn't mean to steal your locket. It's just, you know—"

I jammed Gnaghi's bean-shooter into the small of Joey's back. That shut him up real good. "If you say it's nothing personal, I'm going to put a bullet through your spine. And when the docs come—if they come, because I hear respectable folk don't come around to the Mat much—and they ask you how it happened, if you happen to still be alive and not in my condition, you know what you can say?"

He was too terrified to say anything. There was a kid who really cared about living. It was nice not to have those sorts of worries anymore.

"You can say, 'It was nothing personal,'" I said. "Because I don't give a shit about your spine, Joey. You know what I do give a shit about?"

His tongue sounded like sandpaper as it limped out the next three syllables. "The locket."

"The locket," I agreed.

That was about enough of his funny business on the stairwell. On the top floor, he reached up and fiddled with the dangling white plastic knob to the attic folding stairs. He fiddled with it so long I knew he was scared. I wanted to grab the knob and stiffen it for him to make him feel bad, but I couldn't reach. Instead, I pulled back the hammer on my gun. He got ahold of the knob real ricky-tick then.

I had a moment of worry when he scrambled up the fold-down steps and was out of my sight as I climbed them. I stopped, pointed the gun up toward the attic entrance, and sat, waiting for the rock or trophy or boiling oil or whatever he was going to dump on me.

"Joey?" I asked loudly.

"Yeah?" He was still invisible.

"Let me see your head."

He popped his head back out of the attic, grinning like a child who had realized his mistake.

"How's about you stay right there?"

"Sure, Mister…?"

He was prodding me, but I didn't finish his sentence for him. The little punk could go on calling me just "mister." I should have known better than to think he was smart enough for any funny business anyway.

The asbestos peeled away from the garret walls, and a single boarded-up window faced Ganesh. I could see the city in the spaces between the boards, and it seemed almost peaceable from up there. Someone lived in the garret, or maybe had and didn't anymore. There were cracker crumbs and cheese curds scattered around the floor that the mice had only recently started to nibble. A mattress with a massive yellow stain lay on the floor. Other than that, there were no furnishings, just cardboard boxes and foot lockers and trunks.

Joey didn't have to look at all, which was good, because none of the boxes were marked "Christmas Decorations" or anything like that. I wondered what they would be marked in that den of iniquity. "Mootah" for one and "Hot Crap" for another and "Heaters" for a third, maybe. All their loot was in one particular trunk, the only one with a padlock. He thumbed the combination into the tumblers and threw open the little treasure chest.

I almost whistled in appreciation at the load those little pack rats had squirreled away. The locket took a little scrabbling to find, but it was the only locket, which was good. Otherwise, I wouldn't have been able to identify it. I had no idea what Miss Claudia's husband looked like. The rest of the chest was filled with mementos: silver picture frames and diamond rings and tie tacks and just about anything you could pluck off a corpse.

Each hot rock, I supposed, was a life ruined or wrecked or maybe just made a little more miserable. I should've said something brave, should've taken it all. But I didn't. One step at a time.

I made him walk in front of me all the way to the back door. I stopped before I hit the door though. "One more thing. You'd be better off to stay away from the graveyards."

He said, "We don't go there anymore. Too many of your kind now."

"That's good. Now forget you ever met me."

He closed the door behind me and waved as though we were old friends.

1. Who stole Miss Claudia's locket? Two gangsters for the Infected, Ed and Joey.

Case closed.

Before I went back into Hallowed Grounds, I crossed the revised first numbered question out of my notebook. It's the little things that make a difference. "*Why did they bump me off?*" was number one again. Time to get cracking on that.

Baldy was still at Hallowed Grounds, of course.

"You know where I'm going," I said.

"Password?"

I stopped and thought for a moment. I wanted to take a swig from my flask, but there was nothing left. I turned it upside down. I could only shake out a few drops. I even coveted those. Even though the man may (or may not) be blind, I didn't want to drop to the ground and lap it up in front of him. I just had to get through and get more.

"Come on, let me through, stretch."

"Not without you giving me the password, stretch," the old fence responded.

I took a deep breath even though, functionally, I didn't need it. It was just one of those things we do, I suppose. Same way Miss Claudia kept crying even though her tear ducts were all shriveled up and useless. We're nothing if not creatures of habit. People, I mean. If we are still people.

I fingered my gun and considered using it on a blind man to scare him to death for the second time in three days. What was I becoming? Was I really the monster that greeted me in the mirror every morning?

No. I closed my eyes and stared at the backs of my eyelids. Lazar, that damn absentee landlord, had never mentioned a password. He couldn't have guessed I would've muscled my way into the speako the other day. That meant the password had to be something all of our kind would know or guess. Something we would see and remember if we hadn't woken up in a pool.

"Resurrecturis," I realized.

He smiled. "Go on back."

Once inside, I took a quick look around the speakeasy. She wasn't there, of course. That would be too much to hope for. I bellied up to the bar anyway. Same old gorilla in shirtsleeves was there.

"Well, the man they call Braineater."

"Damn straight," I said. "I'm a braineater and proud of it."

The gorilla shook his head and wiped at his favorite spot on the bar. "What can I do for you?"

I sighed. Another one of those physiologically meaningless gestures.

Whoa. Where did all that fancy talk come from? Maybe I was a professor in my old life.

"I don't suppose you would comp me," I said.

"No," the bartender said.

I held up my hands imploringly. "Well, could you ask the owner?"

The gorilla scowled. "You do not"—each word thudded like a boot stomp—"want to bother *him*."

I perked up. Lazar! Had to be. Whatever he called himself to the help, I had a feeling it was him. "No, I do, in fact. I want you to ask the owner."

To my surprise, instead of going up to talk to Baldy or pulling out a telephone, he disappeared down into the floor. I leaned over the counter and saw a trapdoor lid hanging open with a ladder leading tantalizingly down into some secret, subterranean lair. I listened as the big gorilla descended into the sub-basement and came back up holding a pickle jar. I felt a stabbing pain like an ice pick through my eye. A painful headache of memory. I had seen something like that before at a sideshow, except it had had two heads. The image was clear as day in my mind, and another one was on the counter in front of me. A pickled human fetus floating in something. Grain alcohol maybe. A joke, no doubt.

"What's this?" I said.

"It's the boss," the bartender assured me.

I looked into his eyes. No hint of caginess. A good joke maybe. Then the little baby opened its eyes and put its hand against the wall of the jar. The little beastie motioned to the bartender.

The gorilla opened the top of the jar and pulled the little guy out. He put it down on the counter where it stood, wobbly, on its stumpy little flippers. It was definitely soaking in moonshine, or something equally potent and disgusting.

"This is the boss?" I asked, looking at the bartender.

"Don't talk to him," the fetus grunted. "He's just the help. Talk to me."

"I'm new," I said, hoping that would explain it all.

The little guy shook his head. He took a few steps and shook the booze out of his nonexistent hair. He snapped his fingers, and the bartender immediately dropped a martini in front of him. He could've taken a bath in that damn thing. "They call me the Old Man. Kind of a joke, I guess. Ha ha."

"What's your story?" I said.

"Oh, it's like that, eh?" the Old Man said. "Grilling me in my own place? My mama aborted me with a coat hanger in an alley. Does that shock you?"

"Not really," I said.

"Yeah, I thought not," the Old Man said. "If there's one thing I don't trust, it's bitches. Can't stand 'em. Can't stand to be around them. All they ever want to do is be near me and cuddle me." He shuddered at the thought of a kind woman showing him some affection.

Somehow, I doubt that anyone would want to be near him for any reason, being as I had the heebie-jeebies just talking to him. But you never know. Skirts are weird.

Suddenly he became alarmed. He looked around, panicked. The soft, sloughy flesh of his neck made him look like a fish on a tripod. "There aren't twists in the bar, are there?"

"No, sir," the big gorilla said in his best approximation of a soothing voice.

The Old Man relaxed into a wad. "Don't like 'em near me. They're all like my mama. But what that whore didn't know when she buttonhooked me was I was one of us and not one of them. The doctor who scraped me out sealed me in a formaldehyde jar and kept me on his shelf. That's where I learned English, all that good stuff. That was all… damn, twenty years ago."

"He's the oldest of us," the bartender said.

I looked from the giant servant to the tiny master. The Old Man tipped over the martini glass and gave himself a little shower, most of which went into his vestigial mouth.

"Why? How long do we usually last?" I asked.

"If you're not kept in a pickle jar?" the Old Man said. "Five years. Ten tops. But, as I always say, the brain can last longer."

"Is that what you keep down there?" I pointed with my chin toward the trapdoor leading to the sub-basement. "Pickled brains?"

"How's about you get to the point?" the Old Man said. "I'm getting a little pruny out here in the air." He grabbed his forehead with his flippery little arms. He looked more than a little pruny. He looked as if he was about ready to collapse.

"Uh, can I have a drink?" I said.

The Old Man looked me up and down. "I like your spunk."

"I am full of spunk," I agreed.

"But too much of a good thing can be bad, Sonny Jim."

"I will watch my spunk output, sir."

"Give him a daiquiri," the Old Man said, "then a boot in the ass when he's done. Now get me back in my jar."

And that was that. Luckily, Miss Claudia came in eventually. God damn, did I ever nurse that daiquiri. The gorilla knew it too, but he didn't call me on it. She was so overjoyed to see me—and she gave me a stack of money—I felt as if I was on cloud nine. I wanted to head out and get my old room at the Three Rivers.

A hand stopped me. "You did good."

It was Lazar. We sat down.

"I was beginning to think you weren't real," I said.

"In which sense?"

"So I learned you're not the owner."

He perked up. "Ah, so you met the boss. Well, I never claimed I owned the joint. I'm nothing more than a salesman."

"You mean a pusher."

He shrugged. "Names." As if that explained everything.

"How is it that a fetus makes a fortune, anyway?"

"Same way the rest of us do, I imagine," Lazar said, avoiding the question. "Are you starting to get a grip on your situation, I wonder."

I couldn't be sure whether that was a question or not. Didn't sound like one, but it did. Hard to say. "Well, I got a few bucks in my pocket."

"Yes, I heard. Claudia is quite taken with you. She's singing your praises to everyone who'll listen."

I looked around. It sort of looked like that. She was sure pointing at me a lot.

Lazar—or whatever his name was—leaned in toward me. "We are a very small community, Jones. Or more accurately, I should say a close-knit community. It doesn't take long to make or break a reputation. Helping Claudia Winston is a reputation maker."

"You mean Baumer? Maybe you were behind it, huh?" I said. "You told me to come here, but I haven't seen you in days. Just so happened when I got here that she's here and crying."

"You can't lead a horse to water, and you certainly can't make him drink. But I'm a bit of a junior gambler, Jones, and there's one thing I do know. You can always arrange things in your favor. What comes out of it, though…" He shrugged.

I nodded and stood up. "Well, thanks for everything. I'm going to go check into the flophouse, I think." I made a circle over my right eye with my thumb and forefinger and tipped it forward in a salute. "Be seeing you."

I was halfway to the door when he said, "Why not stay here?"

I turned back. "In the bar?"

"Not in the bar," he said. "Above it."

He tossed a keyring on the table. One key was marked "FRONT DOOR," one was marked "FENCE'S CAGE," and one was marked "OFFICE." I noticed there wasn't one for the bar. There was a difference between being trusting and being crazy.

"Isn't that where Baldy lives?"

He stared at me for a moment, his face unchanging though his pause suggested he was thinking deeply. "Oh, Homer. No, he doesn't live here. I did, but I've moved recently. Maybe you'd like the room."

"I don't got that much money," I said.

Lazar looked around the room. "You might, given time. You know how the police treat us as pariahs. You could be a policeman of sorts, for a price."

"You mean a private dick," I said.

"That I do," Lazar said. "I'll cover your rent. I'll even keep you in booze, to an extent. Well, let's say I'll give you a small working discount." He placed a small bottle of Crow on the table.

I'd been feeling a little fuzzy lately. Not that fuzzy, though. "What's the catch?"

"Ah, yes, the catch." Lazar nodded. "You just have to do a few things for me. Otherwise, any cases that come your way, take them."

"Braineater Jones, P.I.," I said.

Lazar raised a glass. "Shall we drink to it?"

NOVEMBER 5, 1934

The apartment had apparently been Lazar's workspace. It had a desk, a foldout bed, and not much else. It suited me just fine after a couple nights in the Three Rivers and out on the streets.

I glanced out the window. All I had a view of was the grimy street below. It made me, weirdly, long for the garret above Ed and Joey's place. I shut the window, then put my hand through the holes where glass should have been. It's a good thing the cold didn't bother me.

I spotted a deck of cards snapped in a rattrap. Either the rat had been smart enough to use a decoy or someone had carelessly tossed the deck on the floor. I carefully extricated the deck, then flipped the cards out one by one onto my desk. There weren't quite forty, not even enough for a proper game of Patience.

So I practiced tossing playing cards into my cap. Not much else to do. I meant to lay low for a while and settle into my new life. Then I would get into the business of who killed me and all the other mysteries that had been cropping up since. But for a while, I simply wanted to relax in a little peace and quiet in a place I could call my own.

I went down to what passed for a consignment store in the Mat and bought a suit that fit and even a trench coat. At Hallowed Grounds, I found a few bullets for Gnaghi's boomstick—well, I guess it's my boomstick now—and arranged to have Lazar send up a few bottles of mostly Crow to my room. After that, I was just about tapped. But what else does a man need?

So later that morning, I sat, still not playing Patience, tossing cards into my brand new fedora. I should have thought to buy a new deck while I was out. My solitude was inevitably interrupted.

It was a dame of course. She had legs up to her eyeballs. Literally. She was carrying a pair of legs, one over either shoulder. I shook my head in wonder, but it wasn't even the cockamamiest thing I'd seen in the last twenty-four hours. "Pawn shop's downstairs. Not sure if they take drumsticks but never hurts to check."

"I'm here for you, Mr. Jones," she said.

"Well, if you think my first name's 'mister,' you ain't here for me," I said. "That was my father's first name." I wish I knew what my father's first name really was. V-V-Victrola?

She threw the getaway sticks down on my desk. The toes were clenching, and the feet kept arching and flattening. Like the girls in Hat Scratch Fever, someone was still controlling the limbs remotely.

Sighing, I put the "deck" of cards down. "These aren't yours. These aren't even a dame's."

"No kidding, Sherlock," she said. "Maybe I came to the wrong place."

"No, no," I said. "Calm down. Tell me what your issue is."

Her name was Kumaree Tong. I might've spelled that wrong. You know how I am with foreign words. She's a real spicy meatball, though. Or bowl of borscht. Or whatever.

In the course of our conversation, I never became quite sure how she had bought the farm. She didn't show evidence of anything. Maybe an aneurysm or something that left no visible marks. Cause other than being dead, her body was about a cock's hair shy of perfect. Gorgeous dame.

I didn't pay much attention to what she was saying. Gist was, her brother had been flopping on her couch. Tough times for everybody I guess, especially when you don't have a rich patron like Lazar. Lucky me.

"One morning I came out of the shower," she said.

She said it slowly enough that I pictured her dripping wet, wearing nothing but her hair up in a towel. That's neither here nor there, but it seemed relevant to my line of thinking.

Anyway, what was I talking about? Oh, yeah, the twist in my office.

"My brother was gone," she said, putting a handkerchief over her face but thankfully not boo-hoo-hooing all the damn time like Claudia Winston.

I nodded sympathetically and poured her some Crow. It obviously wasn't to her taste, but I had already finished the only bottle of Bacardi I had asked Lazar to forward me for variety's sake. Well, she'd make do. A free drink's a nice enough gesture in that burg. "Into thin air?" I asked.

"Well, no. He wasn't totally gone. Half of him was still flopping on the couch."

I glanced at the extra set of legs she had walked into my office. They were lying on my foldout, ripped apart at the seams and still kicking, but minus one owner. I rubbed my temples. It was more an affectation than anything else. "You think he's dead? Well, you know what I mean. Double dog dead."

She gave me a funny look. I hoped it signaled arousal. Probably not, though.

"You mean somebody put him down?" she asked.

"Yeah, that too," I said.

"How long have you been one of us?"

"Long enough." Six days was the real answer to that question. Maybe I don't talk all the jive lingo, but hey, who makes up jive lingo anyway? We do, that's who. So maybe my words'll catch on, and then everybody else will look stupid instead of me.

She started collecting her dead brother's legs. "This was a mistake. I need someone with more experience. Any experience, really. If he was dead, his legs wouldn't still be kicking."

She shook one of her brother's hairy limbs at me. They were definitely still moving. Oof. I really had a lot to learn. The hookers at Hat Scratch had controlled different parts once they were stacked up. Maybe it was like keying a lock. Once a limb was hooked to their brain, they were still connected to it. At least until somebody else keyed themselves to it.

Her brother was still controlling his legs remotely, kicking to let her know he was still alive. Undead. Whatever. It was a signal, a distress call, an S-O-S by L-E-G.

Damn it. She was halfway out the door before I had worked through all that. I called after her in a desperate attempt to keep her from going, no matter how much I was enjoying watching her leave. "You don't know what I did before I was turned."

Ooh, threw out a fancy deadhead word for you there, didn't I?

That seemed to calm her down. Of course, I didn't know what I did before I was "turned" either. "Well, that's true," she said. "What did you do?"

I shrugged. "What I'm doing now."

Sitting. Probably technically accurate. Talking to dames. Probably also true at some point.

"Well, will you take the case?" she said.

"Let me look at my schedule." I picked up this notebook and flipped through it a few pages. "I'll see if I can squeeze you in, but I need to know a little more. You know anybody who might like your brother…?" I made the choppy-choppy finger across my neck.

"No," she said. "Nothing like that. He was a pussycat."

Yeah, I'll bet. "What did he do?"

"Well, he used to work in the textile factory," she said. "But as he started to, you know, decompose, he had to get work in the fish market."

"A lot of our kind work there." Just a guess.

She nodded though, confirming my suspicion. "Lately he wasn't even getting regular work. You know how it is in the breadlines. When they catch our scent, well, you know."

"Run us off," I guessed again. "Or worse." Funny how on the nose I could be after six days. I guess human nature never changes, only targets do. Or whatever.

"So his name was Tong, too?" I asked.

She shook her head. "Oh, no, he wasn't my brother in life. He was my, you know, morgue mate."

Buried at the same time? Woke up at the same time? I'd ask Lazar later to be sure. "I see." I drew a cartoon owl as a way of pretending to take notes. "And what was *his* name?"

"Skaron," she said. "Ivan Skaron."

"Anywhere else Ivan spent time?"

"No," she said, then corrected herself. "Actually, he went to the library a lot. Researching our condition."

I raised my eyebrow. If there were books about our kind, that was something I'd have to look into. "What'd he find out?"

"Nothing we didn't already know," she said.

I shrugged. Damn, but that dame played her cards close to the vest. I learned a little something about our physiology after she left. We sleep, we drink. Other things still happen.

I went to the fish market. Having been around our kind for a couple of days, I could finally identify one of us by smell. I could at least tell our kind from theirs, though some of both wore eau de cologne and perfume that complicated the matter. Not to mention all the fish in the air complicated matters, but that was probably the reason our kind liked hanging out down there.

As I had suspected, a lot of our kind were at the wharf. Good place to remember when dead ends start cropping up in future investigations. "Dead" ends. Ha!

I wandered for a bit, smelling at folks and trying not to be too obvious about it. I finally spotted a cat I was 100% sure on; he wasn't wearing flower water or anything. Black rubber covered him head-to-toe. Massive galoshes poked out under his slicker and a hood more than covered his face. Sure, it was November on the high seas and all, but the sun was burning bright and not another longshoreman was bundled up as tight. I followed him until he turned down an alleyway between row upon row of packing crates.

Instead of a kewpie doll, that lucky contestant earned my hands around his scruff. I threw him against the pine wall the crates made. "You got a bullet hole under there?" I hissed into the empty void of his hood. "Or maybe a Gloucester smile from ear to ear?"

There was abject silence and a distinct dearth of motion for about as long as it takes for the world to end. He wasn't breathing; that was obvious. He could've been eyeballing me, but I wouldn't have known either way.

A nondescript voice finally wafted out of the blackness where his face should've been. "I don't know what you're talking about."

He tried to wriggle out of my grasp, so I took the opportunity to bounce him off the crates again. "Oh, come on," I said, leaning in a little too close for either of us to be comfortable. "You show me yours, and I'll show you mine."

I let go of him and, with one finger, tugged my blouse open and showed him my mortal wound.

"Whaddaya want?" he asked finally.

"Looking for someone," I said, "a day laborer."

"There's a million of them on the docks," the shrouded man said, pointing back to the mouth of the alleyway. "No need to turn queer on me in an alleyway. Some'll work for five bucks a day."

"I'm looking for a particular one," I said. "Ivan Skaron."

That's when I caught a brick to the gut. I looked around. I had been so focused on accosting the poor longshoreman that I hadn't noticed his friends had crept up to defend him. Our kind definitely sticks together, on the docks the same as in the Mat.

Some of them were swaddled head to toe, like my good friend the Grim Reaper. Others were a little more passing, but only just. A few definitely had the pale, sickly skin of the recently drowned. Others were bloated and waterlogged as if, whatever their original cause of death, they had been fished out of the bay a few days or maybe weeks later. One had an industrial-sized hook through his chest, sawed off at either end and just barely recognizably curved.

The next blow fell from behind and took the knees out from under me.

"You think I remember one day laborer out of thousands?" the Grim Reaper asked, laughing. "You must be dumber than a Portuguese man-o-war."

"Yeah, I get that a lot," I said. One of the longshoremen hoisted a crowbar over my head. I remember thinking that that was the end.

The Grim Reaper held up his hand though. "Wait, he's one of us. Even if he is sticking what's left of his nose where it doesn't belong."

"Thanks," I said.

He looked me over. I wasn't sure beneath all that rubber, but it was either that or he was just standing there. At least he didn't say, "Don't thank me yet."

"You new?"

I nodded. "Pretty new."

"We stick together."

He gestured at all of his friends with a back-and-forth motion of his left thumb, but I guess he meant all of our kind, even including a dummy like me.

"That's why you get to walk away. But you come around asking questions, you don't act like you're part of the community, maybe we make an exception for you next time. Capiche?"

I nodded.

"Put the boots to him medium-style," he concluded.

They proceeded to beat the ever-living fish heads out of me, but I gathered not as badly as they might have.

I went home smelling like fish. Homer didn't like it. His cat loved it, though.

NOVEMBER 6, 1934

Only one lead left in the case of the fabulously swinging chickadee's missing brother or whoever.

Welcome to the Mat Public Library. What a steaming garbage pile. I've seen more variety of books in piles outside Nuremberg.

Wait. Have I? Or is that just an expression? Seems like an odd turn of phrase.

Librarian was your usual type. Gray as a ghost, hair up in Manchukuo-style chopsticks or some such, glasses as thick as my thumb. I would've laid it on a little thicker, but I knew how gray and sallow my skin was getting. I wasn't much to look at. Still passing, but not much to look at. My gums were black enough to scare breathers, and when I wasn't paying attention, my neck sometimes twisted at awkward angles. That wasn't too bad in the grand scheme of things. Some of our kind ended up at the point where they couldn't even go out anymore, like the Old Man. Though, to be fair, he had never been at a point where he could go out.

"Ma'am," I said, tipping my hat.

"You might take your hat off when you're indoors, young man," she said.

Right, right. I took it off.

I hope my hair isn't getting too thin and stringy. I might have to get a little Brylcreem. Actually, I might have to get a rug if things keep going the way they seem to be going. How do Kumaree and Lazar look so good when I look so bad after only a week?

I cleared my throat. "Ah, listen, ma'am, a friend of mine used to come here. Ivan Skaron. Maybe you remember him?"

She stared daggers at me.

"Anyway," I went on, "I was wondering—Ivan is such a bookworm—I was trying to figure out what to buy him for his birthday. Coming up, you see. Any chance I could see what the last few books he checked out were?"

As it turned out, I didn't really have to turn on the patented Braineater charm. She didn't give a shit. She handed me his old record. After a few minutes of figuring out that fancy wooden card catalog, I sat down with a stack of books that probably left that little rattrap library looking bare.

Liber Mortis, *Malleus Maleficarum*, *De Vermis Mysteriis*, *Naturom Demonto.* Are any of these in English? Even a play about some guy wearing yellow. Who knows?

Funny how little there is describing our condition. Ivan scoured those books. Notes in the margins and everything. A lot about wampyr. That's not really us, though. Those guys go back to their graves and drink blood to stay alive. Closest bit was maybe about a revenant, who only has to drink a bit of blood. They say Jesus turned his blood into wine. We have to drink liquor. I might be stretching it there.

Ivan highlighted this passage everywhere it appeared:

That is not dead which can eternal lie,
And with strange aeons even death may die.

Interesting.

There's a lot of other weird stuff that Ivan seemed really into. Voodoo witch doctors down in the island of Haiti. I guess they create beasties called jumbee. Never heard anyone in our community call it that before, but Ivan kept circling the word and highlighting it. That was where his research was leading him. Crazy bastard.

I wonder if there are any voodoo witch doctors in the city. The sour librarian, of course, refused to help, but luckily a helpful stewbum didn't mind pointing me toward Little Haiti in exchange for a zozzle of Crow.

Little Haiti smells, if anything, worse than the fish market. Even in my short existence, I had learned there are parts of the Mat people go to and parts that people don't go to, even one of us who doesn't care about getting aced. Little Haiti was one of those places people don't go to no matter what. If you're on fire running down the street, and no one will douse you, you take pains to avoid that ghetto.

I felt as if I had crossed an invisible line and every eye in the slum was on me. Oh, well, what would they do, kill me? Stay away from the salt and the bread; that's what Ivan's books told me. Of course, I suppose they could fill a shotgun shell with rock salt. If that even kills us.

A beggar held out his hands at me. I think he said, "Sergeant?"

"What do you want?" I said.

He rubbed his fingers together. I pulled out a coin. That seemed to excite him quite a bit. "Okay," I said, "but tell me where I can find a witch doctor. You understand me?"

He did not. I checked my notes.

"Bokor," I said. "Where's the bokor?"

"Bokor?"

He seemed to understand that. I waved the coin at him. He shook his head. I pulled out another. He shook his head, waved his arms, and took off running as if he had never run before in his life.

"Shit," I said.

"Murder," somebody behind me said.

I turned. "What about murder?"

It was a woman. Pretty bird. Would've been more striking if she weren't so damn skinny. Her ribs damn near poked through her shirt. I wanted to buy her a Polish sausage right then and there, but I don't suppose the cart guy comes down that way.

"Not murder," she said. "That's shit. You don't speak French?"

"I don't speak jibber-jabber, if that's what you mean," I said. "That sure don't sound like no damn froggy talk I ever heard."

"You are an ignorant man," she said.

"Yeah, I never said otherwise."

"You come into our neighborhood. You disrespect us. You ask about things you don't understand."

"Listen, girlie," I said, "I don't care much about any of that stuff. As you can tell. I'm trying to help somebody, save somebody's life—erm, well, limbs, anyway. If there's a voodoo priest here who can help me, great. If Lucifer himself will help me, great. I'm just trying to do my job."

She stared at me. I assumed there was a little bit of a language barrier between us, but she couldn't possibly have missed my gist.

"I'll take you to the mambo," she said.

"That's the good witch," I said. I had read it in some of Ivan's books. The girl nodded. "What about the bokor?"

"You"—she paused—"you would do well not to ask about that."

She led me up the street, past the newspaper blowing by like tumbleweeds and the derelicts splayed out in the middle of the road where no jalopies went by. There were car parts and former cars set on concrete blocks, but no functional people movers came to that part of the Mat. I didn't think things could get bleaker than they were in the deadhead section.

She led me into a tenement building with a tar paper roof and garbage piled up against it that the denizens had simply dumped out their windows. Inside, some folks were sleeping in the halls. Others were doing more than sleeping. She pointed me up a stairwell. I went first. That was my first mistake. I stomped through one of the stairs with even my light step.

The door was smeared with–well, I don't want to know what it was smeared with. But there were symbols, words. Some of the smeared I-hope-it-wasn't-excrement looked like a chicken skull. Another mark was a snake eating its own tail. Curious. I probably stood there rubbing my chin too long because the girl poked me. So I knocked.

"Entrée," somebody inside said.

"I don't know," I said. "Chicken. Or beef. Probably better go with the beef."

I hadn't eaten in a week. Literally. I hadn't even stopped to think about it.

12. Can we eat? Is alcohol enough?

"Come in," the voice of some old lady inside said. Then she said some words in mashed up pidgin that I couldn't figure out word for word but didn't seem any damn good.

I opened the door real slow, partially because it seemed covered with some kind of goopy grease. The inside of the apartment resembled a caveman's circle, leastways what I figured a caveman's circle looked like. Gutted animals lay strewn about haphazardly. They used the corners of the room for jakes, and that wasn't jake. She had a fire going in the center of the apartment. Wasn't too cold out either, not even for November.

Shadows danced along the walls in a million funny and scary shapes. I would say "arcane," but I never was 100% sure what that word meant. It was almost like a shadow puppet show. I wondered if she set up the room special that way.

She tossed something, dice maybe, onto a rabbit pelt. It seemed to have been freshly skinned, although what do I know about stuff like that? The old lady was bundled up in a hundred layers of scarves and pearls.

"Welcome to Port-au-Pauper," she said.

I didn't get it. "I don't get it."

"You come for answers," the old lady said. Her voice sounded like a rock dragged across a chalkboard, and her face was covered.

I didn't much like talking to someone I couldn't see, and for good reason. "Well, I didn't come looking for questions."

"What do you want to know?" she said.

"Looking for a guy," I said.

The old lady laughed, and it was awful. Like listening to the lost souls on the *Lusitania* screaming. "You like men. Cities are funny places."

"I'm not a fairy," I said, then I stopped to think about it. "Well, I don't know. Maybe I was. Who knows?"

"You don't know?"

"No, look, it doesn't matter," I said. "I'm looking for a particular guy. Business reasons. Name's Ivan Skaron."

She shook the dice. I guess they were chicken bones, based on what she said next. Maybe the chicken part was optimistic.

"You want the bones to show you? Five dollars, I answer any question."

I waved my hand. "No, I'm not here for fortune-telling. This Ivan cat was interested in voodoo. I think he might've come here looking for a bokor, and you're the furthest I've gotten so far."

The old lady seemed really scared. She reared up like a beached whale. "I am a mambo. Clean Vodun. You had best stay away from the dark arts."

"Yeah, that's what everybody keeps telling me," I said, jerking a finger behind me to indicate the girl. "But it ain't getting me any closer to finding my client."

The old crone gestured for me to come toward the fire. "Come closer, then. Let's see if we can find your wayward friend."

As soon as I took a step, I regretted it. A shot rang out, and my trench coat was perforated. I had a new hole, an inch below my unbirth hole. Son of a bitch. Couldn't have just shot me in the same place twice, huh? I whirled around.

The younger girl, the one who was a dead ringer for a skeleton, stood there with a Colt .45 and an expression like I had just stepped on her grave. The gun was already shaking. "What? How?"

"And here I was thinking you were nice," I said. "Guess that from cradle to grave you can't trust a twist."

Then suddenly my arms were up in the air like Jesus on the cross. I tried to fight, but there was nothing there to grapple with. No gorilla holding me back, no rope, no nothing. I simply couldn't move.

The old lady talked. Only, she wasn't a lady. "Don't be foolish, Francoise," "she" said. "You can't hurt this one like that."

I turned my head as far as I could. The "old lady" was shedding layers. When he was down to nothing but a loincloth, I saw he was as skinny as the girl. I should've known better.

"You need one of these," he said. The witch doctor waved a funny little sack doll in Francoise's face. The doll's arms were tied up in the air. Supposed to be me?

Funny, if I wasn't already a walking corpse, I wouldn't have believed in magic. Didn't, really, even after all that. "You must be the bokor."

"Delamort," he said, tipping his lidless top hat in my direction. "And what are you? More and more of you keep coming, but you're not mine."

"I was sort of hoping you could tell me that," I said.

"Well, let's talk somewhere more comfortable," Delamort said. He made the doll's legs move, and sure enough, against my will, I walked into an adjoining room. At least three or four deadheads were in there. A couple were down to heads in jars, so I didn't know if they still counted as our kind. Sure enough, one of them was missing nothing but his legs.

"Hey, how's it going, Ivan?" I said.

"Who are you?"

"I'm here to rescue you. Your sister hired me."

"How's it going?" he asked.

"Not well."

Delamort made me sit. If the main room was like a caveman's hut, that place was like a mad scientist's laboratory. All the deadheads were in varying states of experimentation. I assumed the ones down to their heads had been there the longest.

"So you know each other," Delamort said, pointing between us.

"I've never met him before," Ivan protested.

"Somebody hired me to find him," I said.

"Kumaree!" A wave of relief washed over Ivan's face. "So she got all my messages?"

Uh… "Um… what messages?"

"In Morse code," he said. "With my toes. Don't tell me you didn't notice."

So that was what all the random twitching was. The old bokor looked as if he wasn't buying it, but he decided to table the discussion. He picked up a doll that was missing its legs, like a gingerbread man bitten in half on Christmas morning. Real quick, like it was nothing, Delamort sewed over the doll's mouth. I looked over. Ivan couldn't talk, as if his jaws were glued shut.

"Son of a bitch," I said.

"I'll do it to you, too," Delamort said. "Be… what's the word? Civil."

"Civil?" I said. "Sure. I can be civil with a kidnapper and a killer."

Delamort laughed. Turned out the creepy old lady's laugh was real enough. I shivered a little bit. Like I said before, funny how much physical stuff is a matter of habit.

"You cannot kill what is already dead," the bokor said.

"Yeah, but you can blow it to chunky kibbles," I said.

"Dead is dead," he said.

"'That is not dead which can eternal lie,'" I said. "Ah, hell, I forget the rest."

Ivan stared at me, jerking his head as if he wanted to say something. I guess Delamort didn't notice.

"You've been studying," he said, "like him."

"Are we jumbees?" I asked.

Delamort shrugged. He stood and walked around the room, looking at the other deadheads as though they were wax statues in a gallery. I've got to admit, he had a good point, and I might agree if I wasn't one of them.

How can you feel bad for a walking corpse? How natural is it to be one? But then, how natural is chocolate milk for that matter? Doesn't make it bad.

"It's a word you could use," the bokor said. "But you are unlike any jumbee I have ever met… or made. Walking dead, yes, but your minds are intact. If I could harness that power somehow, who knows what I could do?"

Sorry, I know I ought to keep writing, but the pen is shaking so much I can't even read my own words anymore. I must be alcohol deprived and exhausted. Gonna grab a shot of Crow and go back to bed for a while. I'll finish the rest of the story tomorrow.

NOVEMBER 7, 1934

Didn't do anything much yesterday. I'm still recuperating from my ordeal. I went to the bar, then back to the room. I just realized I never finished my last entry. Where was I? Oh, yes, finishing up the story about that S.O.B. Delamort.

Anyway, Delamort had me locked up or paralyzed or whatever it was in his little dungeon of doom and gloom and torture. Ivan, the client, was there too, as was a whole stack of other deadheads I wasn't getting paid to help. I'd be damned if I wasn't going to help them anyway.

"Hey, listen, Delamort," I said, "I'm dying for a square. As long as you've got my arms like this, you think you could do me a favor?"

He stared at me as though I was talking some hippidy-bippidy mumbo-jumbo.

"Cigarette?" I simplified.

"Oh," the bokor said, nodding. "Yes."

He reached into my jacket pocket and pulled out the pack of Luckies and my lighter. He stopped and stared. "Luckies," he whispered as though it was the name of Jehovah or something.

"Yeah," I said. "How about lighting me up?"

"These"—he flashed my pack in my face—"are for the baron." He left the room. Crazy Haitians.

I yelled after him, "Yeah, well, I hope the damned baron brings them back!"

"Hey, shut up, bigmouth!"

I looked up. One of the heads on a shelf was speaking to me. "What?" I said.

"He's out of the room, stupid ass," the head said. "Now's our chance."

"You can talk," I said.

"Well, sure." He was struggling like a lunatic to throw himself off the shelf. "He never sewed my mouth shut."

"What are you doing?"

"Why don't you take my advice and shut up for once in your misbegotten death and look!"

I looked down. Sure enough, Delamort had run off so fast with my squares, he had left one of the little fetish dolls on the ground. Mine, maybe? The head on the shelf was rumbling forward like a motorboat, shaking and rocking and rolling for all he was worth. Thankfully he was one of the ones who hadn't been stuffed into a jar yet.

The other heads on the shelf started jumping—if that's what you can call it—up and down to help move their buddy. Delamort, meanwhile, was chanting or something in the other room. I was keeping my trademark wit in check so as not to call attention to us, but it was hard to bite my tongue. Then I started to smell some of that cool, soothing Lucky smoke.

"Son of a bastard," I muttered.

Then the chanting stopped. Shit. The head fell on the floor. Double shit. Loud noise. That's no good.

"Come on," I said. "Let's go."

"I'm trying!" the head said. The head still had all of his neck and what looked like a chunk of his torso scooped out from between his collar bones. It sure hadn't been a clean cut like with a guillotine. It looked more like someone had chiseled it out with a machete.

Between his neck and his head, he rolled back and forth from one ear to the other. The bottom chunk of his neck twisted up like a kid twisting up the chains of a swingset, then slowly reversed. He kept rolling, trying to pick up momentum. The doll was maddeningly close, but he couldn't get to it without any limbs. I heard some froggy talk from the other room, and it wasn't no chanting.

"Francoise!"

That word I could identify, then some more shouting. "Shit!" I said. "Shit shit shit."

"Not… helping…" The little head case was rolling for all his worth. I was in one of those panicky moods where I could've pissed my pants, except I haven't pissed since I was unborn.

Funny. That's in spite of all the extra booze I've been drinking. Where does it all go? Evaporates, I suppose.

Then the starving girl was in the doorway. Damn. "What's going on?"

Oh shit. Some luck. At least she didn't look down and notice the head rolling around on the floor.

I didn't look down either. "You got me, chickadee. What are you looking for?"

"What's going on in here?" She waved her gun around again as if it mattered.

Funny what creatures of habit we are. What does it take to break us of our habits?

"Nobody here but us chickens," I said.

Then she screamed. What, like she never saw a decapitated head rolling on the floor, tangling with a fetish doll using only its teeth? Pff.

"Uncle Delamort!" she yelled, only it sounded more like "ankle." I just kind of guessed she meant "uncle."

Delamort came running. He wore his top hat and his face was painted white. Weird.

"Come on, come on, come on!" I said.

"What's the matter, darling?" he said, clutching his niece to his bosom.

The deadhead finally gnawed through my doll's bonds. I jumped up and, in one swift motion, grabbed the head, doll and all. Francoise fired off a round, missing my head by a hair's breadth.

"Watch the head!" the head in my hand said.

Another shot rang out.

"Put the head down," Delamort said.

"Why should I, shaman?" I said. "You got something to offer me?"

"Let's talk about this. You want to know more about yourself. I can tell you more."

"Yeah, somehow I'm not so interested in what you have to say anymore," I said. I took two tentative half steps backward.

"Kill them," the bokor said, tapping his niece's shoulder.

"I'll be back for you, Ivan," I said, "I'll be back for all of you." Then I went out the window.

NOVEMBER 8, 1934

I forgot I stopped halfway through the entry yesterday. I guess I did that the day before, too. Across the street from Hallowed Grounds there's an old abandoned haberdashery some of our kind have shacked up in. They're loons, mostly, the kind who can't handle the change but don't want to be put down, either. The Old Man sends them a case of fortified wine every week or so to keep them from making the rest of us look bad.

One of the crazies fell asleep with a Lucky in his mouth, and the next thing you know, the whole building was toasted. Ganesh has a professional fire company, but they just laughed at me when I called. I guess they're really only for the Altstadt. So those of our kind who were around and willing started up a chain of buckets to try to put out all the boxes of outdated hats and moth-eaten overcloaks.

I guess the bucket brigade was a success. The only one of our kind who was put down was the one who started the fire. The rest of the crazies reoccupied the burnt-out haberdashery like nothing had happened, and the Old Man sent them two crates of E. & J. Gallo and called it a kindness.

But where did I leave off before the fire started? Oh, yeah, my three-story vertical express train with the end of the line being Ground Central Station. I remember that plummet like it was yesterday.

So I'm walking down the streets of Port-au-Pauper (meaning?) with a head in my hands. All the Haitians were looking at me, but I just shrugged if one of them caught my eye.

"Thanks for getting me out of there," the head said.

"Well, yeah, anytime," I said. "I feel like kind of a screw-up though. You're not exactly my client, and there were others back there, too."

"Well, what are we going to do about it?"

"'We'?" I said. "You are going to sit on my desk. Maybe in a fishbowl. I'm going to have to figure something out."

"You're a jerkoff," he said.

"You're a head."

"I'm a person."

"Are you?" I asked. "No, I really want to know. Am I? Are any of us? What's the definition of a person? I'm nothing but a walking corpse."

He made a noise like a big wad of oatmeal getting sucked up a puckered anus. "I hate philosophy."

We walked on in silence for a while. I guess I must have started to swing him, because he asked me to stop. We got back to Hallowed Grounds eventually. I slapped the head down on my desk and leaned back in my chair to take a swig out of my flask.

"You want a taste?"

"Yeah," he said. I gave him a little tipple. "That's enough," he said. "I was a teetotaler in life. Guess I don't drink a whole lot now, either."

"Well, you're nothing but a head," I said. "Not as much to preserve."

"Get bent," he said.

I sat there for a while taking sips. I must've looked pretty pathetic. A has-been detective who never was. Solved one case and then screwed up royally when it really counted.

"What's your name anyway?" the head said.

"I don't know," I said.

"Says 'Braineater Jones' on your door."

"Huh?" I took a look. Sure enough, Lazar had painted it on. More likely he had paid somebody to paint it on. Whichever. "That's just what they call me."

"Mine's Alcibé," he said.

"I didn't ask for your life story!" I shouted and turned the head around so he was facing away from me.

After a while I turned him back. "Spanish?"

"Honduran," he said.

"Oh," I said. I didn't know what that meant. I waited a while before speaking. "What were they doing in there anyway, Alcibé?"

"Anything and everything," he said. "I was whole before I got in there."

"Yeah," I said, "must be rough."

"I'm dealing with it," he said. "So what are we going to do about the others?"

I thought about it. Not much I could do. I should've called the police. Fat lot of good that would've done. But then, I guess I was supposed to be the new sheriff in town.

"You know what they used to do in Wyoming in the old days?" he asked.

I shrugged. I couldn't remember what had happened last week, let alone what some folks had done in Wyoming in the old days.

"Something like this happens," Alcibé said, "and there's no law, except the law of your own hands and your own community. They'd bring together a posse and go lynch that son of a bitch."

I stared at the head on my table. "I don't know about that. I don't see a whole lot of get-up-and-go from our kind. They mostly just try to stay out of trouble."

"You think after you tell them what you found in there, they'll still act that way?"

I grinned. I must've looked like the Cheshire cat. Or else some kind of horrible beast flashing its teeth. "Maybe if you tell them."

I walked into Hallowed Grounds and slammed Alcibé down on the bar. The room wasn't crowded or anything, but everyone stopped to look at us.

"This is Alcibé," I said.

"Who are you?" some heckler said.

I slammed my fist down on the bar.

While drowning my maggots and conditioning my hair in the tub yesterday, it occurred to me that I could have said, "I'm your worst nightmare" or even "I'm the guy with the gun." Nothing clever occurred to me at that point, though. Come to think of it, I could've even said, "I'm the guy carrying around the head." Ah, damn it.

"We've come from Little Haiti," Alcibé offered. "I've been there for three weeks. I was whole when I got there."

Folks started to get up and gather around. Even the gorilla bartender stopped rubbing the little white spot into his countertop.

I think the same heckler asked, "What happened?"

"Some Haitian Frankenstein has taken an interest in our kind," Alcibé said. "He's been running experiments."

The gorilla behind the counter said, "Somebody oughta do something about that."

Alcibé tried to look up. He clenched his eyes shut and even tried to rock around on his neck stump. I saw he was having trouble, so I grabbed him and turned him to face the bartender.

When he was positioned properly, he said, "My thoughts exactly."

An hour later, we were walking down Keene Avenue, about thirty strong. Even the gangsters and derelicts scattered. I wondered if it was the first time we'd come together as a community. Intellectually, I knew it couldn't be, but I wished it was. I had a gun. No doubt a few others did. Most, though, were carrying cudgels and bricks and likewise.

Little Haiti was like a ghost town when we got there. I had taped Alcibé on my shoulder like a parrot, so some of the breathers were probably scared of the two-headed corpse. I pointed at the bokor's building.

"There," Alcibé said.

I wanted to go in charging, gun blazing, but I wasn't even the first one up the steps. A girl who had probably been no more than eight when she turned—but looked to be toward the end of her unlife—was the first through the door. Lamely I followed her, and the rest of the crowd behind me was pushing so hard up the steps, I barely had to move my own feet.

When we got to the apartment, Francoise was cooking a pot of something unsavory on the naked fire in the center of the room. I thought to tell my group maybe she didn't deserve to be torn limb from limb, but the crowd was out for breather blood. The little/old girl leapt on Francoise and clenched her leg like a parasite.

The bokor's niece hopped on one leg, trying to shake off the girl with the rapidity of a hummingbird. I wanted to step in and separate the two, but before I could, a brick flew through the air and smashed Francoise's face in. Maybe I didn't want to separate them that bad after all. The newly dead girl's teeth littered the floor like kernels of corn under a scarecrow.

Delamort was sequestered in a closet chanting a cadence, haunting and eerie. I tried to put my shoulder into the door, but that made Alcibé yelp in pain.

"Watch it, you buffoon!" the head shrieked. "You almost staved my skull in."

Turn the other cheek. That's what I should have said to him. Ah, well.

Unable to come up with a pithy remark, I slapped him for cutting wise. I turned my other shoulder to the closet door, but after one or two mostly useless slams against it, I felt a massive hand descend on my headless shoulder like a dark shroud.

"Let me," the big gorilla said.

I turned to see the whole angry crowd had stopped whaling on Francoise's corpse and were watching my futile efforts with the door. I slid aside while gesturing to the door, like the lost Marx brother. The bartender smashed the door to splinters in one blow with the heel of his fist.

When the door burst open, we saw Delamort trying to pull on his old lady disguise while furiously jabbing needles into a hundred fetish dolls at once. I guess it's hard for someone to split their concentration like that. The bartender palmed Delamort's head with one hand and tossed him out into the round. I wouldn't say I shed any crocodile tears for Delamort exactly, but it was tough watching the gang of deadheads rip him up like confetti.

As I watched the crowd satisfy its bloodlust, I realized the big gorilla was not watching them, nor was he joining in. His eyes were squarely on me. I didn't turn to catch his gaze because I had an ominous feeling in the pit of my empty, non-stomaching stomach that if I turned away from the blood orgy and caught his gaze, he would've caved in my skull like it was nothing. Creepy. But finally the crowd finished its work and the moment of dread was over. The gorilla and me were just like we had been before: nothing to each other.

We had to rip apart the fetish dolls before the prisoners were free. I wish I could say there were a hundred happy reunions that day, but for the most part, nobody had ever met. They didn't bother to thank me, and I didn't mind. A lot of the escapees tousled Alcibé's hair and bowed down to kiss his nonexistent feet, which I guess were my feet, being as he was mounted on me. The rest had to be carried out.

Ivan, though, remembered me. At least, he remembered I had been there before. He limped over to me on his hands, being as he had been separated from his lower appendages some days before.

"Well, it's good to see you boys," he said. "I think the bokor was about to liquidate his stock."

"What's that mean?" I asked.

"Guess you never worked in retail," Alcibé sighed.

I shrugged. I had no idea one way or the other.

"Let's just say you fellows got here in the nick of time," Ivan said.

"Well, now," I said, "it's not that I'm a glory hog, but you know, only one of us walked out of here and walked back in."

"Why don't you pull that stick out of your ass, Jones?" Alcibé said.

"I'd say whoever pulled it out of yours pulled too hard, head," I muttered.

"Well, listen," Ivan said, "what do I owe you two? You said before I was your client."

"Oh, yeah, that," I said. "Well, your unbirth sister, or whatever you call her, was going to pay."

"What? Are you stupid, Jones?" Alcibé whispered in my ear, though I'm sure the poor legless bastard could see some kind of conversation was going on. "Let him pay twice."

"No, I insist," Ivan said.

"See, Jones, he insists," Alcibé said.

"Well, I ain't going to refuse you, Ivan," I said. "Oh, that reminds me. I've got something for you. I wonder if they'll still work?"

"What?"

"Your legs."

NOVEMBER 9, 1934

I was back to my old game of tossing cards into my hat. I was finally playing with a full deck—don't say anything—but a game of whist with the new head on my table was exhausting, so I inevitably gave up and went back to the old toss.

"You ever been to Hat Scratch Fever?" I asked after missing the jack of spades.

"I've heard of it," he said.

"Did you ever think about—"

"No."

"You don't even know what I was about to say."

"You were going to offer to treat," he said, "and I don't care. I never paid for it, and I never will. That might work for you, Jones, but where I come from, we have a little more pride."

I looked him up and down, the full foot and a quarter of him. He wasn't smiling.

"You're putting me on," I said.

He finally cracked a grin. "Yeah. Were you getting at buying me a new body?"

"Yeah," I said. "Or I know this scaredy-baredy at the graveyard who would probably dig us up one for free." Whoa. My aim was way off that time. I set off a rattrap and wrecked the ace of ones, all in one action. The noise warned all the rats and sent them scampering.

"I don't know, Jones," he said. "I've thought about it. But it wouldn't be my body, you know."

"So what, you'd rather be a useless head? Want me to find a plaque and hang you up on the wall? 'Braineater Jones's Hunting Lodge, no prey too small.'"

"I don't want to be a head, but I want my body back. I don't want some weird body that I don't know what the previous owner did with it. What if he was a self-abuser with big hairy knuckles?"

"Who said we're getting you a man's body? I don't let anybody flop with me but ginchy dames."

"Any body?"

"Heads are okay. Where is your body, anyway?"

He shook his head so hard it looked like he was about to topple over. His neck didn't quite stand him up perfectly. "I don't know. Honduras, maybe."

"Where's that?"

"South of Mexico."

I whistled. "Well, we'll try to find your body right after I find my murderer."

"Who says we have to solve your case first?"

"The one who's not a useless neck pimple."

"Well, we'd better get started, then. Have any of your memories come back?"

I looked up. "How do you mean?"

"Well," he said, and I suppose if he'd been whole, he would've leaned back in his rocking chair and lit up a pipe or something. "When I was first turned, I was having real memories again after about a week. From what you've told me, it's already been almost two."

"Ten days," I said. "I'm sure it's different for everyone. Like puberty."

Alcibé grunted. I couldn't get any more cards in the hat after that, so I stopped tossing them.

I sighed. "Well, I get these flashes sometimes. Like a big thumping migraine. But they still kind of feel like they're somebody else's memories. And sometimes words and thoughts and phrases pop into my mind that don't make sense. Like somebody else would've said them, but I did."

"If we were still alive," the head corpse said, "I'd guess you had some kind of brain injury. But as we're dead, I know that's not true."

"Why not?" I said. "Lot of things cross over. Sleep, for instance. Why does a corpse need to sleep?"

"I don't know about that," he admitted, "but I can tell you that any real brain trauma, and you'd be put down."

"Dead dead?" I said.

"Dead dead," he agreed.

I grunted. Maybe so. There were a lot of things I still didn't understand. "Does anybody ever not get their memories back, period?"

He thought for a moment. Strangest thing I ever saw, a disembodied head thinking. Like watching a bust come to life right before your eyes. "I don't think so," he said. "But my experience is not all-encompassing."

"No, I guess not," I said.

"How do you feel about this partnership?" he asked.

I threw the whole rest of the deck up into the air. The cards tinkled down in a little flurry of spades and diamonds. "What partnership? What do you bring to the table aside from that wet spot there?"

"Experience, and I've got a good head on my shoulders. Well, you know what I mean."

"I hate to break this to you, Alcibé," I said, "but you're about as useless as Dr. Watson. And I don't have a soft spot for you, like Holmes did for his boy."

We both sat silently for a moment. One by one, the cards appeared back in my hand.

"So you've read Doyle," he said after a while.

"Yeah, I guess so. But everybody does, don't they? Kids and such."

"Perhaps," he said, "but can you remember reading Doyle? Actually remember doing it?"

I thought for a moment. I felt a white flash before my eyes. It hurt, but yes, there it was. Yellowing, tea-stained pages of a book resting on a floor, myself supine and kicking my legs while reading it. "I can, actually."

"That's good. We have a tangible memory to start with. It could be a clue to your past life."

"What, that I was a kid before I died? Let's alert Hearst."

He shrugged or whatever they call it when someone without shoulders tries to shrug. "Maybe it's nothing. Or maybe you were an English professor. In any case, unless you were a kid with a lot of money, you probably went to the library more than once."

"I didn't say I remembered every story," I said, "only that I knew who Dr. Watson was."

"Fine," he said and gave his little non-shrug again. "Never mind then."

NOVEMBER 10, 1934

The next day I was back in the library. The place was looking threadbare as usual.

"You might think about getting a library card if you come in here much more often," the librarian said.

I was the only one in the library, of course. No busy crowds to hide behind. Damn it. "Uh, yeah, sure. How much is that?"

"A nickel," she said.

Highway robbery! I checked my pocket. Only about twenty bucks left from the Little Haiti caper. Not sure I wanted to spend it on that. "Well, ma'am, it's tough all over. I don't have that much right now—"

"Maybe you ought to come back when you do," she said.

A squawk came from the covered birdcage strapped to my shoulder. "Rawk, pay the nice lady, rawk!"

I slammed the cage with my palm. Stupid corpse head.

The librarian's eyebrow near about crawled up into her dusty 'do. "You ought to listen to your… parrot."

Hmph. Hell of a place the Mat must be where you can take your pet any-damn-where. Well, I'm sure she must have seen stranger with the winos and wannabe gangsters wandering in and out. I tossed a nickel on the counter.

"Name?"

"Jones," I said.

She tapped her pencil angrily against the counter. "First name?"

"Look, lady—" I started to say.

"Don't you call me 'lady!'"

"Rawk, don't call her 'lady,'" the birdcage agreed.

I slammed my palm against the cage again. If a real bird had been inside, a flurry of feathers would've flown out. I sighed. "No first name."

"How about you get out?" she asked.

"How about Brian?"

Thank God that brutishness was over. With a brand new $0.05 blue library card with a metal strip in the middle, I wandered into what passed for the stacks in the Mat's library. Once I found the mystery section, I flipped the cover back on the birdcage.

"So, what's your plan?" Alcibé asked.

"This was your plan, chum bucket," I said. "What do you think?"

"I guess you should grab all the Arthur Conan Doyle and see if any of the covers strike you as familiar."

I turned to look at him angrily as best I could with him sitting on my shoulder. "How do you expect that to work?"

"That's how memory works," the head said. "It's all flashes, underneath the surface of the conscious mind. After we're done with all this, there's a book by an Austrian guy you should read."

I grabbed stacks and stacks of Holmes books. I was surprised and impressed by how many there were. Considering the guy had, what, two full-length novels, it's incredible how many different combinations of short stories there were by different publishing houses and in different orders and with different covers. I took them over to one of the wobbly tables with the plastic kiddy chairs and spread them out like the pieces in a puzzle. More than one had the usual dark silhouettes in an alley. One cover featured an empty deerstalker hat and a still-smoking pipe. I ran my fingers over another with the title embossed in gold and no other decoration, but the feel of the letters didn't stimulate anything in me. I must've been peering at them too long for the head's taste.

"Anything?"

"Shut up," I said. I looked around the room. Nobody there but a few drunks sleeping off last night. I pulled Alcibé out of his cage and laid him down on the table. There was something about the books. Something that tickled the back of my neck.

"Something's coming back to you," he said. "I can see it."

"Yeah," I said, "like when a word is on the tip of your tongue and you sit there for the rest of the day, and then it comes out a week later in the shower."

"Ah, one of those," he said.

I stood there scratching my head until I took off a chunk of my scalp. Muttering under my breath, I tried to stick it back on, but it was as if it was glued to my finger. I finally wiped it off under the table with all the wads of chewing gum.

If I keep falling apart like this, there won't be much of me left to crack the case. I'd hate to think of a time when I'd envy Alcibé.

"You'll have to do something about that," he said.

"I've been thinking about getting a rug," I said.

"Don't you even think about it, my magnificent undead brother," he said. "Be proud of who you are."

"Yeah, whatever," I said. "How do I kickstart this under-the-mind process bit?"

Alcibé stared at whatever I suppose he was pointed at, but his brow was furrowed with thought. Finally he spoke. "You ever play one of those little penny puzzles? You know, the one where you have a picture of, I don't know, a boat, only there's nine segments and only one hole and the boat's all mixed up?"

"Yeah, sure," I said. Then reflecting on it, I added, "I think so." I started moving the books around. I flipped one over. I moved them faster as if I was playing three-card monte. It occurred to me that I'd found another cover I had never seen. I flipped that one over. It became easier and easier. The books were a blur, but I could spot the ones I had never seen before. After a few minutes, I was left with three. I sat staring at them.

"Well," the head kid said, "take a look."

I opened the books and flipped through them. No notes in the margins. The pages were a little dog-eared. Nothing special. I looked at the cards in the backs of all three. Something struck me. He must have seen it.

"What is it?" he asked.

I actually pulled out this notebook and threw it down to the first open page. I pointed. "Look!"

"That's your handwriting," he said.

There was a name in all three of the books—Billy H. Must be me. Billy H.

Not sure I can handle that name right now. Of course, it's only a jab in the right direction. How many Bills or Billys are there in the city? Millions? It's the H that I've got to figure out.

The librarian was, of course, no help whatsoever. She may have been a fixture there since time immemorial, but it wasn't as though she would remember some kid from ten, fifteen, maybe twenty years ago. And no, they didn't keep records like that, naturally. It was the Welcome Mat, after all, where people go to disappear and never return. Even the library was like a whirlpool.

I have a little more to go on today than yesterday, though. I grew up in the city, in the Mat. I knew my first name. A few more days like this, and I'll get to where I need to be.

NOVEMBER 11, 1934

Armistice Day. Hard to believe. The head was up before me this morning.

He was staring out the window from his perch on my desk. I picked him up and moved him to the sill so he could get a better view, but there wasn't much to see. The parade in the Welcome Mat was pretty sad. A few downtrodden, middle-aged men in their business suits with medals pinned on from the Great War. A couple of older geezers from Spain and the Philippines trailed them in wheelchairs.

"Does all that mean anything to you?" he said when I came into the office.

I didn't really come anywhere, of course. The mattress was in the corner of the office, but we liked to pretend there were a variety of rooms. When he was in the foyer, for instance, I couldn't hear him over in the billiard parlor.

"All what?" I asked.

"All this," he said, clarifying nothing. "In Flanders Field the poppies grow, I watch them, count them, row on row, and so on so on, on we go."

I flopped down into my chair. I had my first drink of the day. That sparked me up a bit. I checked my holes, weeded out a few maggots. It was getting to be a routine. They crunched like popcorn when I bit into their heads, and they tasted like nothing. The worst day had been the first, when they really founded a new Shanghai down there. Since then, it was only a little cleanup work daily. "You got a real lyrical mind, Alcibé. No, I guess it don't mean anything to me."

"It means something to me," he said. "I'd march in it if I could walk."

"You were in the war?"

"Yup. I was at the Somme."

"And you can remember all that?" I said. "Like it was yesterday?"

He turned his face and pointed his eyes as best he could at me. "Like I'm there right now."

We sat silently for a while. The Mat really is a miserable little place. That was all we could muster for a parade. I had no doubt that somewhere in the Altstadt, the fat generals who had done nothing but send good boys to die were having their own parade. They were rolling down the streets in something nicer than the one Model T our boys could muster.

Of course, I couldn't see any of our kind. That is, assuming they let our kind march. I could picture the railroad bulls with staves in their hands, making sure not to let the deadheads mingle with the breathers. I couldn't say I blamed them. Might've been a bit appalling to have a dead man march in an Armistice Day parade.

"How old do you think I am? Was, I mean?"

"Who knows?" the head replied. "You're all corpsed up now."

"I remember it a bit, but I don't think I was there. Like, newspapers and such."

"Maybe you were young," he said. "Like the Old Man."

I did some arithmetical calisthenics in my head. "He woulda been in his bottle, what, four years when the war started? I doubt I was that young. I woulda been reading the funny papers still. He's a weird little shit, isn't he?"

"Weird, yes," Alcibé said, "but on my worst day, my shits were bigger than him."

"When you had an asshole, maybe."

"It's all right. I found a new one."

"I don't like that guy," I said, generously ignoring his wisecrack. "I wonder why someone doesn't just squish him."

"I used to say the same thing about Hoover."

"Seriously, though, why doesn't somebody just…?" I trailed off, just throttling a bit of drumstick with my dickbeaters.

"Well, did you ever see his bodyguard?"

"Yeah, well then, why doesn't that big mook just…?" I squished a can between my palms as I imagined what that gorilla could've done with the Old Man's Mason jar.

"Would you give up a steady-paying gig like that?" he asked.

"I have no idea," I said.

"I'm sorry about your memory, Jones. I don't know what'll kickstart it."

"Maybe nothing will," I said. "Then again, maybe that's for the best."

We sat there for a moment, watching the men until they trailed away into history. I was too far down in the dumps to do anything else for the rest of the day.

NOVEMBER 12, 1934

It was a good thing Lazar walked into my office. I was down to maybe a third of a bottle of Old Crow. I was reduced to drinking beer and mouthwash to keep up my alcohol content. Alcibé was listening to the radio. As usual, I was tossing cards into my hat.

Lazar walked over and turned off the squawk box. He was carrying a leather suitcase.

"I'm glad you're here," I said. "I'm about dried up. "

"I heard about what you did for Ivan Skaron," Lazar said.

"Yeah," I said, "well, I'm just glad they could sew his legs back on. Didn't know they'd still work. We're funny creatures, you know that?"

He seemed to be trailing his finger along the layer of dust on my wall. What was I going to do? Clean it? Why bother? What difference did hygiene make to our kind? It wasn't as though I was going to catch typhoid and die from it. The dead do not clean.

He picked up my bottle of Crow and shook it. "No more freebies. Time to earn all this." Lazar raised his arms to encompass the vast domain of my one-room crap shack in the middle of the Welcome Mat on top of a pawnshop and a backroom dive bar.

"You've got one of those nonpaying gigs for me, I take it," I said. I tossed another ace in the hole.

"You and your partner, yes," he said, glancing at Alcibé.

I had given up trying to protest the head being my partner. He had his—occasional and limited—uses, and he didn't cost much money.

Besides, if he got out of line, I could always stick him in a fishbowl somewhere.

"Tell us what your game is, Lazar," Alcibé said. "You don't smell right to me."

I had already grilled the head, but he didn't know any more about my mysterious patron than I did. Went by Lazar, probably a joke on Lazarus. No one knew his real name. He was a prime mover and shaker in the deadhead community. No one knew where he went at night after he moved out of what had become the Braineater Jones Detective Agency. All in all, he was a mysterious and powerful deadhead. But not to be trusted. I had more to find out about Lazar.

Question 10 remains on the list. *Who is Lazar? What is his real name?*

"No game, my little friend," Lazar said. "Just a simple task." He placed the suitcase on my desk. It was one of those fancy jobs with two metal combination locks. "I want you to deliver this."

"What is it?" Alcibé asked.

"That is none of your concern," Lazar said.

"Oh, contraire, mon frère," the head growled. "That is very much my concern."

"Then let us simply say that it is not within your purview," Lazar replied.

That seemed to shut the little neck blister up.

"Where to?" I asked.

"To the docks. Here's the address." He handed me a crumpled piece of paper. 101 Gateway Lane. Didn't ring a bell, but that didn't necessarily mean anything.

"Don't do it, Jones," Alcibé said. "It could be anything. It could be illegal."

I shrugged. "What difference does that make?"

"Well put," Lazar said. "And I assure you it is nothing illegal. Incidentally, let's consider the completion of this task your rent for the month. So long, darlings."

What a weird cat. He left, but that didn't stop the head talking. He had a million objections, each stupider than the last.

"What if it's something dangerous?" he asked.

"What do I care?"

"Wouldn't you be bothered if you were responsible for people getting hurt or even killed?"

"I'm already dead," I said. "I don't care about a whole lot of things. But I'm kind of interested in exactly what you think is in here." I thumped the suitcase with my hand. It wasn't very thick. What did he think was inside? A bunker buster? Big Bertha?

"Information can kill the same amount of people," he said. "If it's not something dangerous, why do you think he's asking you to deliver it?"

"Busy man, maybe. Or hell, maybe he just doesn't want to be seen down by the docks."

"I don't trust him," the head said. "I'm not going."

"No one asked you to. Not that you could stop me if I wanted to take you." He bared his teeth and reminded me of nothing so much as a fighting terrier. I waved my hand in dismissal. "You're more of a hassle than a help anyway. Feed the fish while I'm gone. Oh, wait, you can't."

I stomped out. I felt idiotic, like an old woman quarreling with her daddy. I don't know why I even let that stupid corpse head get to me. He's nothing to me. Less than nothing. He had a funny point, though. I stopped on my way to the docks and dove into an alley. I think maybe I was partially worried about repeating my run-in with the longshoremen, and I wanted to find any excuse to procrastinate. Still, the contents of the suitcase were calling to me like a shiny red piece of candy.

The locks on the suitcase weren't exactly like cracking into the First National Bank. I fiddled with them. I grabbed a shard of glass from a broken bottle and tried to jimmy them open. All I got for my trouble was a shredded-up hand.

I sat for a while thinking about what the combination might be. I didn't know Lazar that well. I didn't know any of his fancy numbers–birthday, anniversary, kid's ages, if he even had any. It was pointless fiddling with the dials without even a guess at the numbers.

8000. No. 8674. No.

I probably spent longer guessing than I should have. I stood up. It was simple enough, really. Deliver a package and free rent for a month. What was the issue really?

Stupid fucking head.

The docks stank like seaweed and calamari as usual. I heard a couple of sailors yelling at each other in some funny language. Something was familiar about it. I had a thought. I pulled out this notebook and walked over to them. I was fairly certain—though not 100%—they weren't of the same crowd that had put the screws to me before.

"Hey, you recognize this?" I said.

They looked at it. The first one shook his head. He pointed at himself. "Portuguese." Then he pointed at the notebook page. "Italiano."

"Eye-tie? Thanks."

That was a start. At least I finally knew what language the graffito tag in the Welcome Mat was written in. It seemed like the least important of my numbered questions, but for some reason, it pressed the most heavily on my mind.

There it was. 101 Gateway Lane. A nondescript sort of loft. I checked my pocket real quick. The gun was loaded, at least. The door had one of those old-fashioned knockers, shaped like a gibbering face. I knocked.

The door opened, but they hung back in the shadows. "What do you want?"

"I got a delivery for you," I said.

Long pause. "Slide it in."

I did so. Then I waited. The door didn't close.

"Am I supposed to pick something up?" I said. "Some kind of receipt, maybe?"

Another long pause. "No."

The door closed. And that was that. With my head on swivel, I walked home to find a bright, beautiful new bottle of bourbon waiting for me.

NOVEMBER 13, 1934

The head didn't talk eye-tie. And if he did, he wasn't helping.

I tried the bar. The gorilla wasn't a dago, either. Neither were any of the regulars. I didn't ask any of the nonregulars, but they weren't looking promising. Hell, I even tried old Homer in the fence. He was no help. I would've tried his cat, but it was sleeping.

The library was worse than useless. I found one battered, old English-Italian dictionary. Trying to figure out the tag from that was like trying to decrypt the Rosetta stone with a crystal ball. The old hag gave me a funny look, too.

I'm about exhausted dealing with her.

Little Italy was an option. It was in the nicer part of Ganesh, though. We weren't talking about going around the corner of the Mat, like Port-au-Pauper. The garlic eaters were a little richer, at least richer than the deadheads and Haitians, and they found a grudging niche in the wider city.

"You want to get some spaghetti?"

The head didn't even look at me. But then, he was facing the opposite direction.

I tromped down the stairs a little louder than necessary. I had been pondering whether it was worth the hassle to try taking the trolley. Today was my day. According to the transit map, all the trolley stops in the Mat were "temporarily suspended." According to the locals, "temporary" meant longer than anyone except the Old Man could remember. It was a few blocks out of the Mat to the nearest trolley stop, but I figured that was better than walking the whole way to Little Italy. Even though the day was a little hot—or what I would've considered hot when my nerve endings were still at 100%—I wore my hat and my trench coat.

When the trolley came, I turned up my collar to cover as much of my face as I could. I tossed a nickel in the bucket and sat as far in the back as I could. I didn't look back. I hoped nobody was watching. When I finally stopped to take a look, of course they all were staring at me. With my fist, I wadded up the bullet hole Francoise had put in my coat, but that gesture only seemed to invite more unwanted lookey-loos to see what I was trying to hide.

I waited. And waited. The trolley made its stops. After a few people got off, most of the folks weren't interested in me anymore. Only one kid still stared at me.

"Hey, kid," I said.

He didn't say anything, just sat there chewing gum like a motherless little bastard.

"Wanna see something?" I asked. I opened my coat and showed the kid my bullet hole. Luckily for me, I had laid off the booze a little that morning and a worm had found his way in. The kid turned around. Even though the trolley was moving, he ran up to the front seat.

I vowed that would be the last time I would take public transportation, even if I had to walk the whole length and breadth of the city. It's not worth it.

Eventually we stopped in Wopville, and I got off. Ritzy. Upscale. Not at all like the Mat. I guess some ghettos can move up in the world.

Maybe once me and my kind showed up, we bumped the eye-ties a few rungs up the ladder. Or maybe not. I walked into a butcher's shop.

The butcher was easily three hundred pounds soaking wet, and he wore a white apron and a tiny white paper hat like teddy bear clothes. He just stuck one big sausage of a finger at the door. "Get out."

Didn't need to tell me twice. Damn. I was starting to worry that I wasn't passing for human anymore. Some folks still talked to me, but others sussed me out right off the bat. Some folks stared at me, like on the trolley. I felt unwelcome, exposed.

I sat down at one of those little outdoor cafes—I guess they call them beast-rows—with the red and white checkered tablecloths. A jug of wine with a candle stuck in it sat on my table, still unlit. A couple of shady characters sat here and there, smoking, looking at me, and eating only the occasional pastry.

Under their glare, I tried to retreat as deep into my clothes as I could, like a turtle hiding from his old lady. I finally understood why the longshoreman on the dock had hidden so deep in all his fishing gear.

A waiter in an apron splotched with yellow stains appeared eventually. He was smiling, and he had such a greasy moustache, I guess he could've buttered all the garlic bread in the joint with it. He stood in front of me, pencil poised over a notebook, and his smile didn't disappear. That was a start, anyway. "What'll it be, buddy?"

"Hey," I said, "you speak Italian?"

He gibbered on and on in Italian. I guess he misunderstood.

"No, no," I said, "I don't speak it. I wonder if you can tell me what this means." I threw the notebook down to the right page.

He cocked his eyebrow, but he picked up the book and stared at it. He nodded like a broken sipping bird. "Very nice, very nice. Is Dante. Classic. You probably know this line, actually, in Inglese."

Alighieri. That usually meant the Inferno. Nobody ever read the other two, anyway.

Maybe I was an English professor. I certainly wasn't no Italian professor.

"You want I should translate it right here?" he asked.

"Go to the next clean page," I said. I took the notebook from him when he was done.

THROUGH ME THE WAY INTO THE SUFFERING CITY,

THROUGH ME THE WAY TO THE ETERNAL PAIN,

THROUGH ME THE WAY THAT RUNS AMONG THE LOST.

ABANDON EVERY HOPE, WHO ENTER HERE.

I held out a five-dollar bill to him. The waiter waved it off like it was nothing.

"No, no," he said. "It's nice to help. So you want anything?"

"Yeah, sure," I said, and I ordered.

4. *What does the cryptic entrance sign mean?* It's a quote from Dante, apparently, the sign above the entrance to Hell.

I wonder if all the threads in the tapestry were coming together. Not really. I have to get down to some real gumshoeing.

It was a long walk back that night, longer than I had figured when I had hopped on the trolley. I threw a box down in front of the head. He had moved from his position that morning. Not sure how. Maybe Homer came up and moved him, or more likely the bartender.

He eyed it warily. "What's that?"

"Spaghetti," I said.

He looked up at me. "Everything tastes like ash, and we don't need to eat."

"No, I guess not," I said, "but sometimes it makes you feel human."

He had to slurp his like a disgusting child. I ate with a fork and pretended not to notice the pillow of masticated noodle slowly elevating him off the desk. Good thing my gag reflex doesn't work anymore, I suppose. We talked for a while, like two ordinary eggs having a meal.

12. Can we eat? Is alcohol enough? We don't have to eat. But it sure feels nice sometimes.

NOVEMBER 14, 1934

I was sitting in Hallowed Grounds watching a fly buzz around one of the light bulbs. A glass of rum sweated in front of me. Normally I only drank Crow, but lately I'd been thinking about spicing up my life. Someone plopped down in the chair next to me. I didn't turn.

"Nice to see you here," Lazar said.

"You don't come around much these days," I said.

He laughed and gestured at the bartender. There was some unspoken arrangement between them, I suppose, because the big ape immediately poured some kind of frothy orange mixed drink with rum, pineapple, a cherry, and an umbrella. "I just wanted to say good work on the delivery the other day."

I grunted.

"Your curiosity didn't get the better of you, did it?"

I let the question hang. He rubbed his hands together like a kid on Christmas and gratefully took his drink from the bartender.

"Where is your annoying little companion anyway?"

"The head?"

He nodded.

"He's upstairs," I said. "Sleeping it off from last night."

"Overdrinking can be dangerous," Lazar said. "Almost as dangerous as underdrinking."

"Wasn't that," I said. "Son of a bitch ate a whole bowl of linguini. I spent the rest of the night cleaning it up off the desk."

"Strange," Lazar said. "I wouldn't think that would make him lethargic."

"Jaw muscles," I said, pointing at my own. Mine were practically poking through the skin of my cheeks. I had to wonder how some of the skirts stayed so good looking, Kumaree Tong and the bunch. Must take a lot of cosmetics and even more booze. Maybe there was some other secret. Lazar, for one, always looked immaculate, and by all accounts, he should've been getting pretty long in the tooth. "How do you always keep looking so fresh and minty, Lazar?"

I don't think he could've looked more stunned if I had asked where his mother kept her combat boots. I watched him slowly, carefully swallow the mouthful of fruity drink already in his mug.

"I'll give you the address for my scratcher." He scribbled down an intersection on a bar napkin.

"Scratcher?"

"He'll get you fixed up," he said, stuffing the napkin in with my handkerchief. "Now about last night."

"Yes?"

He clapped me on the back. "Well, I just wanted to say thanks. We may look forward to a bright future working together."

"I don't suppose I've earned any answers," I said.

He snorted. "Hardly. To be honest, I feel like most of the goodwill and effort put forth is on this side of the table. You're like a baby and I'm like your papa. That doesn't make us equals."

"Okay, pops," I said. "How about you at least tell me what you are."

He dropped his finger into his drink. Not literally, not like it fell off. I imagine that happens for us sometimes. He just dunked the end of his fingertip in and swished it around a little. "Well, you already know that, Jones. I'm a bootlegger."

"Do you still call it that when Prohibition's over?"

He smiled. "I suppose so."

"A bootlegger, then. That could mean anything. You could be Al Capone or you could be the Great Gatsby."

"A reader of literature," he said, luxuriating over every word. "You really are full of surprises. I'd wager there was a little education crammed into that head of yours before it was buried."

"You're good at running conversations off the rails. If I didn't know any better, I'd say you were a politician."

He leaned back on his stool. Being as there was no back, he didn't have very far to go. "Maybe I am. But I assure you, I'm more of the East Egg school than the Chicago outfit."

"Not a whole lot of booze you can fit into a suitcase," I said.

"Well that depends on whether it's airtight or not," he said.

I nodded. Not much chance I was getting anything out of him. I hoped maybe a little more might come out another day, but it's impossible to tell things like that.

He picked up his drink and pointed at nothing in particular behind the bar. It was a nervous gesture, I guess, to make him look important. "I've heard you've been taking on some extracurricular activities. I mean, beyond your paying cases and my little favors. It's not wise, you know, to get too mixed up in the affairs of your old life."

"Are you telling me to back off?" I asked.

"It's not a threat," he said, "just a warning. I don't want your heart to get broken, Jones."

"Don't worry about my heart," I said. "It doesn't even beat anymore."

"That doesn't mean it can't get broken," he said. "There's a saying in our community."

I waited for what seemed like a solid minute. "What's that?"

"Huh?" He looked at me. "Oh, well, just what I just said. Just because your heart doesn't beat doesn't mean it can't get broken. That's the saying. Really, now, Jones, you must try to keep up." He stood and littered the counter with bills, no doubt to cover my drink and his own. Goddamned gorilla double charged me anyway.

I stomped back up the steps after the speako closed down for the night. Funny that an illicit gin joint has to stop serving, but I guess everybody's got to clean up at some point.

The lights were out. Strange. The head should've been up. I fiddled to get my keys out. I had taken to locking the shop up when I was gone. There was no point.

The door was already ajar. I pressed it open, hoping it would be silent, but of course it had to creak. It was a creaky, old, piece-of-shit door. I drew my piece.

"Alcibé," I said, "give me a noise."

A voice cut through my chest like an icicle. "He's not here."

I turned and fired at the figure silhouetted in the moonlight. There was a gargle, and the figure clutched its chest and fell backward. I flicked the light switch on and off. No power. Or else they had gotten to the fusebox.

I stood over the intruder. She was laughing. She.

"Is that any way to greet an old client?"

I squinted. My dark vision wasn't real great. Couldn't have helped that my eyes were rotting out of my head. "Kumaree?"

She smiled. At least, I think she smiled. She was wearing something black and lacy, like out of a Tijuana Bible.

"Where's Alcibé?" I broken-recorded.

"The head took a walk," she cooed.

I looked around the room. What was going on? Was she setting me up? Somebody sending in a dame to take me off the balls of my feet? "Why do I find that hard to believe?"

"He agreed," she said. "He's staying with a friend. I gave him a little scooter to ride."

"Assuming I believe you"—I waved the gun in her face—"what are you doing here?"

She got to her knees. It must not be as big of a foe pa in the deadhead world to shoot somebody as it is in the thinky breathy world. "I realized that I never thanked you for saving my brother."

I lowered my gun. Tentative, but I lowered it. Any mook in the shadows would've made his move by then. I think. "I got your payment. Matter of fact, I got his, too. Got paid twice for the job. Very lucrative."

She touched my leg. I guess my nerve endings weren't completely dead after all. "Paid, yes," she said, "but I wanted to thank you."

She stood. I looked around the room. What on earth was she wearing? Like something out of the back of the Sears catalogue or something.

"Did you turn out the lights?" I said.

She took my head in her hands. She nodded.

"Are you hurt?" I said.

She laughed and stuck her finger into the hole I had so recently provided her with. She leaned in close and put her tongue in my ear to speak. "Nothing a little plaster won't fix."

Plaster. So that's how the women did it.

"Meanwhile," she said, "I have a new hole, if you're interested."

I didn't know what to say. I wasn't much good at pillow talk. Or maybe I was. Who knew? I stuck the gun in my belt. "I might be more interested in one of your older ones."

Hey, I said I was bad at pillow talk.

I was lying on the mattress, smoking a Lucky. I lit one up for her too while I was at it.

She took it. "I normally smoke Chesterfields." Just like a twist to complain about a favor.

"Yeah, well, I normally…" I couldn't think of anything to say.

"Sleep alone?" she suggested.

"Yeah, I guess so." I put out the cigarette on my wrist. I didn't really think about things like that anymore. Probably disgusting to a bird, though. Damn it.

Probably to make me feel better, she put hers out on her tongue, then swallowed it. I guess there were advantages to feeling next to nothing, because something weird like that seemed dead sexy. I kissed her. She didn't object. Would've been disgusting if I had been alive, like kissing an ashtray. As it was, it was a whole new world. I leaned back again.

"I didn't know our kind could do that," I said. "I guess I'd heard rumors…" I trailed off again. I'd been doing that all night. I didn't think it would be real wise one way or the other to mention my experience at the Hat Scratch. She must've thought I was positively medieval in prudishness.

Actually, I didn't come up with that turn of phrase. She told me as much later on in the night.

"Of course we can," she said. "Wouldn't be any fun if we couldn't. Who would want to unlive like this? Just don't look at the stain afterward."

I lifted my eyebrow but refused to take the bait directly. "Wonder how it all works."

"Wonder all you want," she said. "The living don't know how anything works either. They blame it all on God."

"Don't you believe in God?" I was trying to be sly since I had my own thoughts on the matter, but it's hard to tell when a twist might turn out to be gaga for Jesus. Heavy talk for the sack, I know, but don't we all get like that sometimes?

"No, I guess not," she said. "Something about being promised life after death and getting this instead. Sours most of us to God."

Funny, the same thoughts had occurred to me, too. "So there are no religious deadheads."

"A few," she said darkly, "but you want to stay away from those. Fanatics. Worse than the worst living ones."

I nodded. I'd file that away to find out more about later. Or not. Nothing seemed to matter much that night. I took her into my arms and kissed her a bit around the neck. "So I guess you'll be a repeat customer," I said.

She pushed me away. Dames. Who can figure them? "Don't flatter yourself, Jones. I only do virgins. You're no good to me anymore."

I folded my arms. "That's not what I meant."

She laughed at me and stood to get dressed. I guess she had some real clothes around the apartment after all. I surreptitiously lifted the covers to look at the stain. It was green and slimy, and a bit like a fungus. She was right. I wished I hadn't looked.

"You're terrible with double antennas," she said. "But sure, if one of my morgue mates goes missing again, I'll be sure to call." She ran her hand along my desk. "Oh wait, you don't have a phone."

The door closed not with a slam, but with a miserable little creak.

NOVEMBER 15, 1934

I left the "bedroom" feeling as if I'd been plowed over by a steamroller. Alcibé was back, struggling to eat some pancakes. I'd finally gotten him into the habit of sitting in a bedpan when he eats so I don't have to clean up afterward. There was a stack for me, too, covered with fruit and still steaming. I sat at the desk and popped the cork on a new bottle of Crow.

"How the hell'd you pull all this off?" I asked.

He gave one of his customary nondescript shrug-like gestures.

"I suppose you had help," I said.

"I do have friends other than you, Jones," he said between munches.

"Sure you do," I said.

"Hey, I did have an unlife before I met you in Port-au-Pauper, you know."

"What the hell does that mean?" I said. "The bokor said that, too."

"It's just a pun," he said. "Don't worry about it."

I shrugged. No sense worrying about it. I had enough questions on my numbered list already.

"So, ah"—he was as reticent about the subject as I was—"your old client stopped by last night."

"Yeah," I said, tinkling my fork on the plate.

He nodded, or he would have if he had more of a neck. "Not much on under that trench coat, I'll wager."

I said nothing.

"I had a sex life of sorts, before Delamort got his claws into me," he said. "I suppose I still could. You know, it would be limited in certain ways."

I slammed my fist on the table, fork and all. "Enough. I don't want to hear about a head giving head."

We ate in silence for a moment.

"Grumpy," he remarked.

I heard screaming through the window and a few shots rang out. We stared at each other. I grabbed the head and my revolver and ran out onto the street in nothing but my socks, drawers, and bathrobe.

One of our kind was staggering down the street, arms out like a Frankenstein and slobbering. A crowd of breathers had gathered around to form a circle but were giving the deadhead a wide berth. Some of the men were shakily waving torches and knives at him. Within the circle, a young girl sat flat on her behind, petrified with terror. Her fingernails were ragged and bleeding from scrabbling backward along the macadam. None of the brave breathers were doing a damned thing to protect her.

"It's like he's rabid," one of them said.

Somebody else countered, "You ever seen a rabid person?"

"What's going on?" I whispered to the head as I stuffed him inside my jacket as though I was hiding a stack of schoolbooks from the rain. I recognized this was no situation for us to be mistaken for what we really were. I guess Alcibé realized that too, because he didn't protest being jammed up against my fetid armpit.

"It's one of our kind," he whispered through the terrycloth. "Shoot him in the head."

"Shoot him?" I said. "That'll kill him. For real kill him."

"Yes," Alcibé hissed. "He's too far gone now."

"The hell happened to him?"

"He's either off the sauce, or he's reached the end of his time. That's a real braineater, Jones."

"Who in the blue blazes are you talking to?" some old guy said, turning to look at me.

I grunted and pointed at the lump under my robe. "Ventriloquist."

The old guy gave me a look like I had raped his two-year-old. "This hardly seems the time."

"Out of the way," I said, practically knocking the old guy over.

I pushed my way through the circle of breathers. I got down on one knee to help my aim and pointed my pistol at the braineater. Unfortunately, I guess the breathers took that as a signal to back off. Without the knives and flames in his face, the braineater lurched forward and grabbed the little girl.

Before she could scream, he took a huge jagged bite out of her skull. I could see the teeth marks in her head, like in a Felix cartoon.

"God damn it," I whispered as I blew his brains out. I had never seen one of our kind dead before. Incredibly, the crowd of breathers up and disappeared. Nobody claimed the girl. She wouldn't become one of us. That had been preempted by having an apple-sized chunk of her brain bitten into and splattered on the street.

I dropped the gun to the street, and my hand went instinctively along my jawline. I felt thick, ropey muscle there, thicker than a regular human's, and a thick knot of it at the joint. Dazed, I released the head from his hidey-hole and held him by the hair. He didn't protest.

"I didn't know we could bite through bone like that," I said. "Did you?"

"Yes," he said, "but don't start on me."

I plucked a thick, brown glass bottle off the street—a piece of debris—and put it between my teeth. Tentatively I bit down and sliced through the glass as though it was butter. Absently, I chewed a bit, then spat out the glass, thinking that the next time I saw Kumaree, she wouldn't appreciate jagged glass if we went French-style. I didn't believe that bit about her only shacking up with virgins for even a minute.

Some of our kind wandered onto the street at that point. They had been hanging back, I suppose, waiting for the breathers to leave. I felt betrayed.

Someone clapped me on the back paternally. "It had to be done, Jones."

I didn't know him. "Get fucked," I replied.

They picked up the deadhead and the girl. Cops didn't come to the Welcome Mat. There'd be no investigation unless I performed it myself. I wondered briefly who the little girl was, with her blue dress and white apron and perfect little blond curls. Didn't much matter, I suppose. Just another dead human.

"This is why they hate us," Alcibé said.

"This isn't us," I said. "This is…" I was at a loss for words.

"You understand now why you shouldn't call yourself Braineater?" the head asked.

"Fuck that," I said.

It's a badge of honor. After a fashion.

NOVEMBER 16, 1934

I flopped down into my usual seat at the bar. I flipped through my notebook then stuck it back in my pocket. The gorilla came around eventually.

"You're not here to drink," he said.

"No," I said, "but you can hit me anyway."

He gave me some of that clear Russian stuff, and I threw it back. I kept giving the "come hither" signal with my finger when the glass got empty.

"What do you know about Lazar?" I asked.

The gorilla shook his head.

"Come on, damn it," I said. "You know who I'm talking about."

"Sometimes he goes by Lazar, sometimes by Russ, sometimes by—"

"Lazarus." I already figured that.

"Other things, too," the gorilla said. "I don't trust a man—even one of our kind—who can't settle on a name. Like he's always hiding something."

I waited. "That's it? That's all you know?"

He shrugged. "Used to live upstairs. Left a little while before you came. Kept to himself. I don't know his business. I don't care to know. He and the Old Man talk a lot."

I stroked my chin. Felt strange not to have any stubble. Or did it? Muscle memory, maybe. Must've had a beard when I was alive or didn't shave much. Contrary to popular belief, our hair and fingernails do not continue to grow.

That wasn't really my line of thinking at the time, though. At the time, I was putting it together that Lazar—or whoever he was—was the one keeping the speakeasy in business. He had some kind of arrangement with the little abortion. What was the arrangement? Some kind of kickback thing? If not, why didn't Lazar simply run the speakeasy himself?

"Let me talk to the boss," I said.

The bartender nervously polished his hands with his dishtowel. I noticed for the first time that he had lost one of his ears. I wondered if he had ever had it since I met him, or if he had lost it at some point and I was just noticing. Didn't matter much, I guess, but might go a long way toward telling me what kind of detective I am.

"I don't think he'll want that," he said.

"What, do you speak for the Old Man now?" I asked. "I ain't asking for an audience with the pope. Now bring that little shit up here."

I wonder if I was a papist before. Kumaree was right, after all. There wasn't a religious bone in my body after my physical conversion. Only thing that twist was right about it.

The gorilla tried to pull one over on me. He went through all the motions of clomping down into the little basement and then clomping back up. "He's busy."

I flung myself over the counter and grabbed the big mook by the lapels. Probably not the best idea, someone as tiny as me taking on a gruesome monument like him. But it seemed like the thing to do at the time. "You get that little jar of crap and you bring it up here."

It worked. God damn. At least I had the instincts to know he was bullshitting me. He climbed back down, and the jar containing the Old Man popped up out of the trapdoor, resting in the big gorilla's palm. The Old Man gave me the "come hither" fingers.

I followed the gorilla down through the cellar door. It was the first time I had been into the sub-basement of Hallowed Grounds. I wouldn't have believed the place existed if I hadn't seen it with my own eyes.

It was one of those wine cellars like in the old Poe stories. Bottles and bottles of wine lined the walls, covered in cobwebs and worse. Candles sat atop human skulls, and piles of bones sat in some corners. We're not talking about a serial killer here. Those bones had been there since the city was founded. Decades, centuries. Then again, maybe that was where deadheads crawled off to die when they felt the urge to eat brains.

We were crawling down twisting and turning tunnels. I might've believed there was a whole underworld beneath Ganesh.

"Hey, I don't like this," I said.

Next thing I knew, I had a piece in the small of my back. He must've kept it in his apron all the time. Big, round barrel. Seemed familiar somehow.

"Just keep walking," the gorilla muttered. "You've stepped in it now. The boss wants to see you."

Careful what you wish for, huh? By the time we reached a dead end, I was so turned around, I was nervous that I might never see the surface again.

If Eli Whitney had been a big fan of narcotics, he might have dreamt up the crazy machine I saw down there. The gorilla screwed the Old Man's jar into a holster in the great machine that looked as though it had been specially crafted for that purpose. The jar apparently had two flaps in the bottom, and two levers from the machine fit through perfectly so that the Old Man had controls, like on a bulldozer.

"I'll be off then, sir," the gorilla said.

"What is this?" I asked, looking around in awe.

Something grabbed me around the neck. I reached up and tried to loosen myself, but it was like a vise grip the size of a surfboard. The Old Man was pleased as punch, sitting there pulling and twisting those levers.

I tried to say something, but my windpipe had been crushed. The Old Man lowered a microphone down into his jar. His voice sounded a little wet but otherwise normal. Well, for a twenty-year-old fetus. "You like playing games, Mr. Jones? How does this one strike you?"

The hydraulic arm—or whatever it was—jerked me forward, right in front of the jar. He looked in my eyes. "I can see you're wondering what's going on."

I shrugged as best I could. Couldn't say much. The claw released me from its vise-like grip, and I dropped to the floor like a bag of wet laundry. I wanted to suck in air, but of course, I didn't have to. It was a purely instinctual response. I tried to talk, but my windpipe was flattened. I struggled to jam a fist or a finger down my throat to open the airway up a bit so I could talk again.

"This is our future, unfortunately," the Old Man said. "I've been working on this for a long time. It's just a prototype, of course. No legs and no real tactile control. A brute. But the next model will be a little better."

As I fiddled around with my neck, I felt a crunch. I didn't know what the noise was, but I could talk again. I might have to get a doctor to look at it later. Or, well, whatever the equivalent of a doctor is in our community. A mortician, maybe. "I don't want any trouble." My voice was audibly hoarser.

"Don't want any trouble?" the Old Man said, bringing his ridiculous mechanical arms together like an elderly woman tenting her fingers. "That's why you threaten my tavern keeper? That's why you insist on interrupting my work? You act awfully strange for a man who doesn't want any trouble." One of the mechanical arms grabbed me by the collar. It dragged me up in the air.

"Okay," I said, "I get the point. You're an important guy. Size doesn't matter. I won't make that mistake again."

He stared at me for a moment. "No, you won't, will you?" He dropped me to the ground. "What was so important, after all, to disturb me about?"

"It seems silly now," I said, massaging my throat to try to get my voice back in order. "I'm trying to get a bead on Lazar."

"Lazar?"

That's when I saw the strangest thing I ever imagined. The little fetus sitting in a fishbowl full of booze and controlling a massive clockwork machine was odd enough. When the mechanical hand went up and scratched the top of the jar, just like a man scratching his head, it was too much for me. In any other circumstance, I would've burst out laughing. As it was, I was smart enough to keep that on the inside.

"I guess I know who you're talking about. I wouldn't worry too much about him. He's making his way out of the community. He already lives in the Altstadt. Consider him untouchable, if you will."

The Altstadt. That was… news.

He shooed me away with his huge claws like a man shooing away a cat. "Go on, now. Find your own way back. And Jones?"

"Yeah?" I said.

"Don't you ever ask to see me again unless I invite you," he said.

Don't have to worry about that.

I wanted to kick in a few doors, ask a few questions, find out where in the Altstadt Lazar lived, but it turned out I had one major problem: I could barely talk.

The collapsed throat was a lot worse than I initially thought. After reopening it initially, I had a relapse. It must've really folded closed, because I could hardly communicate at all. I had to break out this notebook and scribble most of my requests.

That method was not conducive to getting the kind of information I wanted from the kind of people I had to ask. Half of them are illiterate, anyway. I decided instead to ask a few folks about how to get my throat fixed.

As it turns out, there are a number of "doctors" who specialize in our kind. Some are members of our kind and have real humanitarian (or corpsitarian?) motivations, but most are the med school dropout types who wander into the Welcome Mat with hangers looking for a few back-alley, knocked-up prom dates. They take on our kind, too. Why not? Can't hurt someone who's already dead, and no one can call the cops or sue. Most of our problems are cosmetic or functional, like my collapsed throat. They're more like tradesmen than professionals. They treat a deadhead like a house with a leaky roof or a broken window. Not like waiting for a human being to heal.

The scratcher Lazar had recommended had a real vibe going. He wore a white lab coat that was yellowing at the edges and a big shiny reflector on his forehead, big thick birth control glasses, a toothy grin, and a light European accent. Foreigner, immigrant, something? Scratcher, anyway.

"What can I do for you?" he said, only it sounded like, "Vat ken I do for vu?"

I will forgo the accent in writing for your benefit and my sanity.

I pointed at my throat. He took a pocket lantern of some sort and none too gently pried open my throat. He could fit both of his gloved hands in my mouth. No kidding. Alive, I would've choked to death. He knew exactly what my limits were, of course, and our kind's high, almost nonexistent pain tolerance.

"Trouble with the voice box?" he asked, shining the lantern down my throat. "Well, the whole esophagus is highly infected, but that's normal. However, it is also pinched shut, and that is less so." He leaned back on the cardboard box that served him as a chair. The guy acted like any other sawbones in a nice, clean office. It was a funny juxtaposition being in a back alley. He snapped off his gloves, sending a puff of talcum powder into the air. "So, let's discuss my fee, shall we?"

It wasn't exactly what I'd call a discussion—in polite company, anyway. More like he dictated to me that it would be twenty-five smackeroos. What a scam. I could've practically seen a real sawbones for that, if he wouldn't have noticed my missing pulse and started whacking away at my chest and trying to give me the lips of life.

I fished into my pocket. Funny. My wad of cash was still there, but it was wrapped in a rubber band. Someone had stolen my damned billfold. Naturally. But who would do that and leave the money? Oh well, the scratcher didn't care where I kept my money, so I handed him the greenbacks.

"All right," he said, "sounds good. Let's get started."

So out this guy pulls—I shit you not—a bicycle pump and one of those long balloons like a clown uses to make balloon animals. Why he had those objects, I don't know. Seemed a bit nonstandard, even for a back-alley scratcher. He started feeding the balloon into my mouth, so naturally I pushed him away.

"Swallow it," he said to me, like I'm a dog. "Swallow it."

He started stroking my throat. Like, to loosen up my dead muscles? I was about to walk away right then and there. Let him keep my twenty-five clams.

"I know it's going to be difficult, especially through the fold in your trachea, but you must swallow this so I can reinflate the airway."

What the hell, I figured. At least I'll find out what I'm paying for. It took a while, but I got it down. Then he started pumping away with the bicycle pump. I imagined the kind of pain I would have been in had I still been breathing, and I was fully aware of the humiliation I was feeling even though I wasn't.

As he blew up the balloon with the bike pump, I did feel a change in my throat. I guess I understood his theory, but there must have been easier ways.

"Now we're going to keep doing this until we hear a crunch," he said. "Let me know if you hear it before me."

Not exactly reassuring. But sure enough, a little while later, I felt it more than heard it. I motioned to him.

"All right," he said. He let the balloon deflate then pulled it out of my throat like a strand of spaghetti. "How's that?"

I took a tentative, totally unnecessary breath. "Feels better." I was pleased to hear what I thought of as my own voice again. "Well, it doesn't really feel like anything. But you know what I mean."

"I'm glad," he said. "Now is there anything else I can do for you? Patch up your hair a bit, perhaps, or anything peeling or falling off?"

I thought briefly about my bullet hole, but I decided I planned to avoid that sort of work as much as possible in the future. I waved my hand like I was folding a bad blackjack hand. “Thanks, I’m good.”

NOVEMBER 17, 1934

The Altstadt is the fancy part of town. Closest thing to a gated community we get in Ganesh. Even if I hadn't forsworn the trolley, I couldn't've gotten there. The trolley didn't make stops there. If you couldn't afford a taxi or—God forbid—your own jalopy, you certainly weren't allowed in the Altstadt.

Despite his protestations, I didn't bring the head. It wasn't going to be like hanging out on the streets of the Mat where nobody gave a damn if you had a parrot on your shoulder, or hell, a talking decapitated head. That was where the Rockefellers and the Roosevelts rubbed elbows with the Carnegies and the Capones.

It was one long, endless walk from the Mat to the Altstadt. Unsurprisingly, it started to rain about halfway through so I could get nice and wet, then it stopped right around the end so I could slosh about in wet clothes for the last few blocks. Alive, I would've been furious. Dead, it was just a bit of a nuisance.

I clenched an address in my hand. It had taken a fair bit of talking to get. First the gorilla, then Homer, then a few other bar patrons. I had to move my circle a little bit wider and wider. It took almost the whole rest of the day yesterday. Between that and getting my throat reopened, it was a long day.

Every other building in the Altstadt was a steel-frame skyscraper. Some of them seemed more glass than stone. The nice ones would've had penthouses and maybe kidney-shaped swimming pools on the roofs, but I knew I'd never get high enough to see for myself. The other buildings were opera houses and fancy restaurants with one-dollar steaks.

44 Bow Street. Apartment 3C. It didn't sound special. In the Altstadt though, it had to be a penthouse at worst.

As it turned out, it was all but a skyscraper. I half expected to see a giant monkey crawling up the side. The folks coming in and out were über-ritzy. All top hats and monocles for the men and fur coats and opera glasses for the dames. It half made me want to retch, but aside from the fact I had no bile left in my ducts, I didn't want to make myself stand out any more by being covered with puke. I decided to go for it.

"Hahem," the doorman said as he closed the door for me.

"Come on, buddy," I said.

He looked me up and down like looking at me was making him dirty. Shitty little Napoleon in his tin soldier clothing with shoulder boards as big as donkey calves. Look down at me? Where does he live? If not the Mat, sure as shit not in that damn building. "I'm sorry, sir"—he sure made it sound like it pained him to call me "sir"—"but I can only let in residents and guests."

"That's me," I said. "I'm a guest. So I guess we're all done down here."

He didn't move. He steeled his jaw like he was Dick Tracy or something. Big fat, jowly, drippy jaw, and he tried to stick it out at me. I wanted to slug him, but sometimes I've got to suppress my wants. The real options, as I saw it, were to pull out my billfold— well, WH's billfold—or to pull out my gun. Oh shit, I forgot my billfold was gone. Rubber band, then. I was leaning toward the gun.

I stuck out my own chin, except I pointed at the telephone. "Why don't you pick up that squawk box, bub, and call 3C?"

He lowered his voice to a barely discernible growl. "I think you're the one that's a bub. Why don't you beat it before I beat it for you?"

That was it. Screw the gun. Screw the cash. Time to throw down. I grabbed the doorman by his big, lacey lapels, but he already had his hands wrapped around my throat. Aside from collapsing it again, though, he didn't know that it didn't bother me. I guess our scuffle was about to get untoward.

"Manny!" somebody yelled.

I recognized the voice. Shit. So much for being clandestine.

The doorman let go of me and readjusted his uniform. He did all but pull out a lint brush and start brushing me off. "Yes, Mr. Bethany, so sorry about all the trouble. I was about to escort this gentleman off the premises."

Lazar stood in the stairwell, his feet straddling two steps, his face hidden in the shadow. "It's all right. Let him in."

"Quite so, sir, quite so," the doorman said.

I gave him one last look and pointed my finger at him like a gun. He mouthed something back to me, probably, "It's not over."

I followed Lazar up to his apartment. There was an elevator with an operator dressed like a little Horatio Nelson to complement the Napoleon at the door.

Where am I getting all this from? History must be bleeding back to me, but not more than a moment or two of my own history.

Nevertheless, Lazar seemed to prefer to walk. I wondered why. Maybe he was "passing" enough to walk down the street and not get noticed, but two minutes on an elevator and Uncle Moneybags and Auntie Aristocrat would suss him out. Maybe he had a wretched smell in confined spaces. Then again, maybe he just preferred to walk. Who knows?

He kept his door locked. Must be nice. The spread was immaculate. Paintings on the wall—real, not prints—from fancy European venues, no doubt. The sitting room was a pit in the floor with carpeting and plush couches, like a dried-up hot spring.

He tossed his keys into a little Polish pot near his door and stepped into the bathroom before I saw his face. "So, spying on me, I see."

"That's my job, ain't it?" I said, adding, "The one you gave me."

After a few nonexistent heartbeats, he reappeared in the bathroom doorjamb, illuminated by the fluorescent lights behind him. He looked much less passing than usual.

"Not strictly," he said. "The key difference between a regular flatfoot and a private detective is that the one investigates everything and the other investigates only what he is paid to. Typically that doesn't involve spying on your patron."

Lazar, or Russ, or Bethany, or whoever sat down in the sitting pit. He tapped the chair next to him with his palm. Reluctantly, I joined him.

"What can I say?" I said. "I guess my curiosity got the better of me."

"Or more likely that head has been feeding you ideas." He examined his fingernails closely. "We'll have to take care of that one day."

I picked up a piece of lint from the couch. Must've been the maid's day off. "I don't need anyone else to give me crazy ideas."

"Yes, I heard about your exploits with the Old Man," Lazar said.

"Already?"

"I do have ears, and I listen. You'd be wise not to hassle the Old Man. Consider that free advice, and I give that rarely."

I stood up. I never could sit for long, but listening to someone blow smoke up my ass made me even more antsy. I took a walk along the foyer wall, pretending to admire the paintings and pottery.

"What do you need to know about me so badly?" Lazar asked.

I didn't bother to look at him. I just stood there, admiring some wooden chunk of pregnant African lady or something. "Thing is, according to the Welcome Mat's public library—"

"Font of all wisdom," he said.

"It's got its faults," I said, "but it's got books and blats, too. And here's a fun fact: Prohibition ended last year."

He smiled. I could tell without even looking. I looked, though. Ruined my cool-guy stance, but seeing him all smug like a Cheshire cat was worth it. It was worth it to make me angry. Sometimes it's nice to feel abused. It made me want to punch the teeth out of his head.

"True enough," he said finally.

"So how is it that you're a bootlegger? What's going on here?"

He sighed the kind of sigh that made it sound like the story would make *Gilgamesh* seem like a short anecdote Mark Twain had jotted in a spare minute or two. He stood and poured himself a glass of something fancy and clear. "Drink?"

I didn't say anything, but I took the glass.

He settled back down into his seat. "Ours is a funny little city. Not to put too fine a point on it, but the reason that Ganesh is still dry is you and me." He took a sip.

"Our kind," I said.

He nodded. "The rich, they don't care. They can get anything they want. A gin and tonic is no bigger deal than a day's tuition for the kids at boarding school. Cops will turn a blind eye if your wallet's big enough. Half the time they don't even need to bribe. It's an understanding."

"Selectively enforced Prohibition," I said.

He pointed his finger at me. On the nose. "So the barrels keep flowing into town, no problem. It's not even as hard as it was before. We don't even have to go to Canada anymore. All I have to do is step outside the city limits. Bootlegging is like taking a nice walk. Only…"

As if to prove a point, he turned his glass upside down and poured his expensive liquor all over the rug. It started to evaporate immediately. I could've lapped it up, but I didn't want to look like his dog any more than I already did. That, and I still had my own glass.

"When it comes to the Welcome Mat, it all dries up. That slum is the great Kalahari of the U.S. of A. Draw a circle around it on a map, and you'll have a good idea where all the police checkpoints are. You ever notice there are almost no automobiles in the Mat? And the trolley doesn't even run anymore? They've got us cordoned off. Quarantined, you might even say."

"They're trying to smoke us out," I said.

He shrugged. "More like they're hoping the problem will work itself out. This city's leadership is beyond corrupt. Officially, there's no position on the walking dead, and rumors are just that—rumors. Urban legends. Unofficially, cut off the booze and the stinky deadheads collapse."

"Except we don't collapse. We turn all braineater and we rip into them."

"Personally, I'd prefer not to see the city turn into the Somme. So I do what I do."

"So that's it?" I said. "You're our little Robin Hood?"

He shrugged, but I could tell he liked it. "I wouldn't go that far. The Old Man does more…" He broke off that thought before it even began. "I'm in the business of—to torture an already stretched metaphor—building watering holes. A little oasis like Hallowed Grounds keeps our people alive. They can't stray too far, but I do my damnedest to keep the hooch flowing and keep prices down."

"You just can't stand the sight of us," I said.

He smiled. "I live here for more pragmatic reasons. Believe me or not, I don't care. It's easier to bribe the chamber of commerce when you're seen with the commissioners. The Altstadt is where things happen. I simply can't do as much from the Mat as I can from here. Now, would you care to spend the night?"

I put the glass down on one of his potted plants. It was empty. The glass, not the plant pot. I figured he had a bullet for my brain, or failing that, a screwdriver. It wasn't that I didn't trust him, but damn, did I ever not trust that son of a bitch.

"Thanks," I said, "but I'd better get back. Wouldn't want any of your real friends to see you with the likes of me."

"At least let me pay for a cab, Jones." He stood and walked toward the door.

I stepped out into the hallway. I scratched the back of my neck. A little chunk of it came off under my fingernail. Damn. I turned back around to face him. "No, I'm good. The walk'll help me clear my head. Oh, just one last question, Lazar. Or maybe I should say Bethany."

"It hardly matters," he said flatly.

"Yeah," I said. "What was in that suitcase you made me deliver? Bribe money?"

"Now, now, Jones," he said, "a man could get killed asking questions like that. Twice."

He slammed the door in my face.

NOVEMBER 18, 1934

I woke up to a flurry of knocks at the door. God damn it.

"Jones!" Alcibé yelled. "Get the door."

"Get it yourself, head," I moaned.

Another flutter of knocking. God damn it.

"God damn it," I said, and I pulled myself up. I wouldn't say we get hungover. That doesn't make much sense. More like we get sleep deprived and the closest thing I can compare it to is being hungover. I was out most of the night walking home from Lazar's penthouse. Still not clear why we need sleep. Or why we can have sex. I went to the glass door. "Gnaghi?"

"Thank you for answering," the old gravedigger said, near breathless. "Please let me in."

"The door was unlocked," I said, pulling it open. "The door's always unlocked. This is a place of business."

The big blue goon hurried in, and I sat him down in front of my desk. He looked as if he'd seen a ghost. Occupational hazard, I guess. I noticed my desk drawer that contained the gun I had… er… "liberated" from him was open. I shut it, real nonchalant-like.

"I don't have much to offer you," I said. "Drink?"

He waved his hands in front of his face, as though he couldn't be bothered to think about drinking right now, or indeed, ever. He looked as though he was going to fall over.

"What the hell is wrong with you?" the head asked.

It's a testament to Gnaghi's capacity to stomach the bizarre that he saw a talking head on the desk and didn't think anything of it. He pointed his shaking finger at me. "The two graverobbers you asked me about?"

"Ed and Joey," I muttered.

He stared at me blankly. Obviously he didn't know the hoods' names.

"Go on," Alcibé said.

"They attacked me," he said. "Said you came poking around. They beat me up. You took my gun!"

I rubbed my chin. Alcibé gave me one of those looks. Gnaghi didn't look like he had anything else to say.

"Fair enough," I said. "What do you want me to do about it?"

"I want you to fix this," he said.

"How?" Alcibé asked.

"Talk to them, kill them, I don't care." He shook his head with his hands.

I lit up a smoke and offered the pack to the one-and-a-half others. No takers. I leaned forward on my desk and gave Gnaghi my all-business voice. "Listen, Gnaghi, I'd love to help, but I don't really take on living clients."

He was quivering again, but that time it looked like it was with rage. I briefly did the mental calculus to see if I could take the big blue ogre one-on-one. Even if I couldn't, the gun was in the desk drawer. His gun.

"This is your fault!" he screamed. "Your fault, Braineater Jones! You took my protection. You brought those two down on me. I had to ask a hundred corpsies to find you, but I found you. Now you make this right!" He slammed his hand on the desk. It nearly sent poor Alcibé flying.

I leaned back in my chair. "I suppose this will be *pro boner*, then."

Gnaghi stared at me as if I had just killed his kitten.

"I don't suppose you'll be paying me," I said.

"Me?" the old gravedigger said, thumping his chest. "You should be paying me. But take care of this, and I call it even."

Alcibé, back in his traveling cage, said, "Did you really take that poor sucker's piece?"

I jammed my hands into my pockets as though I was digging around for something. "What of it?"

"You never take a man's piece," Alcibé said. I could feel himself shaking his head, or rather, shaking himself. "That's dirty pool, old chap."

"Yeah, well, that was before I met you, so you could be the annoying good angel on my shoulder."

He peeked through the cover. I guess he grabbed it with his teeth.

Note to self: ask him how he does that.

"Hold on," he said. "We're on Infected turf here."

"Yeah, I know," I said. "That's where the graverobbers live."

"This is crazy. We're not taking on that gang by ourselves and for free. Turn back. Just tell the cryptkeeper you took care of it."

"I thought I took care of it last time," I said. "They promised they wouldn't come back."

He really laid on the sarcasm with a trowel. "Oh really? You mean two street hoods lied to you? How difficult to believe."

Actually, looking back in my notebook, I realized that Joey had only promised they wouldn't go back to the boneyard. That didn't mean the groundskeeper was off limits. He must leave sometimes, at least to get shack spackle and tiny wind bells. Maybe they jumped him then. Or maybe, like the head said, they just didn't keep their word. That would break my unbeating heart.

"Hey, I'm trying to figure out this job as I go along!"

"I can tell. You're making a terrible muck of it."

"A muck?"

"That's what I said."

"What does that mean?" I asked.

"It means you're an idiot. You're not taking any precautions. Have you even thought this through?"

Precautions. Precautions. I looked around the street. A worker was spot-welding a lamp post. Of course, this being the Welcome Mat, that wasn't the whole story. When there weren't any peds around, he turned back to his real task: cutting bike chains from a rack. I walked over and tapped him on the shoulder.

"Hey, buddy."

Kneeling over his "work," the man flipped over on his back, startled, when I tapped him. The blowtorch clattered to the ground and went out, hissing as its gas continued to pump. He crabwalked deftly out from under my shadow.

"Hey…" I repeated.

The man flipped his welding mask off and revealed himself to be a dame and a breather, too. Why not? In coveralls and a mask, everybody looks alike. Times must be tough when a breather's down in the Mat stealing our crap.

"I'm sorry!" she said. "I didn't mean to do it!"

"Sure, whatever. Look, I just want to see if I can borrow—"

She leapt to her feet and beat pavement away from me. Luckily, the mask caught the wind and somersaulted back off her head, and it landed with a clatter at my feet. I bent down, wiped the dust off of it, and stuck it on my own melon.

"There's your precaution," I told the head.

"Another robbery boldly foiled by the Braineater Jones Detective Agency," Alcibé said. "Or should I say, 'committed by'?"

"Clam up."

We pounded the few blocks to Infected territory.

To my not-at-all surprise, ass-eating pink snakes littered the walls the closer we got. It took me a minute to remember the place, but when I spotted the garret where I had found Miss Claudia's locket, I knew.

"This is the place," I said.

"Be cautious," the head warned.

"Let's be bold. We have nothing to lose but our brains." I pulled the boomstick out of my pocket and flicked it open. Six rounds. Good enough. I flipped the mask down and raised my leg to kick in the door.

"Stop!" Alcibé fairly yelled. "Perhaps a little stealth is in order? At least sneak in and get the drop on them."

I thought about it for a moment. "Nah." I kicked in the door.

I guess that frightened them because they started shooting at me almost immediately. The place looked like an opium den, littered with gangsters, pillows, and garbage. I assumed the one guy was Ed. A few of the others scrambled behind couches and overturned furniture.

The hail of gunfire was withering. A few rounds dinked off the birdcage. It must've given the head quite a fright. Somewhere his ass was shitting itself.

"Jones!" Alcibé shrieked in my ear.

"Don't worry," I said. "I've got my precaution on." A few bullets whanged off the welder's mask. The rest punched through me. The gangsters must've thought I was a maniac on narcotics or something. I could hardly blame them. I did have a birdcage on my shoulder in the middle of a firefight.

"What about me?" the head yelled after a third and then a fourth near miss.

"Oh, yeah," I said. I put the birdcage on the ground and kicked it behind a couch. That seemed to shut the little shit up, anyway. Then I simply waited until they ran out of bullets. It seemed like the best way to take advantage of my situation. I took my mask off. "Any man who doesn't want to die better clear on out the back." I waved in that general direction with Gnaghi's piece.

Joey and another trouble boy who must've been Ed were the first two on their feet. A couple of real fearless heroes, those two.

I pointed at the two Infected. "Not you two. Ed and Joey stay."

The two gangsters looked like I had cancelled Christmas. The rest of their brethren abandoned them lickety-split. There were a couple of girls with them too, prosties apparently. They all took off out the back door.

"And you'd better not go back around front!" I yelled after them. "I expect to leave unmolested."

I fired a shot at the last guy's ass to put the point across. It probably didn't hit him. I didn't pay much attention. For the first time, I looked down at my chest. I was pretty well ventilated. I might have to go see the scratcher again. Or buy a can of spackle.

Ed and Joey, heads hung like bichon frises, turned around and walked toward me.

"Hands up," I said, "Don't look at me."

They turned around and reached for the sky.

"It doesn't matter," Joey said. "We already know who you are."

"Shut up, Joe!" Ed poked his partner sharply in the ribs.

I recognized that voice. "Say that again."

Ed was wary, his voice halting. "Shut up, Joe?"

I narrowed my eyes. It was like something stuck in my head, like a skipping record. I told him, "Say, 'If he's got it anywhere, he's got it in the safe.'"

Ed obliged.

"Mr. Y," I said.

"What?" Ed said.

Alcibé and Joey repeated the sentiment, but I fired a round to get everyone's attention. That left me with four.

"I came here to help the gravedigger," I said, "but I've had a revelation instead."

"What's going on, Jones?" the head asked.

I put the birdcage up on a couch cushion and whipped off his cover. I poked Joey with my pistol. Gnaghi's pistol, I mean. "Say something."

"What do you want me to say?" he asked.

X. Definitely. How did I not notice it before? Because I wasn't looking for it before.

3. Who is X? Who is Y? Those two Infected gangsters Ed and Joey, same as answer to the second number one, *Who stole Miss Claudia's locket.*

"That's enough," I said. "You two have been to Rothering's house."

They exchanged a tortured glance. A lot must've crossed between their eyes because they took off running for the back door. I burned powder. I meant for it to be a warning shot, but naturally it hit Joey in the back of the leg. You know how those things happen.

"Ah, you son of a bitch!" Joey roared as he crumpled to the floor.

That left me with three rounds. I waved the gun in Ed's general direction. Luckily, seeing his partner in crime in pain was enough to root him to the spot.

"Look, we don't want any trouble, deadhead," Ed said.

"Why don't you have a seat," I said.

"On the floor?"

I nodded. I got down on the floor Indian-style with them, like we were kids at a party playing Spin the Bottle. Except that one was a head, and one was grabbing his blood-spurting knee.

"So," I said, "let's talk. Let's get the easiest thing out of the way first. You went back to hassle the gravedigger. Even after I went to the trouble to warn you off."

"Eddie," Joey moaned.

"Listen, man," Ed said, "please let me bandage him up. It won't take a minute."

I cold-cocked Ed in the chin. He didn't really deserve it, but I didn't feel like those druggies were getting the point. "The gravekeeper!"

"Look, man," Ed said, "that guy sold us out. I don't know him. And I don't know you."

"Well you know me now," I said. "Whatever that means. And you know that whole cemetery is off-limits, as is the gravedigger. Only thing is, now I'm starting to think that the only way to keep you two off his back is…" I waved the pistol at them. Message received, loud and clear.

"No, no," Ed said. "Look, we won't bother him, I swear."

"You can bother him if you have to. Just tug on the bellstring."

"I swear!" Ed shrieked.

"I wish I could believe you, Ed, I really do, but your lives kind of depend on the answers you give to the next few questions."

Alcibé didn't say anything, but I felt his glance. "For the love of God, Jones."

Stupid good cop. Ruining my routine. I grabbed a somewhat clean towel and tossed it to Ed. "Clean up your friend. Then we can all have a nice chat."

It didn't take him more than a few minutes to stop the bleeding and apply a tourniquet. I watched, standing as uncomfortably close as I could. When he was done, he held up his arms as though he was surrendering all over again. Putty in my hands. Good.

"So," I said, "the day I was killed, you two idiots were at a certain mansion."

"Look, we didn't mean to shoot at you, man," Ed said. "We were just supposed to rob the joint. We didn't mean to kill you. We saw you running, and we, well, you know."

I stared at him. He was telling the truth. "You didn't kill me. I was dead before I went out the window."

Ed seemed to breathe a sigh of relief. "Well, no harm done, then."

That deserved another pistol-whipping. What can I say, I'm a good bad cop. Or a bad good cop. Either way.

"So, when you were casing the joint, you didn't hear a shot?" I asked. "Didn't see anyone running away? Maybe catch a glimpse of their face?"

"We didn't case the joint that day!" Joey said, and he sounded as though he was in a good bit of pain.

"Dammit," I said, "what did you steal?"

They exchanged another one of those knowing glances.

"Go ahead. Kiss each other. You know you want to."

"We didn't steal anything," Ed said finally. "It wasn't there."

"What was it?"

"A money clip," Ed said. "Engraved with initials."

I didn't even wait for him to say them. "WH."

He nodded.

"You were hired," Alcibé broke in at long last. "By who?"

"One of you deadheads," Joey hissed. "A bird. Good-looking one, too."

I dropped my hand on Alcibé's mop of hair to keep him quiet. "Don't suppose you got a name."

"It wasn't that kind of job," Ed said.

"Where'd you meet her?" Alcibé asked through clenched teeth.

"The docks."

NOVEMBER 19, 1934

After getting fired up like that, I really needed some electroshock. I felt worse than I did the first night after I was brought across. I felt like I could barely move. I used the trick Lazar had taught me about ripping out a lamp cord.

Alcibé chastised me for ruining a perfectly good lamp. He nagged me like every good wife should. "And by the way, you could've given me some protection before we went in there."

"You wanted a rubber, you dirty old sailor?" I said. "What would you have done with it? Stuck it on your ear?"

"You had a welder's mask!" he said. "I could've been put down."

"Put down," I said. "That's such a nasty term. Sounds like you're euthanizing a dog. I wish we could come up with a better word for it."

"Well, it's better than your childish 'double dog dead,'" the head said. "You may as well be ordering a kneehigh from the sody jerk man."

Not liking the lip he was giving me, I flicked the head off the desk.

"Another thing," he added from the floor, his voice coming in waves as he rolled back and forth, "you ought to have killed them."

"I ought to have lots of things," I said. "I don't think they'll bother the gravedigger anymore. You give him a call for me."

"It doesn't matter. He skipped town. Not worth it, you know. Would you want to work in a cemetery with us crawling out of the graves?"

"No, I guess not," I said.

I went to see the pseudo-European scratcher again. He whistled loudly when he saw me.

"You look like a colander," he said in that extra spicy German sauce of his. "You want me to fill in all the holes?" He had a bucket of spackle ready for the task.

"Yeah," I said. "Make me seaworthy."

He got started.

"Wait," I said.

He looked at me expectantly.

I pointed at my first bullet hole, the one that had gotten me into all this mess. It was a little more ragged than the others, and despite near-constant and liberal application of Old Crow, it was becoming home to a nest of maggots. "Not this one."

The scratcher eyed up my hole. It was clearly the worst one. He shrugged. "Whatever you say. No accounting for sentiment."

When I was all patched up, sitting in the office, it started. As I knew it would. No avoiding it with that jack-in-the-box, less the jollity.

"You know what we have to do," he said grimly.

"Yeah," I said.

"You know where we have to go," he added, as if I hadn't gotten it the first time.

"Yeah, I get it," I said.

"Then why aren't we going?"

I looked at him, drink in my hand, Lucky in my mouth. The walls of the office were stale with cigarette smoke, already. At least, I imagined they would be if we ever stopped smoking long enough to let the five-foot-high cloud of smoke clear out. "Why are you so eager to sell her down the river? If it wasn't for her, you'd still be a lab rat in that bokor's clutches."

"There are worse things than being preyed upon by others," the head said.

"Like what?" I sneered.

"Like, for instance, being preyed upon by our own kind."

I stood and walked to the window. A derelict lay on the sidewalk, face covered by newspaper. Two bums came by and picked him up, beat him up, and took his coffee cup full of change. Crippled doughboy according to his cardboard sign, though that was poorly written and could've been a lie.

"You've got a soft spot for her," he said.

"As I recall," I said, "she's got a soft spot for me, too."

"Dames always get in the way," he said. "I've seen a lot of good men, and our kind too, led astray by a pair of fancy gams. She's a traitor. A Benedict Arnold. We should figure out her game and shut her down."

"You know," I said, "those two morons didn't describe her in any great detail. It could've been any one of our kind."

"Fine," he said. "Prove me wrong. Let's investigate. Get me my hat, would you?"

I grabbed his damned Panama hat and plopped him on my shoulder. No need for all the theatrics of the birdcage. We were going somewhere in the Mat, and somewhere where we could get some answers.

Ivan Skaron looked surprised to see us. Surprised and delighted. He threw his arms around me and kissed Alcibé over and over. I hoped he was foreign and not just a weirdo. "Come in, come in. My saviors. Let me make you some drinks."

"We're not here about that," Alcibé said.

"I won't argue with you," I said.

"Good, good," he said.

It was the first time I had really been in his apartment. Not much to say about it. Covered with an inch of dust and two inches of books. I was familiar with a few of them from the Mat Library; others seemed new. He was branching out. Besides history and witchcraft, there were biology texts and quite a bit on astronomy.

"Your legs look good, back on you," I said with a chuckle.

"Thanks," he yelled.

He was busying himself in the kitchen, clattering dishes and putting a teapot on the stove to whistle, when I sat down. I stuck the head on an ottoman. It sure sounded like he was making tea, or maybe what the Italians called "expresso," although neither made a whole lot of sense as a beverage to offer one of our kind.

I glanced at his wall. He was constructing a sort of a word maze on the wall with bits and pieces carved out of books and newspapers. Seemed to me a bit like a minor sacrilege to cut up a book. A penknife sat on a stack of books he had either recently gone through or were up on the chopping block.

"So," I said, "you hear from any of your morgue mates lately?"

"Eh?" Skaron yelled from the kitchen. "What's that?"

"I said—" I yelled.

"I suppose you're referring to Kumaree." Guess he had heard me. Weird. He emerged from the kitchen with a platter of what the Orientals call "socky." Warm. Blech. But as they say in the Welcome Mat, booze is booze. "So naturally I assume when I'm visited by a couple of busy P.I.s, this is not a social call."

"Oh, no," I said. "Don't think that."

He looked over his glasses at me. "Don't be coy, Jones. This is the first time I've seen you here. You've had ample opportunity. I don't mind, of course. I hate being interrupted when I'm conducting research."

"When aren't you doing research?"

"Precisely my point. Tell me, though, what was it you were wondering about a pro po my sister?"

"Anything you can tell us," I said.

"Anything unsavory," Alcibé had to add.

"Unsavory?" Skaron scratched his scalp.

Leave it to the head to ruin a lead. As soon as we left, Skaron would go running to her or, worst-case scenario, telephone and tell her to pack up shop, wherever she was.

"That is to say," I said, "how close are you?"

"Well, we're morgue mates." He added with a laugh, "Whatever that means."

"What does that mean, I wonder," I said.

He waved his finger. "It's an interesting story, actually. Oh, but I don't want to bore you two."

"Oh no, bore away," I said. "What about you, Alcibé? You find 'remember-when' stories boring?"

"Not at all," Alcibé said.

"Well, as you know, we're both from Greater Russia," he said.

"Sure," I said.

Alcibé nodded. Or more accurately, he rocked back and forth on his ottoman.

"We were both in the Ukrainian neighborhood, as it were, when we died. Probably passed each other on the street, but the sort of thing where you never stop to think about it. I always had my nose buried in a book, rushing to and fro, here and about. As it turns out, that was my undoing."

"Hit by an auto?" I said.

"Piano, actually," he said. "They were lifting one of those grand affairs into an apartment a few stories up. There I was, reading *And Quiet Flows the Don*, ignoring that frayed piano rope, and it crushed me. Like the cartoon after a newsreel. Next thing you know, I wake up in the morgue."

"Huh," Alcibé said.

I would've said, "Go figure," but I figured he didn't need his bullshit in stereo.

"Well, I don't have to tell you my sister's a bit ginchy," he said.

I shrugged.

"Hadn't noticed," Alcibé said.

"Anyway, thing about it is, I tried to make a pass at her when we first woke up. Didn't work out so great. The mortician had already gotten to me. My intestines were out of my body and in a scale."

"How did she react to that?"

"A lot better than I did. She's always kept me together, so to speak. Some of the other morgue mates…" He shrugged. I guess they didn't take their responsibilities so seriously. "It was nice, though. We both spoke Russian, I being from White Russia and she being from Georgia."

I scratched my head.

"They speak Russian there?"

"If you know what's good for you."

Must be a big expat community in Atlanta or something.

He continued. "A few others woke up, and we switched to English. But she stuffed my guts back in and stitched me up. You wouldn't think a woman like that would be good with a needle— you'd think she'd get by on her looks—but she sewed me up just fine."

As if to prove his point, he opened his shirt and showed us the gruesome wound from his dissection. Vivisection? Whatever.

"How often do you speak to her these days?" Alcibé asked.

Skaron seemed lost in his own memories. "Hmm?"

"I said—" the head said.

"Oh, I heard you," Skaron said. "Well, hardly ever, honestly. I was actually rather surprised she, you know, hired you to find me. Not, uh, deeply shocked to my core, but you know, we don't exactly talk all the time."

"You don't know where she lives," I said.

It wasn't a question, but he answered it anyway. "Not by address. But I do know she lives down by the docks."

Alcibé and I exchanged a glance.

"A bit unusual for our kind to stray from our watering holes, I know, but she must get her go-juice some other way. I wonder, should I come with you?"

"Probably better that you don't," I said. "You ought to remember her the way she was."

"Dead on a slab?"

"I meant as your beloved sister."

"Well, she'll always be that," Skaron said. "No matter what you do to her."

I hoped he didn't have a gun. He smiled as he showed us out, though.

NOVEMBER 20, 1934

Morning came, and we were both exhausted. We had traded shifts watching the window. It had been too late when we left Skaron's to go to the docks, but we didn't feel safe enough to go to bed. I had gotten less rest though, because the damned head had woken me every few hours to light another cigarette. They were my cigarettes, might I add.

I ended up sitting in my chair, wearing not much more than my drawers and a union suit, drinking a pick-me-up and chewing on a toothpick. There were no more Luckies. In life, it would've been pathetic. In unlife, it was still pretty pathetic. He sat in the windowsill, scanning the street.

I felt compelled to pull out this notebook and flip through it. Something nagged at me, and lack of sleep was making it stick out in my mind. "Why do you suppose we have to sleep?"

"Every living thing needs to sleep," the head said without taking his eyes off the street.

"Listen to what you just said," I said.

He shrugged in the fashion I was accustomed to.

"We don't heal," I said. "We don't dream. What's the point of sleep?"

"Maybe your body isn't the only thing that needs sleep," he said. "Maybe your brain needs it, too. Our brains most definitely function. Maybe booze alone isn't enough to keep it functioning, despite what Lazar would have us believe."

Made sense, after a fashion.

5. Why does a—whatever I am—need sleep? To give those meaty ticking time bombs between our ears a chance to settle down. Maybe.

The hands of the clock made their rounds at half speed. My eyes were drifting shut. I snapped awake but good. "What do you think?"

"Huh?"

"Think we should risk it?" I asked.

He looked at me, first out of the corner of his eye, then he rotated himself to face me with a sickening motion that made the jagged muscles at the stump of his neck ripple like a snail's belly. His method of ambulation was forced and slow, as if to underline the point he was about to make. "I'm no use to you, Jones."

That stopped me in my tracks. A lesser man might've spilt his bourbon. As it was, I just put it down. "What's all that, then?"

"I'm useless. I'm a burden," the head said. "I can't cover your back, can't answer the door, can't even do research unless you turn the page for me. I kept you up all night when it was my turn for watch. I don't bring a whole lot to this organization."

"You bring heart," I said.

"That's not true, either. I don't have one. You ought to have left me with the bokor. Let him dispose of me."

I took a long drag from my toothpick. I would have to go pick up some squares. Not yet, though. Newsstand wouldn't be open yet. "Let's not be stupid. Maybe I don't slobber all over your ass every day, but as you say, you ain't got one, so don't be offended."

"You're not the one who says it," he said. "You don't have to say it. I know it without hearing it from anyone else. A head's just a head's just a head. Worthless. Like a magic eight ball. All full of answers that don't help anyone. You ought to put me out of my misery."

I stamped out the toothpick in the ashtray. I walked to the closet. In the time since I had—what's the word?—"appropriated" Gnaghi's piece, I had bought a rifle. It wasn't exactly convenient to carry around the city, leastways not when I wanted to be subtle, but it had its uses. I pulled it out and pumped it.

"That's right," he said. "Do me." He squeezed his eyes shut.

I was way past telling if it was all just a fun little pity party or if he was really getting drowsy for the big sleep. Either way, I didn't care. I mounted the rifle on the windowsill with a bit of wire and ran the venetian blind cord through the trigger. Messing with the cord didn't harm anything. The blinds had long since been ripped out.

"What's taking so long?"

"Shut up," I said. "No, wait. Better yet, open up."

He opened his eyes.

"Open your mouth, come-rag," I said.

He opened wide and said, "Ahh." I stuck the cord-pull into his mouth.

He clenched down on it. "What's this?"

I spun him back around and pointed him out the window. "Can you move it?"

He tugged on the cord, and the rifle moved up and down, left and right. A bit jury-rigged, but it functioned well enough.

"Now don't tug too hard," I said, "or it'll go off."

"I can't kill myself with this, Jones. The barrel's too long."

I smacked him upside the head, which unfortunately, sent him flying. I had to run and grab him. "Would you give me a break? At least wait to kill yourself until after I've cracked this case. I need you to watch the window. You don't want to go, you've got a death wish, fine. But at least stay here and watch the office."

"I don't think Skaron's coming," Alcibé said. "I think the absentminded professor bit is more than just a bit."

"He's the least of our problems. At least, I think he is. Do me a favor and keep me from coming home to an ambush." I pulled on my trench coat and made sure to stick Gnaghi's piece in my pocket. I made for the door.

"Jones," he said. There it came, the blubbering "thank you," "you're my best friend," and all that happy horseshit.

"Forget it," I said.

"All right," he said.

I got halfway down the stairs to the fence before I turned back. "Forgot my trousers."

"Yeah," he said.

One-oh-one Gateway Lane. Again. I had no idea if that was the place, whether the bird was there, whether there was any relation to anything else in my life. But if Lazar was running something through the docks and the ginchy dame was running something through the docks, odds were they'd convene somewhere. Maybe that was the place. Maybe not. Maybe I'd get shot. Again.

I checked my boomstick for at least the fifth time since hopping off the back of a garbage truck once it reached the fish market. I knew the bullets weren't going anywhere, but it never hurt to check. They were still there. I thumped on the door with the butt of the piece. Nobody came at first, so I kept on a-thumping. Finally somebody came.

They hid back in the shadows like before. I waited. I could wait all night. Let the bastard talk.

"Yes?" he said finally, and his voice reminded me ever so slightly of that back-alley abortionist I had been seeing.

"You recognize me?"

"Yes." Descriptive.

"Boss sent me back around," I said.

"For what?" the European asked.

Finally. New words.

"Hell if I know. Boss says jump, I say, 'How high?' Boss says shit, I say, 'How wet?' You know how it is."

"I most certainly do not," he said.

I shrugged. Maybe he could see. Maybe not. "Well, if you don't want my help, I'll go back and tell him." I turned and started to walk away.

"Wait!" he hissed after me.

The door closed. I heard a lot of clinking and clanking. Then the door opened just a crack and he waved me inside.

The inside of the loft was a lot like the outside. Metal. Stark. Bare. Only the inside was full of crates. Funny thing about the crates was a lot of them were marked with a funny bird holding a circle and a crooked cross. Looking at that load the eagle bore gave me a white, hurty vision of a fat man smiling at me. It definitely meant something to me. I ran my fingers along it. The ink was cool and stood out slightly over the woodgrain.

I looked around. There were a lot of fellows moving cargo. They wore suits, which was strange enough for working men, especially in the middle of working. Stranger still was that all their suits were a bit oddly tailored. Like maybe they were off the rack, not really made for them. The tall ones wore sizes too small; the short ones were swimming in daddy's clothes.

"What's this?" I said, jutting my chin out at the emblem.

The doormonger stared at me. I got my first real look at him. He reminded me of nothing so much as a vulture. Long, sharp, nose, beady little eyes, and a lean and hungry look that put Cassius to shame.

God damn it. There's another flash of memory. What can I say about flashes like that?

"You really are just a useful idiot, aren't you?" he said.

"Watch it, bub," I said.

"No, I think it is you who are the bub," vulture-man said. "We are not stupid here. We know your type."

"I think it's usually translated 'kind,' Popov," I said.

"And what did Mr. Forday send you for?" he asked.

Was that another pseudonym? Who knew he had so many in him.

"Hauling cargo, I guess," I said.

"Well, this"—he tapped the funny symbol—"is a swastika. You will know it very well, soon, I think."

"NSDAP," I said, feeling the words coming to my lips as I spoke them. "Nazi Party."

The vulture smiled. "You've heard of us. Good. Now you can get started over there." He pointed to one corner of the loft particularly well infested with the poorly tailored European types. I didn't much want to go over there. I would've avoided it if I could. Maybe he already had me pegged as a snoop. Maybe not.

I did notice something on the wall. "Now that symbol, I'm a little more familiar with." There was a neon pink snake eating its own tail. Same graffito vandal as did the fancy eye-tie welcome sign to the Mat. Same fellow who marked up the whole neighborhood where Ed and Joey lived. "I suppose that means you're working with the Infected."

"It makes no difference," the vulture said. "We work with whoever is useful. And you, right now, are useful for lifting boxes. Right over there."

He pointed again. I swallowed—an utterly meaningless gesture for a deadhead—and took a step.

I don't think I got more than two paces before he cold-cocked me in the back of the head with a cosh. In retrospect, I was probably lucky to still be unalive. I never really found out how much damage our kind could take before being killed, but it seemed like a simple whack was enough to put me out without putting me down.

When I woke up, guess who was staring at me?

"Hey, sweetlips," she said.

"Hey, yourself," I said. "So, how's the treason business going?" I struggled to move, but she had razor-wired me to the ground but good. I looked around a bit. We were still in the loft, only in the upper part. Downstairs, the mungos were still moving cargo.

"Oh, Jones," she said, "you always know just what to say to get my blood boiling."

I tugged on the wires. Nothing doing. They were looped through big metal hooks in the ground. Cargo hooks, I suppose. I did have the option of slicing my body to pieces. Hey, they had sewn her brother back together. Then again, I didn't know too many friendly seamstresses.

"What are you doing here?" she asked.

"Oh, you know me," I said. "Just trying to get the answers to a few questions."

"Like who took your money clip?"

Huh?

"Huh?"

She pulled the old silver beastie out of her pocket. She waved it in front of my eyes. I guess she intended it to be tantalizing. Then she laid it down on my chest. "Come on, now, Jones. That's a lot of trouble to go to over something so silly. I left you the money."

I struggled against the wires. What can I say? I'm nothing if not a creature of habit. One tends to want to be free. Damn it. What was she talking about? "What? You're talking about my billfold? That's easily the least of my problems right now."

She leaned back and laughed, long and sophisticated-like. Her neck went all the way back, like one of those Egyptian queens. Creepy. "You didn't even think to ask, did you? Where did it go? You're one hell of a detective."

"Hey, now," I said, "there's no cause for a lady to swear."

She was on her knees and over my head in an instant. In any other situation, I would've been thrilled. She grabbed my chin and my neck, though, as if she wanted to tear it off. Just tear the skin off my face.

Something was up. Something was in her. Maybe it was her time of the month. If our kind gets such a thing.

"I'm not a lady"—she slammed my head against the caged metal floor—"any more than you're a man. And I'll swear as much as I damn well please."

She punctuated her sentences with creaming my head against the floor. I wasn't much enjoying it. Not sure how long I could've survived it, either. Probably a while, but I couldn't be sure.

"Listen," I muttered, "I don't know how deep you are in this. I don't care, either. But you know the answers I want. So help me out. Or kill me now."

She stared at me for a while, then picked the silver clip up off my chest. "You're a queer cat."

"You love me," I said.

"Don't"—it was one of those long, dangerous pauses—"make that mistake." The old dame stood up and walked back and forth, her heels clicking across the floor. They weren't quite stilettos. Those would've punched right through the caged steel and ripped her ankles to pieces. They were still fairly high heels though and made loud clanks.She wheeled back on me. "I'll tell you what. How about I answer one question for you—only one—for old time's sake. You seem to have a lot on your mind."

"Any question?" I asked.

"Any question," she said.

"And you have to answer it completely?" I said.

"To the best of my knowledge," she said. "And no games, Jones. This is a courtesy, if you will. No 'what's going on here' or 'tell me what you know.'"

Damn. If a half-remembered lifetime of genie stories had taught me one thing, it was that semantic arguments always outwitted a godlike being somehow.

There was so much to know. What were the Nazis doing here? Was she in charge? Why had she taken the billfold? When had she taken it? No, in retrospect, I guess I knew the answer to that one. What was in the suitcase I had delivered to that very loft a week ago? Why had she hired Ed and Joey? Why were the Nazis in bed with the Infected, of all people? A European gang with an all-American street gang? Didn't make much sense except viewed through a different lens.

And those were just the questions on the tip of my tongue. There was a whole list of unanswered, numbered questions, too.

Unfortunately, that list was in my jacket pocket, and I was strapped to the ground like a bull about to get castrated. Maybe in more ways than one.

"Tick tock, Jonesy," she said. "Time's up."

"All right," I said, and I picked one. "What did Lazar make me deliver to this joint?"

She smiled. I didn't make her uncomfortable at all. Wrong question, I guess. "That is an interesting one. I guess I may as well tell you, Jones."

She disappeared for a few moments. I struggled to see where she went, but all I could get a glimpse of was her gams, working at something offscreen. Still, that was a nice view to get.

When she came back, she threw a thin packet of white powder on my chest. Thin enough to have been in the suitcase. "This."

I glanced up at her. "That's only a partial answer, genie."

She laughed. "You really don't give up, do you? Well, this has nothing to do with anything we're doing down there, so I guess it doesn't really matter. Nothing you say or do matters. It's enough to make a man feel pathetic. And bad in bed. But you already knew that."

If she wanted to get my goat, she probably had it, but I'd never show it.

"Your best buddy's been poisoning you," she said.

"Too late," I said. "I'm already dead."

"Oh, yeah," she said, "I forgot. But what can every other deadhead do that you can't? Still. After… how long's it been? A month?"

"Three weeks," I said.

"Think about it," she said.

"I can't remember my old life," I said.

"Ding ding ding. You win the carton of Camels, the brand more doctors prefer."

I wriggled, I guess a bit like a worm, trying to get a better look at the white powder. "This stuff keeps me dead in the head?"

"Long after you should've been remembering chasing fireflies and your first kiss with Norma Rottencrotch," she said. "Do you get all your booze from the same place?"

The gorilla behind the counter. Slipped a few greenbacks every week to fizz up my drinks and my drinks alone. The rest came in bottles straight from Lazar. I never bothered to check if they were open already or not.

8. For that matter, why can't I remember anything from before I died? Is that artificial, or is it part of the resurrection process? Because the old bastard Lazar is slipping me mickeys. I'll fix his wagon. Somehow.

"I wouldn't bother coming here again," she said. "You're not the only one getting wise to us."

"What does that mean?" I said.

"Ah ta ta," she said. "I told you only one question." She kissed my forehead. "Love you. Miss you." She slammed me with the cosh again.

Awake. Warehouse empty. The wires were gone, thank God. I rolled over. The pink snake eating itself was sprayed over with black. Nothing in particular. Just a big meaningless inkblot.

I searched the place head to toe. Every inch of that damned mess. Not a cobweb, not a fingerprint. No secret "What Our Plan Is" manual, in German or otherwise. It was as though they had taken a blowtorch to the place.

I walked back to the Mat, hands in my pockets, running it all over in my mind. The twist had let me live. If the Nazis wanted me as a fall guy, why had they sterilized the warehouse? I couldn't believe Kumaree had let me live out of sentiment. Maybe she still wanted me pounding the pavement. A pawn that she didn't necessarily want knocked off the board just yet.

Or maybe… more likely… someone else was calling the shots. It was nice to feel wanted, even if it was just as a fall guy. But somehow it seemed like more was expected of me. Somebody up there wanted me to crack the case… or to kill somebody… or just to be a stumbling block. There was no way to know.

I reached Hallowed Grounds and ran my fingers through the cat's hair in the fence. I walked upstairs and dropped into my chair.

"How'd it go?" he said.

I shrugged.

"What does that mean?"

"It means I'm not going to drink the water anymore," I said. I grabbed the already open bottle of Crow. Miserably, I turned it upside down. I think if the head had legs, he would have come running at me.

"Hey hey hey!" he yelled. "The hell are you doing?"

"It's poison," I said. "Our rich Altstadter friend has been keeping me all doped up this whole time. That's why I can't remember. Time to get a new source of firewater."

"I could've drunk that," he said. "I don't have any trouble remembering."

"Yeah, well, it was symbolic," I said. Symbolic, and it left a big puddle of bourbon on the rug. "We'll start drinking clean stuff together. How'd it go for you?"

"Didn't have to shoot anyone," he said. "Couple of times I thought I might have to, but mostly just kids screwing around."

"Damn kids," I said and instinctively reached for my glass. Of course, no glass was there. Well, the glass was there, only it was empty.

"What else did you find out?" he asked.

I filled him in. The Nazis moving strange cargo. The cargo cult packing up in the middle of the night. Kumaree running it, or maybe being a middle-management type. It was all food for thought, but not much else. It didn't bring us any closer to solving the case or even cracking a hole in it.

NOVEMBER 21, 1934

I was dry as a bone. Dying, really. What do our kind do when we sober up? I already knew that answer. We wander into the streets and chew off the top of Little Orphan Annie's head.

"I'm dying, Jones," the head said.

"Shut up," I said. My throat was dusty. I felt a little tickle in my belly. Like a brain might really hit the spot.

What was that all about? What was the fascination? Something primordial in our being that made us go for… No. Got to stop. I'm getting too sober. There must be a clean source of booze in the city.

"What is this junk, anyway?" I said, throwing the packet of white powder down on the desk. She had left me that much at least. Along with a big sloppy red lipstick mark. On the bag, not on my face. Who could figure out dames?

"Give me a drink," he said, "so I can think straight."

I rolled over onto my belly. Everything seemed so hard. I crawled most of the way to the sink and poured a little sip of water into a Dixie cup. When I tipped it into the head's mouth, he spat it out.

"What is this piss?" he croaked.

"It's water," I said.

"I need alcohol!" he yelled.

"This'll have to do," I said. "There's nothing clean anywhere. Got to get out of the city. I don't know." I lurched to my feet. I felt like… I don't know. Awful. Like my worst bender in real life. Not that I could remember that. Even bone-sober my memories weren't coming back yet. I needed booze to function. Clean booze. I grabbed the head and stuffed him unceremoniously under my trench coat. No time for the parrot cage or anything else. I stumbled down into the fence.

Homer and his cat looked up at me. "Jones? That you?"

"Yeah," I grunted.

"You sound awful," he said.

"I'm blind stinking sober," I said. "I need a drink."

"Why don't you head on down?" he said, pointing toward the speakeasy.

I shook my head, but of course he couldn't see that. "No good. They've been spiking my drinks."

"Oh." He made it sound as though he had heard that a hundred times before. Maybe he had. The community was small. I had to assume the fence heard most everything. He reached under his counter, searched around, and pulled out a bottle. Actually, it looked pretty old. Vintage-like. Not Crow, some junky brand, but it had to be clean. Unless Lazar was bribing the blind old fence too, which didn't make a damn lick of sense. "Here." He started pouring the booze all over the counter.

I stopped him. "Thanks, Homer."

I put Alcibé on the counter. He had to be in a tray or turned upside down for the booze to take effect and not just leak out his neck. I flipped him, which elicited a moan.

"Who's that?" the blind man asked.

"My partner. Bottoms up. Or whatever."

We took our drinks. I didn't know about Alcibé, but that really took the edge off for me. Like a warm, burning glow that started in my belly and spread out to my fingertips and toes. Well, hell, it must've been different for the damn head. Probably just felt like some whiskey soaking into his skull.

"Thanks, Homer," I said.

"Why don't you boys take it?" he said, pushing the bottle toward me.

I had to grab it to make sure it didn't tip over. "No, I can't."

"Doesn't bother me. I can't sell it. Not legally, anyway. I don't drink the stuff."

"You sure?" I said.

"Yeah, go ahead," he said. "Consider it a gift. And, Jones?"

"Yeah, Homer?"

"I didn't like you much when you first got here. But you've grown on me."

I could've said the same thing. I didn't, though. Back upstairs, I sat the bottle on the desk. It was nearly full. Homer had clearly given a tipple now and then to special visitors on extra special occasions. But a bottle, well, how long did that last me? Even carefully rationed, it wouldn't last us longer than a day or two. We'd still ultimately have to get out on the street and figure out some other source of booze.

"I'll worry about pounding the pavement for more tomorrow," I said. "Right now, we need to wrap up this case."

"I don't think we can do that with what we know right now, Jones." He added, "Turn me over. I'm good."

I picked him up and put him back right side up. He was a pretty good judge of when it soaked all the way through his brain. None of it spilled out of his neck.

I rubbed my chin. "There's too much going on. Too many pieces that don't quite fit. What are the Nazis doing here? What are they moving?"

"You said the warehouse was empty when you left?"

"Yeah."

"They didn't leave any clues?"

"No, I searched the place. German efficiency. Clean as a Catholic school girl's cooch." I tapped my finger on my knee. Nervous tic.

"Let me see that bag of powder," he said.

I tossed it to him. Of course, he didn't catch it, so it landed on the ground with a thump. Sighing, I picked up the bag and the head and put them in good staring distance of each other.

"Let me taste it," he said.

"I thought you didn't—"

"Shut up, Jones, and let me taste a bit."

I gave him the edge of my finger coated in a trickle of powder. His eyes lit up like a Christmas tree. "What?" I said. "What is it?"

"I recognize this. I do. Delamort made this."

"What is it?"

He shook his head. Or I guess, his whole self. It worked a bit better than his half-assed nods. "I don't know. He called it jumbee powder. Not sure what it does."

"Numbs the brain," I said.

"He used it for experiments on us. Why, though, would Lazar have you deliver a suitcase full to the docks?"

I shrugged. The only thing that made sense was if he wanted me to catch wind of it. I poured a shot of the fancy old whiskey the fence had given us. After a long staring at, I poured a shot for Alcibé, too.

"I'd better hit the streets now after all," I said. "My head is swirling, but one thing I know for sure is I won't get anywhere if I don't get us some good, clean swill."

"That's a good idea," he said.

I got dressed. When I was about to step out the door, he stopped me.

"Although," he said, "you actually do have a good source of clean booze. You just have to skip over the bucket and go straight to the well."

"Lazar," I said.

He nodded, in his own funny fashion.

NOVEMBER 22, 1934

I waited outside Lazar's penthouse. Idecided to stake the place out. There was that smartass doorman, all full of himself like he was cock o' the walk. Nerts to him. He didn't do anything but open the door for rich people. I waited. It seemed like the right time when I saw a gorgeous dame with getaway sticks to die for walk in. I recognized her. She was one of ours. I had known her once. In the biblical sense. I walked up to the doorway.

"Yes, sir, may I help you?" the doorman said.

Then he was down on the ground. One good punch. Well, all right, maybe he didn't need to be kicked in the groin and the ribs all those extra times. But it seemed like the thing to do.

When I kicked in the door to his apartment, Lazar and Kumaree were sitting in his little living room pit, sharing a bottle of wine and laughing like old lovers.

"Well, hey there, kids," I said.

Lazar stood.

"Not so fast," I said. I already had my gun out. I saw Kumaree Tong smirking and looking away. Yeah, she didn't have anything to do with anything.

"You are getting to be more trouble than you're worth," Lazar said.

"Can it, maestro," I said. "Let's have a chat. Have a seat, why don't you?"

He did as he was told. I fished around his kitchen, not letting the gun down. A couple of bottles of the stuff he had been drinking himself were sitting out. A few of them were Crow. Thank God. I couldn't handle too many other shitty kinds of liquor. I stacked the bottles in a paper bag.

"To what do we owe this ridiculous intrusion?" he called out.

"Yeah," I said, "about that. First of all, what the hell is your name?"

"Does it matter?"

"Yeah, it does to me," I said.

"Why?"

"Because it's on a list of questions I've got."

Kumaree decided, for whatever reason, that that was the appropriate moment to pipe up. "It's true. He has a whole list. I've read it. It's cute really."

I looked at her for a minute. It wasn't that big of a stretch to assume she had gone through my stuff. She had taken my billfold, after all. Speaking of which…

I held out my hand. She put the little metal marvel into my greedy palm. I stuffed it in my pocket. "Thanks, darling," I said. "When we get married, I'll have one monogrammed for you."

I whirled on my oldest and bestest buddy in the whole wide world. "So, let's have it."

"Is this some kind of power trip for you, Jones?" Lazar asked. "You burst into my penthouse and start asking questions, waving a gun—"

"How about it's payback for drugging me," I said.

He stared at me like nothing registered in those cold, dead eyes. Only they shimmered with tears, unlike any deadhead I'd ever seen before. He shook his head and opened his arms wide. "What?"

"Sure," I said, "you never heard of jumbee powder. You never had it shipped from Little Haiti to the docks. Hell, once, just to add insult to injury, you used me as my very own mule. You never insisted that gorilla of a bartender slip it in all my drinks. For that matter, you never steamed off the caps of all of my bottles of Old Crow and slipped it in yourself."

For that one, I had an illustration. I pulled an empty bottle of Crow out of my pocket and tossed it at my erstwhile benefactor. He ducked, as did the woman. It wasn't an admission of guilt. I knew that as well as anyone.

"Look, Jones," he said, gritting his teeth as he spoke, "I don't know what you're talking about."

I looked at Kumaree Tong. Her face was impassive. What the fuck did that mean?

"Tell him," I said.

"Tell him what?" she asked, her expression absolutely, positively, 100% neutral.

"You bitch," I said.

Lazar jumped to his feet. I didn't know he had it in him. "Now is that any way for a gentleman to speak?" he said.

I pushed him back down into his chair. "Games, games, games." I dropped into a seat. Seemed like the thing to do. I dangled my gun between my legs. I could've pulled it on either of them at any moment.

I wasn't really sure how good of a shot I was—fairly good, based on my showing at the warehouse—but I figured at that range, I could've popped either or both of them in the head at an instant's notice with no issue.

I tapped my head to try to clear it physically. It made no sense, I know, and it probably looked crazy to the other two. "Okay, I'm trying to put all these disparate pieces together like Lincoln Logs. You two are in bed together."

"I hardly think that's any of your business," Lazar said.

"He means we're working together, idiot," Kumaree sneered.

I looked at her. That was the first time I had seen someone knock Lazar down a peg and have him stay there. They probably were sleeping together. That boiled my nonexistent blood a little, but I had other things on my mind. I had to keep an eye on her, keep her from getting under my skin.

"Only now I'm getting that there's a lot of stuff she's not telling you," I said. "Did you know the Germans are in town?"

He leaned back in his chair and tented his fingers. I already knew what that meant. Man, I could read the guy like a book. "This is news to me," he lied.

Kumaree Tong stood. I rose with her, as did my boomstick. She sashayed away from her chair.

"Where do you think you're going?" I said.

She didn't turn around to answer. Man, that derriere just bounced from side to side. "If we're going to be here for a while, I'm going to fix myself a drink."

"Get me something, too," Lazar said.

She kneeled down at Lazar's sizable liquor cabinet. It was disguised as something else for the benefit of the coppers, a bureau or a nightstand, I guess. I suppose that was where he kept the good stuff. The bottles I had pinched from the kitchen were just for day-to-day use.

"Get away from there," I said. "Sit back down."

"Or what?" She still didn't turn around. Instead, she laughed. It sounded a lot like that one in the warehouse where she threw her neck back like Cleopatra. In Lazar's apartment, though, she didn't bother with the theatrics. "You going to kill me, Billy?"

She finally turned around so she could show me that she was covering her lips with her hand. "Oops, did I say something you didn't know? Just one of a million pieces of information you don't know."

"Joke's on her," I said, turning my attention for a split second to Lazar. "I already heard that name."

That nanosecond was plenty of time. The gun was in the liquor cabinet, I assume, if it even was a liquor cabinet and not just a hidey-hole for firearms. My saving grace was that she wasn't an ideal shot. Not a terrible shot, per se, but not the best shot I'd ever seen.

She stood there with one of those little snub-nosed numbers like dames use, smoke still billowing from the barrel. Man, that oughta be a cover on a penny dreadful. I was still standing, though, so I lifted my own boomstick.

I think Lazar shouted, "No!"

It was instinct. Well, not really. That's a lie. It was a lot of pent-up anger, too. That ginchy dame had to go, from the first moment she started playing me. Unlike her, I didn't miss. It was like she got thrown back by a big, ugly bouncer. There was a hole in her forehead, and chunks of gunk flew forward out of it.

How does that happen when the bullet is going forward? I don't know.

She slammed against the wall and slumped down.

"Well, that's that," I said.

Lazar didn't really lose his composure. I guess he did a little. He went to her body, held her double-dead hand. Sweet. Touching. Ugh. Gag me with saccharin.

"She didn't love you or anything," I said, plucking some greens from my teeth with a toothpick. "No matter how many times she opened her legs for you."

He looked up. I think he might've been crying. Who knows? "I wasn't fooled by her. Not for an instant. Were you?"

"Sure you were never fooled," I said. "What's with the waterworks, then?"

"Just because I could see through her doesn't mean I didn't like what I saw."

Wow. Talk about pretzel logic.

A low grumble came from his prostrate form. "I think you'd better get out of here, Jones."

"Not yet," I said. "I've got a few more questions."

In a second, he was up on his feet, waving the abandoned snubnose around. Not pointing it at me, just waving it like a bowling pin. Tears really were streaming down his face.

Can our kind cry?

"Questions! Questions! It's always questions with you. Do you ever get any answers? Your whole idea of detective work is to wave guns in people's faces. Does it ever get you anywhere?"

"That's not true," I said. "Sometimes I bribe them, too."

"Do you ever try using that thing between your ears?" he said. "You know, maybe Braineater is the best name for you. You're nothing but a mindless patsy."

"I still have to know the truth," I said.

"The truth? Get out!" he yelled, taking a step toward me, "Get the fuck out!" He wasn't even pointing his piece at me.

Grimly, I stepped back and tipped my lid to him. Don't know why I did that. Maybe I meant it. Maybe it was just a sarcastic gesture. I stepped out.

He said one last thing in a tone so low I almost wouldn't have heard it outside his door. He was obviously speaking to me. "Don't bother going back. You're not welcome in our community anymore. You're out."

I poked my hat back around the corner. "You can't do that to me. You don't have the numbers."

"Try me," he said. "Go ahead. Go back to Hallowed Grounds. See how that works out for you."

"You're not the bigwig you think you are," I said. "You're not even one of us anymore, living here in your gilded penthouse."

"You don't know anything about me," he said. "Still don't after all this time. Why waste your time going back? Nobody's got your six. You've made too many enemies, no friends."

The cops were already pooling in the lobby like blood. I had to go out a window. I tried to avoid breaking my neck as best as possible, but it didn't really work out. More importantly, I didn't bust the few clean bottles of alcohol I had ganked from Lazar—or whatever his name is.

I'm on my own now.

NOVEMBER 23, 1934

I didn't go inside. Didn't even know if I could trust Homer anymore. Lazar's point had been made abundantly clear. I was an outsider. I never fit in, never even tried to. He was well respected, well liked. More importantly, he kept that particular watering hole full. Nobody was going to jeopardize that for a half-witted dick like me.

I had to toss pebbles at the office window. I had left the stupid head on guard duty, but I guess he was asleep. Finally, I managed to strike the idiot with a rock.

"Ow!" He looked down and saw me giving the "keep quiet" signal. He stared at me quizzically.

I motioned for him to jump down. He shrugged, or did what I had come to interpret as a shrug over the few weeks of our acquaintanceship. Finally I made a little hippity-hop like a rabbit, and he seemed to get it. He closed his eyes and probably would've crossed himself if he had arms or were a papist. He seemed to be mouthing sweet nothings to God. As Kumaree had told me, our kind tended to be irreligious. Maybe the old faiths came flashing back in moments of tension. Or maybe, again, old habits are hard to break.

I understood why he was faux-praying. If I didn't catch him perfectly, he would splatter his brains all over the pavement, and that was the only way to kill one of our kind. Bye bye, brainy. I held out my arms. Rocking back and forth on his neckstump, he nudged himself over the edge.

Thank God I caught him. Or Whoever. We've been over all that. I stuffed him under my overcoat and took off. That didn't stop it from seeming like I was having a conversation with my armpit as I went.

"What's going on, Jones?" he asked.

"Don't worry about it," I said.

"Stop." He said it in a way as to brook no opposition. I stopped. "Take me out."

"Alcibé, we're in the middle of the street," I said.

"I don't care," he said. "We're going on the lam. I haven't done anything to anybody. If you want me to go, take me out, look me in the eye, and explain it to me."

I sighed. I took him out and held him aloft. He gave me one of those looks, like my third-grade teacher Mrs. Argento gave me the time I hid a frog in her percolator.

Holy shit. I just remembered that whole incident, top to bottom. No white migrainey flash. I think that was a genuine memory. The jumbee powder must finally be wearing off.

Anyway, back to earlier. He gave me that look, you know.

"All right," I said. "I killed Kumaree Tong."

"Why?"

"She tried to kill me first."

"Okay," he said, "why not just tell everyone what happened? You're pretty well liked. Afraid no one will believe you?"

"Well," I said, "it's not just that. After I did it, Lazar banished me. I've got to take that seriously, unfortunately."

He hardened his lips. An old bum was staring at us.

"Something I can help you with?" I growled.

The bum held up his hands and pushed his shopping cart on out of the way.

"Am I involved in this banishment?" he asked.

I had to admit it was a germane question.

"No," I said. "Do you want me to take you back?"

"No."

For some reason, I thought he would take longer to answer. He had probably already figured it all out in his head. He always was the smarter one. I guess that's what happens when you're nothing but a brain in a skinsack.

He sighed, one of those long, protracted, forced, drawn-out sighs where you blow between your teeth like a jackoff. "Well, what've we got?"

"Got my hat and my coat," I said.

"And?"

"And my gun."

"How many bullets?"

I checked. The chamber was full, and I had two loose rounds in my inside pocket. "Only eight."

He did another one of those blowy-draggy sighs. "Okay, what about booze?"

"About four bottles," I said.

"It's a start."

"Hey, Alcibé," I said.

"What?"

"There's something I've always wanted to do."

"No," he said firmly.

"I've got to do it," I said.

"No," he repeated.

I held him up in the air. "To be or not to be…"

"That's not even the right scene," he said.

"That is the question."

Hat Scratch Fever was far enough outside of Lazar's usual circles that I thought I might be able to get a little sympathy. Maybe a cup of warm bourbon. Breathers frequented the joint now and then— not damn near as frequently as our kind, but still, once in a while was better than nonce in an ever—and wherever breathers were, there was the chance Lazar wasn't pulling strings. Or at least that folks might be willing to go against him.

Mighty Dull was polishing dice in the foyer. He breathed on them. Fetid, false, cool breath. He looked up. His eyes were cold, but whose eyes aren't cold in our little circle? His face was pinched. Maybe he was calculating. Maybe he had already calculated.

"Aw, hell no," Mighty said upon seeing me. "You'd best just turn about face and march your hiney out of here."

"Hineys," Alcibé said.

"You ain't got one, head," Mighty said, "and I wouldn't care if you did. Why don't you make like a whore and blow?"

"Who are you talking to?" I asked. "Are you talking to me or to him?"

Mighty got up. That was the end of it. "Damn, cracker, I thought I told you to go."

"Well, you didn't say that specifically," the head chimed in.

"Why don't we discuss it?" I asked.

Out came one of those switchblades like the dancing street gangs on the west side use. "You boys need to take a walk."

Hmm. Was it worth getting in a scrap over? Who even knew if I would win? And if I did, it was all over the chance that I might get to stay. Even then, a roughed-up pimp was probably not going to be conducive to making our stay in his "reputable" establishment all that nice. I tried reasoning with him. "Listen, Mighty, you haven't even heard us out. You don't need to go sticking a knife in my ear just because I came to jaw a little bit."

The blade disappeared. Then it flicked back out again. In, out. In, out. In. Out. Then it was up and leveled at my face. "I don't know you," he said. "I don't want to know you. I've been told I don't want to get to know you. You dig?"

"Hey, I dig," I said. "I'm down."

Maybe I was laying it on a little too thick. Whatever was coming out of it, a few of the off-duty—or whatever you call it—hookers had found their way to the lobby to watch the fireworks. Nice that he took them out every once in a while and let them stretch their legs. Or their mates' legs.

"Give them a chance, Mighty," one of the more—I guess to be charitable—senior hookers said. "Maybe they got something to offer."

Mighty Dull blew an invisible fly off his schnoz. "Bitch, they ain't got shit."

"Watch it, Mighty," the prosty said with a hard edge in her sultry, cigarette-laden voice. "Call me the b-word again. I'll make you regret it."

"Man, shut up! What all you hookers doing out here anyway? Get back to the closet. If you got nothing to do, I'll give you something to do."

They heartily ignored his advice. I shrugged. Alcibé would've probably shrugged too if he'd had shoulders. Mighty's knife hand wavered. Then finally he flicked the shiv closed and pocketed it.

"Shit," Mighty said finally. "Aight, come grab a seat."

I popped a squat in one of the plush, purple-velvet lined chairs that formed a sort of a décor for the cathouse foyer. I tried to put Alcibé on the back of one of the chairs at about eye level, but the damn head kept falling back and I had to run and grab him before he rolled out the door or down the hall. Finally I just plunked him down in my lap, which he didn't like none too much. Well, I didn't like it none too much, either, but a damn head doesn't get much say. That's the end of that matter.

"What you got for me?" the head of Hat Scratch asked when we were finally all settled.

I got nothing.

"A proposal," Alcibé said before I got myself into too much trouble with my silence.

The old pimp burst into laughter. Not the false kind of laughter he seemed to bust out at every turn, either. He seemed to genuinely find the situation funny. "What's that, head? You want a spot in my hat rack? Ain't got no body. Ain't got no legs. Well, we ain't got much demand for homo-heads either."

"There's no need to be crude, Mr. Dull," Alcibé said with more dignity than I would have imagined a dismembered meat skull to be capable of mustering.

Even Mighty seemed impressed. He leaned his chair back on two legs. "All right, so lay it on me."

"We are partners in a very lucrative detective agency," Alcibé said.

"Private dicks?" Mighty interrupted with a cackle.

"Sometimes they call us that," the head admitted.

"Sorry," Mighty Dull said, waving his hand. "Only use I got for private dicks is ten dollars a pop for certain customers. And I don't get those customers all that often. So you two ain't staying here."

"We're not offering our services as… what's the word?"

"Gigolos," Mighty supplied.

"Gentlemen cowboys," Alcibé supplied. I assume he made up a euphemism he preferred right on the spot. "Not at all. What I'm saying is, suppose we put up our shingle here."

Mighty looked from the head in my crotch up to my face and back again. He leaned back and lit up a cigarette. "Get out."

"Come on, Mighty," I said.

"Now, I remember you, first of all. Mr. Braineater Jones, except what the hell is wrong with a deadhead that calls hisself that, hmm? You strolled up in here, steal some time with one of my hos—"

"You offered that to me," I said.

"Whatever you want to call it, big shot," Mighty said. "The idea is the first hit is free, and then you pay afterward. You never followed up with the second part."

"Maybe the product wasn't to my liking. No offense to Brigid," I said. "That's kind of how the whole pusher thing is supposed to work, Mighty."

Mighty had a face like he had just sucked a lemon whole out of its skin. He spat a little tobacco that had gotten loose from his fag on the ground. "Let's make a donut hole in the conversation." Mighty made a circle with his pointer finger. "Supposing I hook you up with a room for your usage and you start working out of my whorehouse. What possible value is that to me?"

"Well, for one thing, you'd have your own personal detectives on staff," I said.

"Bodyguards," Alcibé said. "Bouncers. You name it."

"A head with no fists and a guy with no brains is going to be my bouncers?" Mighty said, "What is you, five foot nothing? You ain't even as scary as half my hookers, let alone my clientele."

"Well," I said, "do you ever have dine and dash problems, if you know what I mean? Pump runners?"

"Now and then," Mighty admitted. "Mostly with Ed and Joey. And you scared them two off. Now that I think about it, you two idiots have cost me customers. And the truth is, you may think I'm an idiot because of the color of my skin and the way I talk and the way I treat the ladies, but I'm not. I know who you is. I know who Lazar is, and I don't get all my booze from him, but he comes around still. He's like a damn patron saint to you and me and ours. So you might be all right with trying to piss him off and run to me, but I ain't. Now get out for real, or I'll break your kneecaps and keep you on the floor 'til Lazar can get here. You dig?"

I did not, in fact, dig, but I left anyway.

Boy. Dayzha voo for him and me and you. How does one find oneself repeating old patterns, going back to old places?

A bridge. The first bridge I ever saw in my unlife. And wouldn't you believe it, the same word-salad spouting underboss was waiting for me. He had replaced my little newspaper hat with a bit of tin foil, the edges twisted into Viking horns.

"Get ready," I whispered to Alcibé.

"For what?" he asked suspiciously.

"Oh holy night," the lunatic cried out. "The beef is coldly sputtering. O-yay! O-yay!"

I didn't wait for him to continue. "Long bomb!" I flung Alcibé at him, not so hard that if he hit the ground, he would splatter or even really be affected. The head bared his teeth in midair or something, because he really latched on to the stewbum's shoulder as soon as he hit.

The loon squirmed and jumped and batted at Alcibé. "Out, out, damn Fido! I don't want your death glove cancer fire brain mojo!"

I could see Alcibé growling and sputtering like a dog. There was something a bit absurd about it. It made me laugh. It was enjoyable watching that son of a bitch get his comeuppance. I didn't think our condition was transmissible. At least according to Gnaghi, it was pretty well randomized. Still, I wouldn't have minded one bit if the captain of the SS Cuckoocloudlander had ended up like me.

He finally managed to scrabble Alcibé off his shoulder and then punted him, but bad. Oh, shit. The derelict went running off in one direction, and my best friend went flying in the other. My fault.

I sprinted toward the falling head. Deadheads didn't historically move much faster than "shamble" but needs must as the devil drives. I wasn't going to make it. That was clear. I dove. Maybe that would do it. Nope.

He bounced once, twice, then came to stop. I crawled toward him.

"Alcibé?" I said. "Alcibé, are you all right?"

Silence.

"Damn it!" I yelled at the sky, "If I ever thought You were up there, I don't now! Damn You!"

Then there was a croak. "Jones."

I rolled over to stare at him. His head was partially flattened, but I guess the brain hadn't been destroyed.

"Yes?" I said.

"I'm starting to regret following you into exile."

NOVEMBER 24, 1934

I went into the five and dime like nothing was wrong. I even got as far as putting my fingers on a glass bottle of delicious, amber-colored Listerine before I heard the shotgun cock. I cleared my throat—there was a roach in it. "Just got a little halitosis, mac." I tried my best to disguise my voice.

"Whyn't you just vamoose, Jones?"

"Damn it," I muttered. I sighed, watching the sweet bottle of mouth rinse—which had been so close to being mine—slip away, back into the shelf that housed it. I turned and looked at the storekeeper. He had real thin wireframe glasses and a white shirt like he was a druggist, but he wasn't one. I couldn't read anything in his eyes. He wasn't shaking, but he was one of our kind, and I don't know that we do shake when we're nervous. It was my only hope anyway.

"Come on, Joe," I said, not knowing his name—although maybe I should've. "You could give me a break."

"Mr. Bethany gave you a break, didn't he? And how'd you repay him? No, you'd better just mosey along."

So that was it. No one was breaking ranks with Lazar, not for a no-account bum like me. In the Altstadt and the rest of the city, I got the bum's rush just for being a deadhead. In the Mat, where I was supposed to be welcome, it was the cold shoulder.

"Please, Joe," I said, putting my hands on the counter, although that was close enough that he could put the barrel of the shottie directly to my forehead. "Just a taste. Just a zozzle. I'm dyin' here."

"Well, then go die out there. Don't die in my store. I don't want a braineater in here, and I don't want to become one myself because I crossed the bootleggers."

The five and dime wasn't the only place to give me the boot, but it was the one I was most hoping wouldn't. I trudged back to the bridge feeling about as low-down as a catfish in a sewer.

The head was jammed, inverted, into the hole of a cinder block for safe keeping. "Any luck?"

"Yeah, I got champagne and Bacardi, whatever you want. Jeeves is bringing it around in the limo."

"What do you say to a bite to eat, then?"

"Won't make me feel any better."

"Maybe it'll take your mind off it."

I sighed and sprawled back against a pile of bricks. "Nah, I don't think so, head."

"Come on," he said. "Thanksgiving's next week. Let's have a bite to eat like we're regular old breathers."

"We can go on Thursday, then," I said.

"Nah, you don't want to go to the soup kitchen on Thursday. Bet there isn't even a line today."

I looked over at him. Alcohol-starved, miserable prisoners hiding under a bridge, fighting off other derelicts to maintain our tenuous control of said bridge. He was just trying to make me feel better, I guess.

"Okay," I said and wrenched him out of the concrete.

We stood in line at the men's mission. I looked around. How many of these were our kind? Were any of them?

It seemed ridiculous, in a way, to take food out of the mouths of living, breathing human beings who needed it. We were just doing it for tradition. But I guess that's important, too. We needed a sense that our universe was grounded in some kind of objective reality.

Wait. What? Was I an astronomy professor or what?

We could've done with a few shots of booze and been on our way, but Alcibé was pretty insistent. I had him in a parrot cage again. Not the nice one we had left behind but one I had jury-rigged out of some mesh and covered with a discarded window curtain. Still, I wasn't the most goofy-looking guy there. One fellow had a shopping cart full of Coca-Cola bottles. Another brought his mangy, flea-ridden mutt in with him. They served us all just the same.

I wandered out into the alley once I had my tray. Had to. Had to if I wanted to involve the head without treating him like a parrot. I made sure to get a little extra of everything.

"No bedpan?" he said.

"Couldn't find one," I said. "We're in an alley. Just eat and let it go wherever."

We sat there for a while chowing down. Turkey, a little bit of filling, some poorly mashed potatoes, and some miserable succotash.

Strange as it was to be sitting in an alley next to a dismembered head and eating food stolen from the poor, it felt somehow normal.

"You think they get swamped with donations this time of year?" I asked.

"I don't know about swamped. I wouldn't be surprised if they're eating gobble-gobble morning, noon, and night for a few weeks."

"What I wouldn't give for a taste of Crow—"

"Don't start that! We came here to get our minds off it, remember?"

"I remember," I said. "I just can't. It's so damn hard."

"You think this is hard? This is nothing. You should've seen the Somme. Bodies stacked like cordwood. Not even a ditch to yourself unless the Hun got your trenchmate. And then you couldn't even appreciate the privacy because you were lonely. This isn't hard. That was hard."

"Were you ever scared?" I asked.

He was munching on some strained carrots or something. He squeezed it through his gullet into some cardboard boxes he was sitting on.

"Huh?"

"Over there," I clarified.

"Oh."

It was a while before he said anything. I stared at a sad little chunk of gobble-gobble on the edge of my fork. I turned it to and fro.

"Yeah, once or twice," he said, "but not as often as you'd think. There comes a point where all you can do is rely on your training to get you through."

I munched darkly on some white meat. "And if you don't have any training?"

"Then you rely on your friends," he answered, without missing a beat.

NOVEMBER 25, 1934

Woke up this morning. The head was gone. I looked around. Had he rolled off? Not likely. Had one of the vagrants come by and snatched him up? I was a heavy sleeper, but I knew damn well I would've heard that. Alcibé would've made sure to yell loud enough to wake me.

If my stomach had still been bubbling and bursting with vital juices, I knew how it would have felt. It would've felt as if a big chunk of ice had plunked down in it. I felt absent not having that feeling. Does that make any sense? Like life was slipping away from me a little more every day. We could pretend when we were part of the community. At least then there were other play-actors acting like everything was the same as it had been before unlife.

I stood up. I knew it wasn't vagrants, not even that King Visigoth Fisher guy. All my bottles were in the brown paper bag, unmolested except for what I had already drunk. Why would they take the head and leave the booze? Why would they take the head, anyway?

No, it was deliberate. Spiteful. To be sure, I checked all around. Nope. Nowhere to be seen.

There was only one place he could be. I waited until noon, when the sun was bright and our kind were not out in the street. We were nocturnal creatures. Not by any biological or societal necessity, but because we hated to be seen. Hated to be noticed. We avoided showing our faces in public. Darkness shrouded everything.

I knew I had to be careful. Homer was blind, but he wasn't stupid. There was a creak in one floorboard, I knew that well. His cat stared at me, waiting. I could've said something, could've put my finger over my lips or something equally asinine. I didn't. What was the point? Cats didn't understand such things. We were all fundamentally prisoners of our own languages, or lack thereof.

Man, am I ever waxing grandiloquent today. Even that word was pretty fancy.

I don't know how I snuck past the fence. Once I was past him, he turned. Heard something, or smelled something, more likely. I inserted my key into the door of the cage as slowly as humanly possible and held the door stiff as I unlocked it. It creaked ever so slightly as I opened it just enough to slip through.

"Jones?"

I stood stock-still. Waited. I would've held my breath if I was still alive. Would've willed my pounding heart to stop beating if it wasn't a shriveled black old husk. I waited for him to turn away, then one-two one-two and through and through went up the steps, snicker-snack.

When I got up the steps, the office door was hanging wide. That was a first. Even when I had visitors, they usually had the common decency to close the door. Something made me pull my piece out of my pocket.

I stepped inside and peered around. Nothing seemed amiss. Alcibé was nowhere to be seen. There was, though, a pink cakebox on my desk. I took a few steps forward and checked out the window. "Head?"

No answer.

"Alcibé," I said, slightly louder.

Shit. I took a look at the box. A note squatted beside it, crumpled into a ball so it wouldn't blow away. I flattened out the note, which was written on a familiar sheet of paper that took me just a second to place.

HOW DOES IT FEEL?

I reached into the depths of my trench coat and pulled out this journal. A page had indeed been torn out. They had been there. Had their filthy hands all over me.

I opened the box. I looked at my hand, the one I had put to the cardboard. I could feel it quaking, but I saw it wasn't moving at all. The memory of a muscle. A feeling. Something like a compulsion. I expected the fingers to quiver, but they lay there, limp, like a squid baked to death by the sun.

The head had been lovingly secreted in the box at a careful angle so that the lid could close. A red pocketknife, like a Boy Scout's or something, jutted out of the soft spot that in the head of a baby grew harder over time but never diminished completely. His jaw hung open like he had one last word to tell me, but probably he had died screaming. And dead he was, or double dead, or put down as our kind so inelegantly put it. Dead as a doornail. Son of a bitch. I closed the box and put it aside.

I buried my face in my hands to think. What do you do with something like that? Chuck it in a dumpster? Try to give him a fancy burial? Maybe cremate it? I didn't know.

There was no reason to be sad, I told myself. The head had never done any good for anybody, least of all me. He had been a nuisance, really. I was well rid of him. Still, loneliness was an unpleasant travelling companion. Just to hear him joke and jibe and tell me everything was jake was a great relief sometimes. He had known more about the community than I did, always had, had proven himself an asset in that arena.

It wasn't like I cared about him. How do you care about a head? Nobody could care about a head. Still, maybe he shouldn't die unmourned. I justified it to myself that way. Nobody deserved to die alone, unmourned. I sat there for a while, rocking back and forth, trying to summon tears. How had Lazar done it? Maybe he wasn't really…

I stood up. It had to be Lazar. I had taken someone important from him, so he had taken someone important from me. He couldn't be satisfied with banning me from what little I had left in my life.

I drew the pocketknife out of my friend's skull, closed it, and tucked what little of his remains remained under my shoulder.

NOVEMBER 26, 1934

I went to the docks. There was a garbage barge taking off that I managed to jump on. As it weighed anchor, I spotted a familiar all-black figure standing by the water's edge watching me. The Grim Reaper raised his hand to his cap and walked off wordlessly. I suppose matters were settled between us.

As I lay amongst the piled eggshells and banana peels, I remembered thinking that I wouldn't have been able to stand the smell if I was still alive. I could still smell it—after a fashion—but it didn't bother me.

I had one last Lucky Strike. Not sure quite what I had been holding onto it for, but I pulled it out. I also pulled out the head and held it aloft. "Alas, poor Yorick." I grinned as I set the head down in a little pile of garbage, on top of a plush red pillow I think was once a dog bed. "See? I knew the right lines."

I waited for a suitably clever response. None came, of course. I couldn't even have thought of what he would say in that situation. I wiped my nose with my shirtsleeve. "You always knew exactly what to say, didn't you? To be honest, I'm kind of lost without you. Shit. I'm glad you're not here to hear me say that."

I took a look at him. Dead as a doornail, but he had one of those looks, a cross between a smile and an "I told you so." I shook my head. Only crazy people talk to the dead. Crazy people and psychics. Which are just a different breed of crazy people.

"I've been thinking about the case. There's one clue we never looked into. I don't know if I ever even told you about it. My first case. Claudia Baumer was the name on the grave. Claudia Winston was the name she used to introduce herself. What do you make of that?" I glanced at the head corpse. Damned if I wanted to admit it, but I really did miss his counsel.

"Yeah, that's what I said, too. A hired actress. Only she had to be a deadhead, so there wasn't much competition. She didn't just forget her lines; she forgot what her damn name was supposed to be."

With the unlit Lucky in one hand, I patted myself down for my flask. I took a sip. "Lazar hires a ringer to hire me to find a locket. Only he knows where the locket is the whole time because he's in bed with Kumaree, and Kumaree hired the Infected who stole it. So all he wanted was to get me in the game. Why would anyone want that?"

I took another drink of the supposedly clean liquor. I lifted the flask toward what was left of him and let a tiny, infinitesimal trickle hit the ground in his honor.

"Insurance against Kumaree maybe. Make sure someone was sniffing under her rocks in case he disappeared. I did kill her, after all. Then again, maybe he wanted to groom me as an enforcer. Like the bartender is for the Old Man. He did set it up so I would owe him everything. Or hell, maybe he just wanted a wild card."

I actually waited for the head to answer for a few moments before I remembered.

"I read a book at the library," I continued. "Not the whole way through. When I was researching the case where you and I met. It was about burial rites around the world. You know there are people in India who put you on a tower and let the buzzards peck at you? That's considered respectful."

Unsurprisingly, he did not respond.

"I thought you'd like this one, though," I said. "Vikings put their fallen warriors out to sea on flaming longboats. Don't know the significance. I'm not much of a bookworm. But it seemed like something you'd like."

I tossed some petrol and pitch on the garbage. I checked to make sure there was a lifeboat and life preservers for the crew. They probably didn't much deserve to have their barge burnt down, but screw them. I've gotten a lot of things I didn't deserve either lately.

I lit up the Lucky.

"Goodnight, sweet prince," I said. Almost immediately, I thought better of it. "That's sappy, isn't it? That's disgusting. How about this? Be seeing you." I made a ring around my eye with my thumb and forefinger, then tipped it forward. I tossed the butt into the garbage. What a way to go. Truth is, you can pretend a garbage barge is a Viking longboat all you want, but that doesn't make it so.

I took a sheaf of plastic, tore it in half, and wrapped up my boomstick and my journal. I stayed long enough to make sure the flame wouldn't go out anytime soon. Then I took a step off the side.

During the long walk back to the docks along the bottom of the bay, I pondered my next move. For one thing, I regretted not wrapping up my shoes, too. They made walking through the silt take twice as long, and I lost one about halfway through. For another thing, I had to fight off some fish and even one rather nasty-looking shark.

Time to put an end to this whole thing.

NOVEMBER 27, 1934

I was already sitting in his pit when he came home. He flipped the light switch, but I had disconnected it. I struck a match. Took it from his pot near the door. Took the smokes, too. Not Luckies, but then, beggars can't be choosy.

I think the flame was probably not much more than enough to light up my face. He stared at me. I guess we were past all the playing around. Brass tacks and all that business.

"You don't get ideas through your skull much, do you?" he said.

"You telling me all that was nothing but a warning?"

"Huh?" he said, like he didn't know what I was talking about. "No, I really kicked you out of the community. That means you're not supposed to come around."

I was talking about the head. He was either pretending he didn't know, or he genuinely didn't know. Who knew with his type. I decided to play along. Why not, right? You always get more out of somebody when they think they know more than you, anyway.

"You said to stay away from Hallowed Grounds," I said. "You never said anything about your penthouse."

He laughed morosely and shook his head. "You really are an obtuse son of a bitch, aren't you?"

"Depends."

"On what?"

"On what obtuse means." Guess my English professor training let me down. Or maybe I just wanted him to think he was smarter than me.

He was carrying groceries—I guess I should have mentioned that already. He walked into his kitchen and put them down. He knew his way around enough in the dark. Everyone does in their own place.

"I don't usually smoke in the house," he said.

"I bet I know someone who did," I said, checking the purloined pack before crushing it. "And she smoked Chesterfields, it seems."

"Yeah, well, she doesn't come around here much anymore being as she's dead."

I jumped in between him and the counter. He should've dropped his bags. A smart guy would've dropped his bags. He didn't. Defiant. He held onto them. I didn't have my gun out, though. It was still a little seasick. But then, he didn't know that. He had to know I was wearing iron.

"Enough to make somebody angry, ain't it?" I said. "Enough to make him want to kill."

He stared at me. Absolutely blank. Expressionless. I reached out and touched his chin. He pulled away, but it was too late. I looked at my fingers. Face paint.

"Makeup," I said.

He put down the groceries, went to the sink, and washed his face. His cheeks were rosy and pink. His eyes weren't sunken in or swollen. Hardly any creases other than normal age and wear and tear.

"You're alive," I said.

"Yeah."

"Why?" Why what? It wasn't a very descriptive question. Just a general "why." I couldn't think of all the things I wanted to know the reason for. Why the deception? Why help our kind?

"Because of her," he said. "I cared for her."

"That's perverse," I said.

"Why?" He turned to me. "What's so different between you and me? A heartbeat? Body heat?"

"A squirrel can quack, but it's still a squirrel."

"Can you fix my lights?" he asked.

"Oh, yeah."

It was a simple wire I had disconnected. I plugged it back in. The more I thought about it, the more sense it made. I'd seen the bastard crying. I'd never seen one of us cry. And he never used his real name, only pseudonyms, and bad ones at that. He was welcome in the Altstadt. Everything seemed to click in place. The lights turned on.

"Is that my shoe?"

I looked down at the mismatched pair and wriggled my toe in his. "Yeah."

He sighed, grabbed the orphan from the closet, and tossed it at me. "Just take the other one. You look like a hobo."

"What's your real name?" I said.

"Does it matter?" he asked.

"No, I guess not."

"She came to me, you know. Gorgeous like she was. I didn't care that what was between her legs was cold. You can warm that up with enough friction. She took care of herself, you know, not like a lot of you deadheads. And she had an idea for me. The Old Man doesn't trust women, still hates his mother, but she was sure she could get the booze. The Old Man was desperate for any supply when he was trying to set up his bar."

"So you put on some circus paint and played the part of the hip urban sophisticate. She got the booze, you delivered it."

"Yeah," he said. "It was easy enough. Free money, practically, for an acting job. Then things got… complicated."

"Complicated how?" I said.

"The Old Man," he said. "He's using the bar as a front. He's keeping money flowing in, but really what he wants is some half-cocked mechanical solution to your kind's fally-aparty problems."

"This I know," I said.

"Yeah, well, did you know he gets his parts from the Germans?" Lazar said.

"That I did not know," I admitted.

"So in addition to booze, she was getting machinery from the docks and I had to deliver it. All because the Old Man hates women. He's positively medieval. Probably because he never grew a dick. Resents the rest of us for having something to do with dames other than play patty-cake."

"So you never actually touched the booze or the parts or anything else. You were nothing but a mouthpiece. She spiked my punch, and she told you to send the suitcase full of jumbee powder to the docks."

He shrugged. “I didn’t ask questions. I just moved shipments. Sometimes I hunted down new customers. Backfired in your case.”

“I think you were looking for a little more than a customer in me,” I said.

He smiled. “Well, I wanted to keep an eye on you. And it’s true, I thought you had potential. Imagine being a blank slate.”

“I don’t have to imagine.”

“Too bad how it turned out.”

“So you didn’t kill the head?” I asked.

“What head?” he asked. “Oh, I remember. Your pet. No. Why would I?”

“I seem to recall you fighting once,” I said.

He shrugged. “I hardly even remember. I posture a lot.”

“More importantly, though, it seemed like a nice way to get revenge for your girlfriend. Or whatever you want to call her. Mausoleum mama.”

He sighed and sat down. He slipped one of her ruined Chesterfields out of the pack I had squished and smelled it. He didn’t smoke it, just moved it along his nose like he was smelling it. The aroma left him with a funny little half smile. “The police came. They don’t even consider it a crime, do you know that?”

I walked into the pit, thought better of it, and kept walking to his camouflaged liquor cabinet. I was pleased to see the snubnose was no longer there. Of course, it might’ve been in his pocket. Or it might’ve been in a police evidence locker. I supposed he was about to tell me.

“Killing our kind?” I said.

"How do you kill that which is already dead?" he asked.

"I've heard that somewhere before," I muttered.

I poured two glasses of Old Crow. I walked over and handed one to him. He waved it off.

"I don't need it," he said. "You know that."

"You need it," I said firmly.

He laughed and took a sip. I suppose a few tears spiked the glass. "Maybe my nerves do, but my liver doesn't. This stuff is killing me. Had to keep up the charade."

"You were saying about the flatfeet," I said.

"Oh, them." He seemed to sag down in his chair. "Yeah, they came. You probably saw them on your way out. They already knew what she was. She didn't look like a fresh corpse. I thought they were going to lock me away and throw away the key. They didn't, of course."

"They know about us," I said. "They pretend not to, but they do."

"Of course," he said. "They rang up the station, made sure her names were already on the books. Didn't even take me downtown. Just gave me one of those looks, you know. Like you gave me a moment ago. About being a pervert."

"It is a little perverted," I said.

"To each his own," Lazar said.

10. Who is Lazar? What is his real name? Some shmuck in over his head.

"If you didn't kill Alcibé," I said after a while, "who did?"

He stared at me. Instead of answering, he said, "That girl? She had a lot of enemies, but not many friends. Only a few people would care if she was gone. Most would thank you for doing it."

"Which camp do you fall in?" I asked.

He bit down on his knuckles. It was weird to see someone feeling emotions so profoundly. Our kind don't feel them or else they're dulled. He was a mess. "I don't know. On the one hand, I could kill you. On the other hand, maybe it's for the best. It means I can finally leave this life. I am just a quacking squirrel, after all."

I nodded. "Well, you helped me out once," I said. "Anything I can do, let me know."

"No, I don't think I'll be coming back to the Mat anymore. And let me specifically say this time that I would prefer it if you would not come back here ever again."

I stood up. "Fair enough."

"Who did kill your friend, by the way?" he said.

"Well, if it wasn't you, I guess that leaves one other suspect."

NOVEMBER 28, 1934

He must've heard me carving into his door. He opened it when I was only halfway finished. He looked at it. "You spelled 'race traitor' wrong," he commented with aplomb.

I shrugged. "I sort of thought I was an intellectual in pre-unlife, but maybe not."

"Maybe a pseudo-intellectual," Skaron said.

I waited. It would've been two—maybe three—heartbeats. I couldn't really count things that way anymore. But it would've been. "Aren't you going to invite me in?"

"You're not a vampire," he said. "You can come in if you like."

I stared at him. Must've been some obscure scholastic bit he had dug up. He gestured expansively with his hand, so I entered his apartment.

"You, ah, left this at my office," I said, holding out the penknife.

He took it. "Yes, I didn't think it would take you this long to find me. You really are a terrible detective."

"Absolutely the worst," I said, flopping down in one of his chairs.

He stared at me as though my actions were totally inexplicable. To be fair, they pretty much were. Who acts like that? Someone crazy, or someone who wants something, or someone too far gone to care anymore.

"Got any squares?" I asked.

He fished around in an empty flower pot and tossed me a packet of stale Players. I lit one with relish.

"I'm starting to piece it all together," I said, making little "piecing it together" motions. "So let's see if you go with me on this one."

He sat down. "I'll bite."

"So this girl dies," I said. "Whether she remembers herself or not hardly matters. What she does know is that as a deadhead, she's a looker. Even kind of ginchy for a fleshy bloody livey type. And that, well that's power."

He stared at me, face of marble, eyes of glass. "Go on." His voice was haunted.

"So a living woman, as you know, might throw her affection around, but for a dead one there's no consequence. No fear of child, no fear of the clap, or if there is, who cares? I'm squirming with a hundred thousand diseases right now, not least of which is gangrene and rigor mortis."

"Rigor is not a disease," he stated simply.

"Fine," I said. "So our girl, the hero of our story—"

"Heroine," he said.

"No, I haven't got any," I said. "Anyway, moving on, the first one she sleeps with, well, that's a nobody to her. A convenience. To get on his good side, she cuts him open while he's sleeping, then sews him back up while he's awake."

"That's what you think?" he asked.

"I'm just playing boy detective here. I'm not exactly Hercules Parrot, as you've pointed out. But let's say the first lover never quite gets over her. Even when her uses for him are limited. Because he's a nobody. A scholar. He protected her in the morgue, but outside of that…" I shrugged.

His eyes were narrowed to slits.

I fingered the trigger of my boomstick in my pocket to make sure it was still there. "She comes up with a plan to get the hooch into our community, which otherwise was floundering. Halfway dead, thanks to the government's mandatory but not really mandatory Prohibition. Only thing is, there was one person she couldn't seduce, and that threw a big old monkey wrench into her plans."

"She couldn't seduce him," Skaron said, "because he was a baby. Not even a baby. Probably not even aware of his microscopic dick."

"Not only that," I said, "but a woman-hater. Misogynist, is that the word?"

"It is," he said.

"So she spurns her first lover, who's about as useless to her as dirt at that point, only the spurning never quite takes in his brain. She finds… get this… a live one. Perfect patsy. He can bribe all the living mayors and commissioners and what have you. She pumps the lifeblood into the community and profits nicely off of it. Only here's where I get a little hazy."

He folded his arms. Stupid move, if he was planning to get the drop on me. But, then again, no one ever claimed Ivan Skaron was streetwise.

"I'm thinking—and like I said already, I'm just spitballing here—but I'm thinking that when a deadhead gets his memory back, he's a lot less dependent on the community. In fact, he might even remember where he used to get booze. Especially if he had a direct source, like say, the same source as our heroine. Yeah, I got the word before. I was just messing with you."

"Like, for instance," Skaron said, "someone directly connected to the Germans. Assuming, of course, it is the Germans that our heroine—or shall I just start calling her Kumaree Tong?—gets her alcohol from."

"Bingo, bango. So the question of memories comes into play. Which I assume she talked to you about."

"At length," Skaron said.

"And you told her?"

"I told her about the bokor, of course. Really the only reasonable source of information about our kind. Or what they call jumbees, anyway."

"She sold you—and you weren't the only one—to Delamort in exchange for jumbee powder. Powder which was supposed to go into the general booze supply at some point, I assume, when the natives got restless or just didn't want to pay her exorbitant costs anymore. Only me, I got to be the test subject. Why do you suppose she kept your legs? To sell to Delamort later when she was cash poor? Or for plausible deniability? Or maybe to get a dick like me involved?"

"You are, if nothing else, a clever one, Jones," Skaron said. "You're right. About almost everything. Some of your details are a little fuzzy, but you are correct. Your direct connections to the German threatened the little criminal empire my morgue mate built. But instead of putting you down, she thought you could be useful as a mindless slave. Little did she realize."

I should've asked what he meant about the German, but I was sure I had finally found my killer so I leapt on it.

"Did she kill me just for that purpose?" I asked, finally getting to the brains and gristle of it. "The living me, I mean."

He snorted. "That's ridiculous. You know as well as I do there's no way to predict who will resurrect and who will not. How could she possibly have known you would come back?"

"Then she had nothing to do with killing me." I'm sure I couldn't keep the disappointment out of my voice.

"I suspect not," he said.

"Who did?"

"How should I know?" he asked. "But I will tell you one thing, Jones, that I find to be an exceedingly amateur mistake. I, like you, am familiar with detective work only in the pages of Conan Doyle and his lesser imitators. But everyone, and I mean everyone, goes back to the scene of the crime at some point for clues. Have you ever done that?"

No, I hadn't. Of course I hadn't. What was keeping me from going back to Rothering's mansion? Nothing, probably. That would be my next stop. Only a little unfinished business there. "So here's the big gap in my whole story, the thing that really bugs me. It just rattles around in the back of my head."

I waited. It was one of those delicious moments.

"Go on," he said.

"She sold you for spare parts, like a car thief," I said. "Why would you care enough to avenge her?"

He jumped to his feet. If he was alive, I think he would've been weeping. "Because I loved her! I never stopped loving her. Not from the first moment. I always tried to cloak myself in scholastic detachment. She was nothing but my morgue mate, right? No, I never stopped caring for her, even if she did just use me."

"And that's why you killed Alcibé? Why not kill me?"

He sneered something so awful that I saw his green teeth and blackening gums. "You should have to live with it the way I have. Losing someone you care about. It's a lot worse than oblivion, isn't it?"

"Well, don't worry," I said. "I'll put you out of your misery, you son of a bitch."

My boomstick had the last word.

NOVEMBER 29, 1934

The rain was gushing down in great sodden sheets, like Jesus was pissing in my eye. Nothing for it.

I checked my boomstick. Six shots left. Every round in a chamber. One extra in my coat pocket. I should've taken a box, maybe two, but I didn't. No place to get extra rounds from anymore. And no one was selling to me.

He killed my best friend, even if he was nothing but a lousy head-in-a-box. That wouldn't stand. There had to be rules, had to be reckonings. That was dealt with, but there was still a reckoning for my own death.

My shoes sank into the river that the road had become and came out heavy. *Slop, splash, squish.* All the way up the road, out of the Welcome Mat, and toward that damnable mansion.

I probably stood outside those gates for far too long, staring at the huge "ER" carved into them. I smoked two of Ivan's Players and drank half my flask of liquid courage. What was there to do? The rain sluiced off the brim of my hat. I had my own personal waterfall in front of my face.

To start a thing is to be half-finished, they say. It took me an age to finally get my feet moving and fling myself over the fence. There was a light on. I recognized the window as Rothering's bedroom. There was the same trellis I'd almost climbed down the first time I was there. His silhouette appeared at the window. I ducked behind one of the hedges and waited. He'd step away eventually, I figured.

No such luck. The window opened. "Who is there?" the fat man called out in precise, measured English.

I said nothing. Staying down, I made my way toward the entrance to the hedge maze. I didn't much want to go back inside it, but it made more sense than going around where there was no cover.

He started laughing. "It doesn't matter to me, thief! I'm warm and dry. And armed. You're out there, and soon my dogs will be as well."

Damn it. I hate dogs. I got down on all fours and started pounding through the mud. It was faster than duckwalking, I figured. Son of a bitch. Wasn't he rich enough to afford goons with guns? I would've preferred getting perforated a million times to getting dismembered and having to crawl around picking my limbs out of the bushes.

Then the barking started. So it wasn't an empty threat. Son of a bitch. I might've been able to find my way through the hedge maze, maybe even during the dark, but at night with those slavering canids chasing me? Less so.

Well, okay, I guess it was down to a question of logistics. How many dogs were there, and how many bullets did I have? After killing all of the dogs—if that was a reasonable outcome—would I have enough lead valentines left over to threaten/kill/maim Rothering if necessary? Hard to say.

I tried to make my way on my hands and knees for a minute. Too hard. Not painful, I was way past the point of feeling pain, just hard to navigate. I took a deep breath. Didn't need it, of course.

I stood and started running. A shot rang out through the night. I looked up just long enough to see Rothering at his window with a rifle before I ducked back down. I was back to crawling or crab-walking through that muck in a labyrinth of shrubbery I'd barely made my way through in the daylight.

"Son of a bitch," I whispered.

Probably a skosh too loudly. The growling started over my left shoulder, real low, like when a Model T is just about to need an oil change but not quite yet. Then there was a *sploosh, sploosh, sploosh* through the mud, and it was a little closer. I had to turn slow, real slow. Get a bead on the beasty before it pounced.

It was standing there, sure enough, and growling so hard its teeth were quivering. I felt like I was in a dream, moving through molasses, only the molasses was the air. Finally, agonizingly, I had the pistol pointed at the bastard.

Blam.

Of course, that brought all of his compatriots running.

"Shit," I said, only with a little more emphasis than I can express with a pen and paper. I decided there was nothing for it. I jumped up. Rothering started shooting at me again, but I figured as long as he didn't get a lucky headshot, I'd be okay. Assuming he didn't know I was a deadhead—assuming he even knew what a deadhead was—he wouldn't be trying to aim for my head. If he hit me in the melon by accident, well, I guess that was about the same odds as one of his slavering devil wolves catching me and ripping me to pieces.

Much as I loved Alcibé, I didn't want to end up like him. Dead or dismembered. I went for it. I darted through that damn maze, bullets flying around my head, and the damned dogs were hot on my trail. I came around a corner, and of course, somehow, one of those Dobermans (Dobermen?) had come around the other side and gotten the drop on me.

He charged and latched onto my ankle. There was no pain, of course; thank God for that. It gave me a minute to think about my options. I swiveled my head back real quick. The other dogs were charging. There really was only one option. I decided to let him have my ankle.

I slammed the butt of my pistol down on my ankle, and for once was glad of the decrepitude of my corpse. The leg bone, starved of calcium from a month of bourbon in place of milk, snapped with one blow. A stomach-churning crunch filled the air, like the sound of a Sicilian grandmother breaking a great big bundle of dry spaghetti noodles in half to fit them in the pot. A seam appeared in the flesh between my heel and knee, and the two parts of my leg sloughed apart like lovers breaking a long and wet Roman kiss.

It was a little slower going without my foot, but I found I could really punch my severed femur into the mud to keep going. I think the foot even slowed the dogs down a bit. They must've stopped to play with it.

A bullet shattered my shoulder. Of course. Not my gun hand, thank God or whatever merciful void is out there. I looked up. I could practically see the whites of Rothering's eyes. There was no avoiding it if he decided to put one between my eyes. It was either that or the heart, but nobody shot for the heart anymore. We weren't in the Old West.

He stared at me hard. The recognition in his face was obvious. I stepped forward with my good leg, then made to punch down hard with the cracked bit of my other leg. Foot or no, there was nothing to catch me. I plunged, face forward, into the swimming pool.

Lying there, I guess I felt a surge of nostalgia, or maybe that's not the right word. Dayzha voo again, maybe. I stared at the bottom of the pool again, and the rain seemed to be not even splashing at all. Wet was wet and wet became wet, and the only difference between that moment and the identical moment all but a month ago was the statue at the bottom of the pool.

The three perfect beauties were wrapped in green. Some kind of slimy residue had enveloped them. I noticed the distinct sting of chlorine was absent from the pool, too. No one had been cleaning it. The angels were monsters, drowning in algae and indifference.

With a few pulls of my arms, I dragged myself to the side and pulled my head out of the water. A living man would've gulped the air, desperate to breathe. It was a habit I had somehow managed to break. I inclined my head up toward the man in his window.

He put his fingers to his lips. What the hell did that mean?

Suddenly a shrill whistle pierced the whole mansion grounds. The dogs stopped barking. Must've been their inviolable signal. The little Pavlovian bastards came crawling out of the hedge maze, tails between their legs. The Doberman that had bit my foot off still carried it in his maw.

"I say," Rothering called out, "is that you, William?"

I looked up at him. What else could I say? "Of course it's me. Now could I come up?"

He was busy cleaning his rifle. "Of course. You'd better grab your foot first."

I stared at the Doberman with no small amount of trepidation.

"Don't worry," Rothering said, "he shan't bite. Again, in any case."

I couldn't feel the warmth, of course, but sitting by Rothering's fireplace almost made me feel like an ordinary human being. I saw the rain-and-pool-soaked fabric slowly drying. It was like magic. A moment later, he appeared with a tray of glasses and a decanter. Fancy, crystal stuff.

"I imagine you'll be wanting some of this," he said.

I nodded. He poured some as I adjusted my foot. I had strapped it back on with a little twine. Intellectually, I knew we could reattach our limbs, the same as Ivan Skaron had done, but feeling it was a whole different thing. I can't really explain our state of affairs. How do I explain what it's like to have a severed foot, and then just not have one anymore?

"What's it like?" he asked, nodding in the general direction of the foot. He handed me a glass. Brandy. Good stuff, too.

I had been thinking about the same question, of course, but how to describe it? "It's like an anthill, I imagine."

He leaned forward. I got my first real look at him in person. First since my unbirth, anyway. He was very continental and more than a little fat. He had jowls like a bulldog and a nose like a pig. But he was friendly enough and wore a pince-nez. What a weird contraption that is. I kept meaning to ask him about it but never did.

"How so?" he asked.

"Well, the ants pour out of an anthill. You put a kid's sucker on the anthill, and they swarm around the sucker. They just incorporate their surroundings into their community. It's like that, kind of."

He nodded. He didn't understand. I didn't really, either. But it made sense in my head, even if I couldn't express it.

"I'm sorry about shooting you," he said. "Of course, I wouldn't have if I had known it was you. Would you like me to take a look at it?"

I pulled my trench coat a little tighter around me. "Not my first."

He stood and put his brandy on an end table. "No, I suppose not." His voice was wistful.

He stared at his bookcase for a while. German books, mostly. Couldn't make heads or tails of them, for the most part. There were a few familiar titles, though, for some reason. *De Vermis Mysteriis. Naturom Demonto.*

He slowly worried his bulk back into his chair. "Tell me what you remember, William."

"Nothing," I admitted.

"Nothing?" He leaned back. "That can't be right. All of your kind get their memory back. If not very quickly, then at least, eventually."

"What can I say?" I said, sloshing the brandy around a little. "I must be special. Or else a freak."

"How did you know your name when I called out to you?" he said.

"I didn't."

He leaned back in his chair and laughed long and hard. I could see the rolls of fat on his neck vibrating. It was disgusting. "Oh, that is simply perfect. Well, tell me what you've pieced together. Maybe I can fill in some of the gaps."

"Well, I knew Billy, though I don't go by it. So I figured William. Last name?"

"Hinzman," he supplied.

I nodded. Suddenly my eyes went wide as saucers. "William Hinzman. WH."

I whipped out the billfold and threw it down. He smiled a little bit and nodded, ever so gently. Smug bastard made me want to slug him one.

"So you knew me?" I asked.

He nodded like a teacher. Pedagogically. Man, where did I get that word? "Very well."

"What was I? Who was I? An English professor? A door-to-door Bible salesman? I get these flashes. Words I shouldn't know. Memories. They're slow to come back, but they're there, occasionally."

"Is that what you think?" he asked. "That you were an intellectual?"

"I don't know," I said. "You tell me."

He nodded. "Well, I hate to disappoint you, but most of what you know, I taught you. When we met in Chicago, you were not much more than a farmboy with a German name. A street rat, and not above doing anything for a few nickels."

"But I suppose you pulled me out of the gutter, made a gentleman out of me?"

Rothering laughed until I thought the walls would collapse. "Oh, William, the day someone makes a gentleman out of you is the day Roosevelt walks. It's true, though, for what it's worth, that I pulled you off the street. I never met a more eager receptacle for knowledge. I would expound upon the Führer's philosophy to you for hours, and you would always ask for more. You lack a certain zeal and passion that I prefer in my disciples, but no one can fault you your voracious curiosity. I recall when we moved here, you spent quite a bit of time at that rundown old library, and you did so love to use what you would colloquially call 'fifty-cent words.' But that was kind of a show."

"I lived in the Mat," I said.

"You did," he said. "Working for me. I am many things, William, but I never made much of a hustler. Nor am I an American. In most of the towns in Europe, all I have to do is put on the airs of nobility and say the word 'Jew,' and I have an army of townspeople at my beck and call. Here, though, all the underclasses hate one another and they hate the wealthy even more. You had a real knack for drumming up support."

"You mean I was a Nazi stooge. A rat."

The fat man shrugged. It was a big to-do, like trying to get Muhammad to the mountain. “A pragmatist. A fan of the finer things in life.”

“You mean I did it all for money.”

“And loyalty, perhaps. We became very close, you and I.”

“Yeah, I’m sure we had tons in common. Doesn’t sound like you were using me at all.”

“Oh, on the contrary, William. I always felt that I was the luckier one in our friendship. I always admired your street sense, amongst other things. You were wise enough not to approach that gang of yours on your own.”

“The Infected,” I said.

“Correct,” he said. “You called in some Italian Fascists to sway their loyalties. You really paved the way for us there in the Welcome Mat. I give you great credit for that. I gave you money, but you were the one who rented that loft in the docks out of which we have been running our operations.”

7. Who or what was I before I died? Some slimeball Nazi sympathizer. Probably better off dead.

“I woke up dead in your pool, which says to me it was some of your goons who did it. If not you personally.”

“Go on,” he said.

“So I came here to kill you, Rothering,” I said, “for what you done to me.”

He took one of those long, deep breaths like when you need a whole lot of air to start a speech. "Well, William, I can certainly understand that conclusion. Of course, I don't think you would say it if you remembered anything of your past life." He stood and walked over to the mantel. He picked up a picture that had been sitting there the whole time, although I hadn't noticed it. He handed it to me.

It was him. And me. Alive me. Arm in arm. Back from a fishing trip. I had a giant bass, he had nothing, but we were both laughing.

11. Who is "WH" and why was his billfold in Rothering's house? Me. William Hinzman. A.K.A. Billy the Kid. And apparently, me and Rothering were thick as thieves back in real life.

"Doesn't mean anything," I said. "People kill people they know all the time. Maybe more often than people they don't."

"Perhaps," he said, settling back into his chair, "but not in this instance."

He must've known I had a gun. Either he didn't care or didn't believe I would shoot him. Probably thought I was so desperate for the truth, I would hear him out to the end, no matter what line of bull he fed me. Maybe he had telephoned some mooks and was waiting patiently for them to come. Hell, maybe he was a trusting soul and just hoped he could convince me not to shoot.

"Let me ask you something," he said, bringing his fingers, shaped like a house, to his lips. "If you killed me, would you dump me in your own swimming pool? Or would you dispose of the body?"

I didn't say anything. I didn't have to.

“Better yet,” he said, “maybe you would try to frame an old enemy. Or at least make life inconvenient for him by having to clean up your mess.”

“Your corpse mess?” I asked.

“Your corpse mess, yes,” he said. “You were killed as a warning to me. Because I cared about you deeply. Because you were important to me. And you were dumped in my pool to add insult to injury. I was to be forced to fish you out and bury you properly without drawing any unwanted attention. What your killer didn’t count on, I imagine, was that you would come back and start looking for him.”

“Who?” I said.

“You know him, I believe. One of your community. That’s what you deadheads call one another, isn’t it? Our community? Our kind? Like the Sicilian mob.”

I had my gun out. I scratched under my chin with it. Probably a little chunk of skin came off. Scratching yourself while dead just isn’t the same as it is alive.

“Lazar,” I said. “That’s why he tries to keep me under his thumb. He’s slipping something into the booze to keep me from remembering. Only he’s not one of ours. He’s a play-actor.”

In that instant, it all clicked in my head. Who had been with me from the start? Who had played my friend? Who disappeared into the Altstadt and abandoned the community? I stared into the glass of brandy.

“I do recommend you get your alcohol elsewhere from now on,” Rothering said. “But I believe the bootlegger was only drugging you for money. He doesn't know any more about you than you know about yourself. He has his own patron, after all."

The Old Man. Why would that little fetus want me dead? It didn't make any sense. I lived above his bar. Why keep me alive, walking, rotting evidence of his misdeeds? "What are you running out of the docks?"

"That whole operation," Rothering said, "is nothing more than a little… let's call it a diplomatic mission. I am, as you've no doubt guessed, absolutely loyal to the regime in Berlin. We've brought in a few loyal Germans, but that will only get us so far. We need Americans sympathetic to the cause. Americans such as yourself, William."

"I ain't no turncoat," I said.

"Oh, on the contrary, America and Germany could be great allies. The greatest. Loyalty to a transnational ideal is, in itself, a higher form of loyalty than one could feel toward a single country."

"Oh, spare me, professor," I said.

It was funny, but I could see the hurt in his face. We really had been friends once, or so it seemed. "It's… a shame to see you this way. I'm glad, don't get me wrong, to see you alive. In a sense. But to have forgotten all that makes you you? That is a sad ending."

"Maybe I'm better this way," I said.

"I doubt it," he said.

"What's in the crates?" I asked.

"Machines, mostly," he said. "Higher tech than what you have here. Our scientists are quite advanced."

"What kind of machines?"

"Mostly clockwork nightingales," he said. "Toys and charms for the rich and famous. To keep the Altstadt indebted to us. We run them through your bootlegger. Those are the proper channels, after a fashion. Other pieces are more useful. Technological marvels."

"What are those for?"

"Bribes, mostly. Some of the crates are simply money. But some of the machines are just there to establish better working relationships within the city."

I stood up. "I ought to kill you."

"Have I failed to answer some of your questions?" he asked, as though he was a child working for a disappointed teacher.

"No," I said, "but I know you're involved in all this stuff."

"Well, I'm sorry to hear that, William. I hope you do get your memory back soon so we can go back to the way things were. If you must kill me, do please do it now. Otherwise, I recommend you search closer to home for your killer."

I pointed my boomstick at him. I put my finger on the trigger and tried to make myself squeeze it. I really did. There was no point. I left.

"Lazar?"

I waited a heartbeat or maybe longer, who can tell? It wasn't like I had a watch. Or a heart. The answer finally came.

"You got the wrong number, fella."

I held the phone and stuck my beak out into the rain. The sky was the color of granite, and the little glass box wasn't keeping out any of the oppression. I came back in and put the phone to my sodden head. "No, this is the right number. I'm looking for Lazar. He might not go by that name all the time."

A heartbeat? Two? Ten?

"Nah, he doesn't live here anymore."

I wiped a juicy sluice of rain out from under my nose. It made me feel as if I still had boogers. The truth was, I was more worried about taking my whole honker off with that maneuver. I did it anyway.

"It's Jones," I said. "I know it's you, Lazar. You can play games and you can play games, but don't ever fucking play games with me."

All the falseness and joy disappeared from the voice on the other end. It became flat, affectless, like a doughboy with a thousand-yard stare. "I told you not to come to me again. I told you that."

"Yeah, well, I figured I'd wait two days."

"You must not have a friend in the world," he said after a moment.

"Yeah, well, that's true. I've got you, and I've got memories. That's about it."

"I ain't your friend," he stated, flatter than flat.

"You ever seen a braineater before?" I asked. "I mean a real one. Not just one of us. One of us after a stint at AA."

I thought I heard him licking his lips, but between the rain and the connection, I'm sure it was just my imagination.

"There's nothing scarier than a sober deadhead," he said. "Nothing."

"I've got a quandary," I said.

"Not my problem."

"It is your problem," I said. "And the problem of every living breather in the city."

"All right, I'm listening."

I took a deep breath. There was no reason, physiologically speaking, for me to do that. It seemed like a thing that couldn't be avoided doing.

"It was the Old Man," I said.

I let that sit for a minute. He'd be thinking. Maybe he didn't know what I meant. Probably did. Probably was mulling over all the possibilities.

"Don't do it," he said finally. "Leave sleeping dogs lie."

"Not a big fan of dogs," I said, glancing down at the severed foot reattached to my shin with twine.

"You nailed it on the head," he said. "What you want, it's not just your problem; it's everybody's problem. Living, dead, and all points in between. You kill the Old Man, and you kill the flow of liquor into the Welcome Mat."

"Maybe it's better that it's not in his greasy little flippers," I said.

"Are you listening? Are you listening, Jones?" That finally got a rise out of him. "You'll lose what little is left of your soul. Everyone you know will turn into a flesh-munching ghoul. The cops won't be afraid to come around the Mat then. They'll put you all down. That'll be it for your kind in Ganesh. A bullet in the head and probably no pauper's grave, even. Maybe you'll luck out, and they'll dump you all in the canal and you can be fish food."

"I'm talking about the man who killed me, Lazar," I said. "My whole reason for being."

"No, no! No! You're Braineater Jones, jumbee P.I. You catch bad guys. You do it because the authorities won't help the dead."

"No," I said, "I do it for revenge. Look, you can help me or you can't. You can make the liquor flow again after the Old Man is gone."

"I can't do that, Jones. I'm done with all that. Too dangerous."

"Then let what happens next be on your head," I said. I let the phone fall out of my hand. I didn't bother to hang it up. I heard his last shouted words as the receiver swung back and forth on its cord.

"You can't avenge yourself, Jones! You don't even know who you are!"

I grabbed the phone again. "Correction: I don't know who I was. I know who I am." Then I hung up.

NOVEMBER 30, 1934

Hallowed Grounds. The big mook was standing behind the bar, and wouldn't you know it, he was rubbing a big white hole in the wood with his bar cloth.

I hated to do it. Hated with every fiber of my being to spill a drop of that precious ambrosia. I did it, though. I smashed the neck of my bottle of Crow, leaving a nice jagged hole.

You might think I screwed up, that I should've taken off the bottom flat part to use it as a weapon. You'd be wrong.

I set the bottle down on the bar, neck up, of course. "Hell of a thing, life."

"I wouldn't know," the mook growled.

I nodded. "Me neither. Thanks to you."

He had one of those looks of surprise on his face, like when you walk in on your old lady screwing the milkman behind your back. It didn't matter because by the time that stupid look crossed his face, I already had his big bald head in both my hands.

I slammed him down as hard as I could. I didn't need to be no karate master to do that. The jagged bottleneck pierced the soft spot between his neck and his chin and plunged all the way through. Destroy the brain. That's the only way to destroy one of our kind.

Never did get his name. Didn't care.

I hated to waste a perfectly good bottle of Crow like that. A few patrons were looking at me. They didn't say nothing, but I could tell they were judging me. I leapt over the counter. "For the record, he's the one who killed me."

2. *Who was the hatchet man?* Physically? The big gorilla. Who masterminded the hit? The motherfucking Old Man.

There was some nodding and generally agreeable noises. In our community, that kind of vendetta was acceptable. Maybe it's acceptable in any community.

I dropped down into the creepy labyrinth below. I didn't really know my way, but I was starting to get a feel for the sleuthing business. The old gorilla who murdered me had left a heavy tread, and he took the same route to the Old Man's little machine every time. I just followed the footfalls.

I had hoped to catch a break, but of course, no such luck. The Old Man was awake, and he was plugged into his Swedish murder machine. He claimed it had no legs, so I tried to stay out of its reach, but then, who knew how far that was.

"Braineater Jones," the Old Man growled.

"Actually, it's William Hinzman."

I could almost detect a spark of recognition and horror on that freak's deformed little features. Like there was almost some give-a-shit that soaked through.

"Recognize the name?"

"I do," he said through that funny aquatic microphone, "but I suppose you still don't have your memories back." He snapped his claws at me.

As I'd hoped, I was just out of reach. I took another step back though, to be sure. "Nope, I've had to piece it all together."

"And you listened to that Nazi scum over an American. And one of your own kind. You should be ashamed."

"Well, you haven't said anything yet. Go ahead. Convince me."

"You think I had you killed?" the fetus said. "You know you were in bed with the Nazis. They took care of you the same way they took care of your boy Röhm. Just a little housecleaning. I took you in and gave you a home and a place to feel like you had a family. Remember that."

He had one of those little pull-wires, like on a bus to signal your stop or in a bank when it's getting robbed. He kept pulling it, real subtle-like, as if I wouldn't notice or something.

"If you're waiting for that big mook upstairs, he ain't coming," I said. "Permanently. What was his name, anyway?"

"Who gives a shit?" the little jar-feeder hissed.

Snap. Snap. The mechanical claws were like dogs on a leash. Reminded me of Rothering's damned Dobermans or something equally ugly and vicious.

"You should know you were a casualty of a war for the future of our people," he said.

"I don't know what that means, and being as I was the casualty, I don't much care."

"It means," he said, "that even I am going to turn into a braineater soon. Just being exposed to the air for a few minutes a day will make my brain turn to goo. And I've got the most longevity of any deadhead unalive. These machines can change that."

I looked around. Sure, we might all live underground like Morlocks, but what kind of a life was that? "Yeah, you've said that before. I don't see it."

"Our kind is nothing but a functioning brain in a meat bag," the Old Man said. I guess he had practiced that speech a million times. "We take out the brain immediately and seal it up in alcohol. Never expose it to the air. Just dump it in one of these metal bodies, and we could live forever, as far as I know."

I scratched the back of my neck. I didn't really want to get drawn into all his mad scientist mumbo-jumbo, but what could I do? A villain's got to have his say. I suppose a hero can indulge him in that. "You may not have noticed this, pops, but you've got two stubby little fins in there to work the machine. A brain has nothing. A brain in a jar rotting? That's not life, that's not even unlife. That sounds like Hell."

He slammed his metal fist against the wall. Those damn hydraulics must've been powerful, because I'll tell you what, the whole chamber shook. The wooden beams holding the place up started to splinter.

"We'll get there! We'll get to where we can plug a brain in. I've been buying stuff from the Nazis. Electrodes and dials, all the stuff I need to make it work. They're decades ahead of us in this kind of research."

"Is that why I had to get shot?" I asked. "Some kind of trade-off went bad?"

The Old Man started laughing. Creepiest thing I've not only ever seen, but that I could ever imagine. Some little festering unborn jumbee baby breaking out into a cackle. Still makes me shiver just thinking about it.

"You don't get it, do you?" he said. "You're a nelly. You and Rothering were lovers. That's why you were there. That's why your money clip was in his bedroom. That never occurred to you to wonder about?"

"I-I-I figured someone put it there." I knew I was stuttering, but I couldn't help it.

"Nah"—he adjusted the machine to make it look like a creepy crouching frog—"you were nothing more than collateral damage. From what the bartender told me, you were taking a dip in the pool, after a long night, maybe. Your lover wasn't there anymore. It was supposed to be Rothering. Always supposed to be him. But after we killed you, he backed off. Hurts to lose a lover, doesn't it?"

I didn't know whether to be angry or confused or satisfied or what. I mean, that was it, basically. The whole shebang. Who killed me, why, who I was before I died. I was William Hinzman, some Nazi's girl on the side. I got killed for being in the wrong place at the wrong time. Left dead as a message.

Only, it didn't feel right. It didn't feel like me. Didn't I love Kumaree Tong? Of course, see how well that worked out. I couldn't deny there was something about Lazar that stimulated me, and it wasn't his sparkling dinner conversation. The little shit had no reason to lie to me about Rothering. Was there such a thing as being half a nelly?

That would have to wait. I shook my head like a kid trying to get the pieces of a jigsaw puzzle to stick together. "So, the big mook turns me over, sees I don't fit the description you gave. He searches the house, finds my billfold, takes my ID, and starts to panic. But because he's a moron, he leaves the billfold where it was, all covered with his bloody fingerprints. So you call in a cleanup crew. Only you don't do it personally, cause that's not how you operate."

"You got it," the Old Man said. "You really ought to be a detective."

11. Who is "WH" and why was his billfold in Rothering's house? Addendum: he was my lover.

1. Why did they bump me off? It was a mistake. But once it was done, they left it done, as a message for Rothering.

I heard loud clanging behind me. I wheeled around. There were about six machines, like miniature versions of the Old Man's giant prototype, only they had legs. They were stomping toward me like the Tin Woodman of Oz.

"What's this shit?" I muttered.

"Oh, I lied before about not having the technology yet," the Old Man said. "I just wanted to keep you talking until a few of my friends came."

"They're just brains in jars," I said.

"Yup," the Old Man said, "and they know who keeps them in axle grease. Kill him, you suckers!"

The Tin Men leered toward me.

"I'm one of you! Your kind!" I yelled.

There might've been some base instinct to preserve the community left in them. They might've just been startled to hear me yell. Either way, they stopped for a second. That second was all the time I needed.

I turned and fired my pistol at the Old Man's little jar. I wasn't exactly a deadeye dick, but I could hit a baby's corpse in a jar from a few yards away. Don't know why, exactly, he never thought to preserve that most important part. But I knew being stuck between a rock and a hard place, I preferred the hard place—assuming the Old Man was the rock. Was that the worst mixed metaphor of all time? Was it even a metaphor?

Unfortunately, I only punctured the Old Man's fragile little body. As the liquor drained out of his jar, he began to choke like a fish out of water. Without hitting the head, he still wasn't dead. I probably made my first mistake right then. Well, not my first mistake ever. Not even my first mistake of the night. But the first mistake in a little while.

I charged the little bastard's jar. That got me in range of his grabbie-wabbies. So naturally, he struggled with the controls and grabbed me. Thank God not around my collapsed neck that time. Just by the shirttail.

"You son of a fuck!" the Old Man spat at me. His face looked bad. He was turning from a kidney bean into a navy bean, like all the blood was draining out of his body. He was quivering in the inch of goo he was trying to stand in.

"What's the matter, preemie?" I said. "You don't look so good. I haven't seen you out of the drink in a long time. Just the once, actually."

He quivered with anger. "I'll kill you!"

It was funny hearing his voice without the microphone. Like a tiny, whiny little girl. Extra tiny, really. Hard to describe. And hearing him so angry, it made me laugh.

"I bet you're reaching the end of your natural life. You can't even stay out of the drink at all anymore. You're a cock's hair from being a braineater, aren't you?"

"I-I..." He was hardly even making words anymore.

But the automatons were walking forward tentatively. They seemed not to know what to do. The other arm of the Old Man's machine—the one that wasn't already holding me—clamped down on my head.

I figured that was the end. But it was a good end. At least I double dog died knowing everything I had set out to figure out. I felt the clamps start to squeeze. In a minute, my eyes would pop out of my head, then a minute after that, my brain would squish out through my ears. Good-bye, cruel world.

Then it stopped. I heard an unearthly moan. I looked over and saw the little fetus, eyes glazed over, little flipper-arms stuck out like a Frankenstein. He groaned again. Goofy looking.

I turned. "Well, are you idiots going to help me, or what?"

The Tin Men all looked around at one another. Yeah, there were definitely meat brains in those metal bodies. It took me some time to wiggle my way out of the Old Man's clamp. No thanks to those traitor deadheads.

"Oh, I get it," I said, once I was free. "You can't talk. You're just brains."

One of them nodded. I walked toward him. He backed away. I showed him my hands to prove I was friendly, whatever that meant. I lifted up the metal mask covering his brain jar.

It was pretty gruesome, even by my standards. There was no way to get them to talk. That required jaw and muscle and tongue and everything. But the Old Man—or some of his underlings—had left the eyes and the ears connected to the brain. They were latched onto the jar in a mockery of a face. They could still see and hear; they just couldn't communicate.

I took a look at his metal hand. Probably couldn't even write. They weren't the most dexterous hands in the world. Who would agree to something like that? Someone desperate, I suppose. As desperate as the Old Man to stay alive.

I held up my gun. "I've only got five shots left. I can take care of each of you, if you want. It just means two of you have to line up. If you want to stay like this, that's fine. But the Old Man won't be here to take care of you—or to give you orders—anymore."

I guess they had all decided ahead of time. Three wanted to be offed, two wanted to live. The last sat in the corner morosely, unwilling to participate. I counted that as wanting to live. Or whatever you call our mockery of life. Then again, who am I, of all people, to judge?

It was lucky, I guess, that only three of them wanted to go. I didn't really want to line them up. That was grisly. I shot two of them about as ricky-tick as these things go. I couldn't let myself get involved. Sure, they were my kind, technically, but they were way past being my kind. For once, I guess I understood how breathers felt about us.

The last one looked at me for a long time. Maybe he didn't look at me for a long time; maybe I looked at him. I suppose he didn't have much choice in the matter. They say the eyes are the window to the soul. I don't know if that's true when the eyes are severed, but still, there you go. He looked terrified and sad. Or I imagined that he did. If it was even a he.

"Don't worry," I said. "Death gives us meaning."

He gave me a quizzical look. Or again, I imagined it. The eyes hung there, attached to that jar.

"Anyway, sometimes it's better to go out at the top of your game. Or just after."

I plugged him between the eyes. Shattered the jar, smashed the brain. The other three followed me, a bit defeated. They were the type in life—or unlife—I imagined were too miserable to live but too cowardly to off themselves. I had to pity the poor bastards. Who knew what the Old Man had done to them? Or offered them?

Speaking of the Old Man, I made the mistake of sticking my hand into his jar. Little braineating bastard bit off my finger. His jaws must have been as strong as mine. That sparked something deep in my neocortex.

I had a recollection, rather clearly, of my youth. My youth as a person, not as a monster, or whatever we are. I worked at a park once. I was quite young, probably no older than eight or ten. Not entirely sure why I was working at the park, but the memory was quite clear.

It was an outdoor park, but to avoid the hazards of bringing folks around wild animals, they had collected a number of beasties in a cabin. One of them was a snapping turtle. Real neat little bastard. It could've bitten the buffalo out of a nickel with those hydraulic-powered little jaws.

We used to have to rake the walkways and paint the benches. Boring stuff, you know. Getting to watch an animal consume another animal was like a little miniature boxing match, Christmas day, and *Amos 'n' Andy* all rolled into one.

Once, it was my turn to feed the turtle. I ducked the worm way too far into his tank. He took a huge chunk out of my finger. Leastways, it seemed like a huge chunk at the time. In retrospect, it was really just a bit of the fingertip. But I had blood spurting everywhere, and it was the only thing that happened all summer cooler than getting to feed the turtle.

It was the first thing I remembered clearly in a month. Maybe it all would come back to me. Maybe it never would.

I grabbed the Old Man around the torso and carefully fished my finger out of his jaws. He was chewing on it like a chew toy, in the fashion I had seen true braineaters gobbling flesh in real life, only miniaturized. Then I squished his little head in. That was the end of that.

I turned to the remaining Tin Woodmen. "Well, the Old Man believed you were the future of our kind. I don't know about all that, but you'll be welcome in our community, for what it's worth. Follow me."

I led them out of the caverns and up into Hallowed Grounds. The place was empty except for the big gorilla's corpse splayed out on the bar top. They must've heard what sounded like a demolition derby twenty thousand leagues under the earth and scampered.

The gorilla slouched back onto the ground beneath the bar, making me think I had missed the mark in putting him down. But no, Lazar was standing there, no makeup on, wiping his hands with a dishrag. He must've pulled the beastie down below just then.

"Didn't think you'd make it," Lazar said. "Thought I might've come down here for nothing."

"I'd hate to think I'd leave you in the lurch like that," I muttered.

Our eyes locked for a moment. I remembered thinking he was a real Valentino the first night I saw him. Without the makeup making him look like one of our kind, he was even gorgeouser. For the first time, I could see myself going with a man the same as with a woman. I still wasn't sure about bringing a breather home to mama, though.

"Who are your friends?" he asked.

I looked at the mute metal men testing the walls and the floor. One grabbed a bottle and smashed it immediately with his viselike hands. They probably had no idea what their own strength was. I held up a finger, and he nodded, knowing that he wasn't going to do it again.

"Haven't really named them yet," I said. "That one's…Clanky."

"Is the Old Man...?"

I sat down at the bar, grabbed a bottle of Crow, and poured myself a tipple. "Double dog dead."

"Good work, I guess."

I sized him up out of the corner of my eye. "I thought you weren't coming back."

He shrugged.

"I guess I have a soft spot for you... I mean, your kind... after all."

"You going to take over?"

He shrugged. "You think they'd accept a breather like me into the fold?"

"Personally"—I stopped only to take a long, effervescent sip of bourbon—"I think we'd take anybody into the fold, assuming he keeps us wet. Case in point being that squirmy little shit I just squished."

Lazar nodded. "Well, it's his own fault, I guess. He tried to squeeze me out entirely. Had to have the whole bootlegging operation or nothing. If he had left me a little slice of the pie—"

"You would have stopped me," I said.

"I might have warned him," he agreed. "But hey, I've got no other way to make a living. I guess I'll have to take over the whole shebang."

"Good for you," I said. "Now if you'll excuse me, I've got to go hang up my hat."

I started to walk toward the stairs.

"Uh, Jones?"

I turned back. "What?"

"Aren't you forgetting something?"

I looked around. A dozen sets of mechanical eyes stared at me unblinking. The three I had saved were just the beginning. More and more were filling the bar, crawling out of the subterranean dungeon the Old Man had incarcerated them in.

"Come on, kids."

DECEMBER 1, 1934

Two pressed suits stood outside my office when I woke up in my chair. I straightened my tie with one hand, and with the other, I reached for my bean-shooter.

"There's no need for that, mister…" The stuffed suit on the right, the one in the inch-thick spectacles, trailed off, staring at my door.

My glass door sign had been smashed in, probably when I first got on the outs with Lazar. There was still a part of the "B" and most of the "I," but otherwise it was gone. Homer had, at some point, cleaned up the shattered glass—though not all of it, as a foot full of glass powder attested—but had never gotten around to replacing it. On the plus side, I didn't have to worry about taking my keys anywhere. On the con side, security was kind of a joke, like my unlife.

"Just call me…" I trailed off too. What was there to say?

"Call you what? Lightning?" That was the one on the left. He snorted like a pig. What an asshole.

"You coppers?" I asked. That'd be a first. Coppers in the Mat. Yah fookin' roight, as our Mick friends would say, if they ever sobered up long enough to say anything. In fact, Righty Tighty said as much.

"Yeah, well," I said, rubbing my ass as I eased myself out of my chair, "not a lot of… citizens dress the way you two do."

"Deadheads, you mean," Lefty said.

"Jumbee, in the parlance of the Caribbean," Righty added.

"Ghouls. The walking dead." That was the one on the left again.

"Christ, minus all the religious bullshit," Righty Tighty tried.

"Oy," Lefty said, crossing himself.

Catholic, must have been. Orthodox maybe. Was it a funny crossing? Who knows. Sure as shit, I'd never seen a deadhead cross hisself, and everything before that is still such a haze. Words, places, gestures… no, I guess it was normal. Probably just a papist.

"I don't care what you call me," I said. "Just don't call me late for dinner."

"Clever." That was Righty.

"Yeah, that's been fresh since before the war." Lefty that time.

"A real joker, this one. You should go on Broadway or something." R.

"I don't think they have jokesters on Broadway. Cohan productions and what-have-yous, maybe, but not so much the stand-up comedians." L.

"Pretty lame for a comedian. You might even say we were being facetious before." R again.

"Now that I think about it, you never ate dinner in your whole unlife, did you, you stinky Red deadhead bastard?" L here.

"Language." R, getting feisty—or more likely faux-feisty—said.

"Hey!" That was me that time. "Fellas! Time out." I made the "time out" signal with my mitts. I heard some cogs clanking and clunking from the broom closet. Not a good sign. They were watching. I glanced around the room real quick. The ones I couldn't stuff in the closet were scattered around the room in various states of repose. Hey, even a robot's got to sleep when he's got a deadhead brain.

So far, the guys who claimed they weren't coppers either hadn't noticed the stack of tin detritus spread around my office, or they didn't care. Likely they both noticed and cared but chose not to say anything just to mess with what's left of my brain.

"Who is you two?" I said. "That is to say, who are yinz?"

"Friends, you could say," the one on the right said.

"Call me Mr. Land," Righty said. "This is Mr. Day."

"Hi," the newly christened Day said.

"That's what you're going with?" I asked.

"Gotta go with something," Land said. "We're looking for a fellow named Herr Hinzman. Know where we can find him?"

"Never heard of the guy," I said flatly.

Day knelt down and picked up a couple glass shards from what had formerly been my door. He held three larger chunks together. "Hey, he's right, Land." Day held the glass toward his partner. "Take a look here."

Land leaned forward.

"Says here his name is Jones," Day said.

"Can't be the same guy we're looking for, then."

"Let's get out of here, partner." Land jerked his thumb over his shoulder.

The two starched suits stepped out of my office. I waited for the sarcastic flourish—from that crackerjack Land, no doubt—that would accompany their return. After about thirty seconds, I stood and stuck my head around the door.

They grabbed me and threw me to the floor. Day put his knee into my spine and his arm around my neck. I heard a loud clanking and clattering, but I still had one hand free to wave the Tin Men into silence. I guess they understood enough to back down.

Land crouched down in front of me, dangling a sharpened screwdriver back and forth between his thumb and forefinger. "All right, here's the scoop, Hinzman. You're going to tell us everything."

"About what?"

"About everything."

"You got all day?" I asked.

Land nodded toward his partner. Day let me go and stepped into my office. I popped my head onto my hand and jammed my elbow into the floor as if I was a teenage girl lounging on her bed with her friends.

"Who do you work for?" I asked. "You with the Boston mob or what?"

"You're the detective," Land said. "You figure it out."

That was when Day stepped out of my office, flipping through the pages of this very journal. "Here, listen to this, Land." Day rattled off a few of my questions.

Land eyeballed me up and down. The shiv of a screwdriver was pressed to my earlobe. "You really don't remember anything?"

"I'm starting to," I said. "Now I'm off whatever Lazar was dumping in my booze. It's coming back in dribs and drabs."

Land stood to his full height and gestured for me to join him. "You know there's a war coming, 'Jones.'"

"With who?" I asked. "The Bolsheviks?"

Day stepped forward and slapped me full across the face with my own diary. The nerve of some people. I rubbed my chin and worked my jaw to make sure it was still all in one piece. I heard a whirring behind me in the office. I hoped I didn't look too panicked or tip my hand as I gestured to the damn robots to calm down.

Land spoke again. "Guess again."

"Well, then I guess I can understand why you might be interested in William Hinzman. Last I heard, the guy was dead."

Day was still pawing through my book. He looked at Land and shook his head as if he had been looking for something specific. Land looked me up and down, glanced back into the office, then down at Homer's fence.

"I suppose if he shows back up—"

"You'll be the first to know," I said. "Leave me your calling card, and I'll be in touch."

They exchanged a glance. Land nodded. Day slugged me in the gut as hard as he could. Damn near ruptured my spleen, I noticed later upon taking it out and checking it.

"What was that for?" I grunted.

"We're going to keep a close eye on you, Jones." Land used his sharpened screwdriver to wipe some fuzz from his jacket. "Like we did outside that phonus balonus deadhead's apartment."

"Yeah, that was us," Day said, nodding. "He sang like a bird, all about you."

"If we can't count on you to be a patriot, we're going to step in." Land drove the screwdriver into my drywall, up to the hilt.

I saw no need for that. I had pretty much gotten his point. But a man with a spike has got to use it, or he'll feel as though he didn't need it in the first place. They took a few steps down the stairwell.

"Hey!" I shouted.

They looked back up. It was one of those looks that said, "You don't want me to come back up these steps."

"Forgetting something?" I asked. Who cared? It wasn't as though they could threaten me with any meaningful bodily harm. There wasn't a whole lot left to take away from me. Except the one thing that bastard was holding.

To his credit, Day, or whatever he was really called, tossed my journal a few steps up from where he was standing. I bent down to grab it.

"Give my best to President Roosevelt," I said, and the door slammed almost as soon as I said it.

Got a caller after the feds rolled out. Mighty Dull. Go figure. Guess he's still in the… whatever business he's in. Lazar referred him. Stolen property case. Mighty had lost one of his girls' favorite torsos. My old friend Brigid. She was furious. Maybe I'd get to see her again during the new investigation. That thought brightened up my day.

Even as the dam was breaking and the flood of my memories with Rothering came back, I was still more comfortable with the idea of carousing with a girl than a boy. It seemed as though when I was alive,

I was only half a queenie anyway—if there was such a thing—and mostly I had gone with whoever could give me the most money. Whatever else he may or may not have been to me, Rothering had always had the most money.

"I'm going out," I yelled, hoping to get past the honor guard of robots before it came together. Of course, I had one foot out the door when a crushing metallic vise got hold of the other foot. Being as it was the one the dog had already severed and was held on with sewing thread, I considered just leaving my left leg behind. I didn't envy making the walk down to the cathouse as a unipod though.

"What do you want?" I said, rolling my eyes back into my rotting skull.

The 'bot on the floor had what passed for a plaintive look on his non-face. I call him Shiny. He must have dived, literally dived, to catch me before I was out the door. His catch had given the other clankers time to swarm out and surround me in a veritable orchard of tin and nickel.

"Look, guys," I said, "I need to work. A, I don't get much work. B, what gigs actually do come my way, I've got to finish; otherwise, I get a bad rep. And a private dick with a bad rep is the same thing as unemployed. And C, I need moolah to keep liquor on the table. You get me?"

Faceless and expressionless as they were, I couldn't help but feel as if I was looking at a pack of cartoon puppy dogs, all begging for my affection. I reached down and, as affectionately as possible, disentangled myself from the junior shortstop who had caught me out at home.

"You cats oughta start a baseball club," I chuckled.

That got them exchanging faceless glances. Confused? Intrigued? Who knows.

"Look," I said, getting a little more down to brass tacks, "I promised I would help integrate you back into our society, and I will. I promise. But Rome wasn't built in an hour, and getting jumbees and robots to get along will take a little time. But I can't do anything if we can't wet our whistles. So let me get some face time down at the brothel and…"

That didn't come out right.

"That didn't come out right. That's not what I meant. It's a case, okay? When I come back tonight, I'll teach you how to play baseball." I looked around the little dump I called my office. And home. Not much sense wrecking what was left. "Only not here."

I was halfway out the wrecked door when a pounding like a baby throwing a tantrum drew my attention. Sure enough, Shiny was kicking and screaming—or whatever passes for screaming in a brain 'bot. I held up my hands. What more was there?

"What?" I said.

One of Shiny's buddies, one I call Clanky, handed him an ashtray off my desk. Painstakingly, Shiny used the ash to scrawl four letters on the floor.

NAME

They didn't know my name? What had the Old Man called me? Or didn't that matter? I opened my mouth to answer and looked at the door. B. I. That was all their evidence of my old life. My first life. My second life, really. What was I now?

Bill. Bill Hinzman. That was my name.

"My given name is Jones," I said, "but they call me Braineater."

I slipped out in the street. Finally.

My little friends need work. I feel like a mother hen trying to herd a pack of jungle cats. Am I mixing my metaphors again? Tough. This is my journal, and I'll mix whatever I damn well please. Ideally an extra dry martini. Gotta pay for it first. That's what the brothel gig is for.

There wasn't much there, but Mighty had a couple of clues and pointed me in the right direction. A hundred clams, plus expenses. Not bad for getting a hooker's heart of gold back, eh?

So I've got a case, I've got a lead, and I've got an apartment full of needy jumbee brains with robot shells.

It's a start.

THE END

BONUS CONTENT:

"THE OLD MAN AND THE SEESAW"

Originally published in 2015 in the At Hell's Gates III *charity anthology, "The Old Man and the Seesaw" is set during the continuity of* Braineater Jones. *It's canonical and theoretically I could have inserted the entirety of this short story into the novel and both would still make sense. However, as it would slow the pacing of the longer work down considerably, I think it's better suited to exist as a standalone. Enjoy!*

NOVEMBER 15, 1934

I'm writing this on a stack of damp cocktail napkins because my regular journal seems to have taken a walk. My legless partner, the severed head, seems to have no trouble getting up and taking walks when it suits him. So, I figure no reason my journal should be any different.

Note to self: paste these napkins in with the rest of your notes. Don't forget.

Anyway, I don't know what's what with my notebook. Normally it's right here in my pocket, but instead, all I've got is a handful of my own peter. At least my boomstick's still here. I can live with my notes being incommunicado for a couple of hours, but I sure as shootin' wouldn't be alive if anyone started shootin' and I couldn't squirt iron back at 'em.

Well, not alive. I'm not alive. Haven't been for…oh, over two weeks now.

Dead.

Undead.

Not dead.

Deadnot?

Dreadnought.

What's a dreadnought?

It's like a sea serpent or something, right? Ah, I can't fuckin' remember.

If I was still alive I'd guess that I'd lost my journal after getting zozzled. I'm already about six—seven sheets to the wind, and it's not even noon. But that's just a normal day for a deadhead. We don't get drunk. We just get pickled.

God, I miss getting drunk. Wait. Do I? I can't remember shit from before I was whacked, but I do feel a definite tickle in my belly and my delicate nether regions when I think about taking a shot.

"Another shot," I just told the bartender.

Eight feet tall if he's an inch. He stares down at me.

"Old Crow?"

"Now what do you fuckin' think?"

He's pouring the delicious brown nectar now. Watching me scribble almost in real time.

Napkin #2.

He may be trying to read what I'm writing. Upside-down. I wouldn't bet on anyone short of Albert Eisenstein bein' able to make heads or tails of my chicken scratch, rightside-up or otherwise. He's squinting real damn hard now. Yeah, you big gorilla, I'm writing about you. Say something if you're going to say it.

"What's eating you, Jones?"

I shrug, such as I can. "That girl today. I mean, nothing. Go away. Go polish the other side of the counter."

The big gorilla shakes his head and takes a step away. With his inseam, it may as well be a mile. He begins wiping at the counter with what I think must be his best friend in the whole world, that raggedy old dishcloth of his'n.

I'm still stewing. That damn girl. Had to put down a girl today. That's what they call it when one of our kind gets dead. I mean, real dead. Double dog dead. Perma-deceased. They call it *putting down*. Like what you would do to a dog.

And I had to do it. She had gone full braineater. That's my name. My nickname, anyway. I have no idea what my real name is. But folks 'round here (grudgingly) call me Braineater. I never saw one until today, though.

At least, I never saw a real one. The breathers, they call us all *braineaters* like the way you'd call a German a *Kraut* even if he never ate a bite of cabbage in his life. We're not all braineaters. Most of us are still smart enough to tip back a little hooch and scrawl our sad little hearts out on wet cocktail napkins.

Napkin #3.

Others of us, of course, are smart enough not to do that, and just stay quiet about it. But, yeah, when you stop drinking for too long, or you miss out on your daily tipple, you start getting all rumbly in the tumbly, and your thinky parts stop operatin'. Then you go on a rampage. Like that kid today.

Pretty girl.

She'd looked like a circus clown with all the blood around her mouth and two fistfuls of squishy brown brains in her hands. They call it *grey matter*, but when it's out and in a little girl's fists, it sure looks brown to me.

I had to drop the hammer on her myself. Nobody else would. And left undealt with, well, let's just say we would've started to have more breathers breathing down our necks than is optimal for a ghetto full of corpses.

"Hey, Jones."

Well, look who it is. My partner, Alcibé, the severed head, has somehow managed to sidle up next to me. Without asking, the gorilla drops a Manhattan in front of him, and a straw (naturally). When drinking or eating, we usually put the head in a pan or on a plate so the comestibles don't just leak out the bottom of his throat, or, anyway, when they do, they're easier to clean up.

"Compliments of the Old Man," the bartender grunted.

"Well, hey, would you look at this?" Alcibé said, clucking his tongue in that damned annoying way he does sometimes. "Tell him I'm much obliged."

If the bartender's grunt was meant to be a response it didn't strike me as much of one.

The Old Man. Now there's a delightful little shit. A real butter and egg man. The main bootlegger what keeps the Welcome Mat wet. And a dry welcome mat would be…well, just full of braineaters like that little girl. So he gets a lot of respect around here. I suppose I should respect him a little more considering I'm sittin' in his gin mill, soaking up his bourbon.

But how much respect can I really have for a buttonhooked fetus?

"Hey, head, let me axe you something," I growl, not familiar enough with my own voice to notice whether something is really off, but still having the odd feeling that it is.

"What's that, Jones?"

"What's that little pint of shit's story, anyway?"

Alcibé cocks his eyebrows. In a full-bodied man, you know, one with shoulders and all, I would take this to be a shrug. As it is, I'm not sure what he's expressing. Confusion, I guess. Or maybe he's just thinking. Yeah, I guess that's it.

"Who? The Old Man?"

I nod, slumping closer to the counter, and trying to fool my eyes into picturing the lowball beneath me as a swimming pool I'm about to dive into.

Alcibé shrugged again, or whatever you call it. "He's just the boss around here, you know?"

Alcibé. Alcibé, Alcibé, Alcibé. When the head wants you to know he knows something, he acts like he don't know nothing. But he knows everything. Unlike me, his summoning sickness is long since gone. Most deadheads have amnesia for a while after turning, but my case is a bit spectacular. Two weeks is way too long to go without an identity—to go with people calling you *Jones* like some anonymous john at a cathouse.

Nah, the head remembers everything, including his life before. And he most certainly knows the score when it comes to all things Mat-related. The Old Man's too big a cheese not to have made an impression on my partner.

"What, do you want me to kiss your ass? I'd have to fly to Honduras to find it. Just tell me what you know without all the pussyfootin'."

"Pussyfooting?" He clucks his tongue at me again. "What does this mean, 'pussyfooting.' Jones, I swear, sometimes it's like you speak some alien language."

"It's just English. Same as Jesus spoke." I guess he was the first of our kind. Deadheads, not Americans.

"You should try a career as a newspaper columnist the way you butcher the language, Jones. 'Pussyfooting,' indeed."

He launched off into a long string of Spanish, but I didn't follow a word. I don't know what I was before, but I sure wasn't a Mariachi. I can't even say *challah* to his liking.

"Har har har. Do you know The Old Man's story or not? I'll bet that's it. I'll bet you just don't know."

It's a dumb ploy. A child's ploy. The sort of playground game that would never work on a grown, albeit decapitated, adult. There is, in fact, no way that he will fall for such a transparent—

"Oh, is that the way it is, eh? All right, Jones. Just so you never doubt your beloved partner…"—I had to snort, and loudly—"…I will tell you the entire score. The score…in its entirety."

If it were possible for a head to look haughty, that's what he did.

"You know the playground? You can see it from our window upstairs."

Ah, yes. Maberry Play Park. Perhaps the saddest patch of dirt and macadam in the whole Welcome Mat. Once upon a time (maybe back when the Mat had still been called Matthew's Parish) the playground had no doubt been state-of-the-art, probably around the time of the Harding administration.

Now it's like looking at a fossil out of time. The monkey bars are rusted right through, such that I suspect if I tried to grab it, it'd crumble to dust in my hand before it held my weight. The slide just has a great big hole in the middle of it. I guess it still works, as long as you don't mind half a ride followed by a fall.

The kids, such kids as there are in the Mat, won't go near it. They prefer to play stickball in the street and…

Damn it. Now I'm thinking about the girl again. "Yeah, I know it."

"Well, you can see the, ah…ah, dammit. How do you say…it's a *subibaja*."

I'd never seen the head at a loss for English before. First time for everything, I suppose. It's not exactly like jungle gyms and swing sets are the kinds of things you learn about in language class. "The what? The merry-go-round?"

The head shook himself as best he could. "No, it doesn't go around. It goes up and down." He stuck out his tongue and mimicked the motion, as though I didn't know what *up and down* meant.

"Like a swing? Or one of those test-your-strength things—with the mallet?"

"It's a playground, not a carnival, Jones. You sit, one child on one end and the other child on the other, and their weight offsets one another…"

I snapped my fingers. "A teeter-totter."

"Teeter-totter? It cannot possibly be called this. A *subibaja*?"

"Oh, a seesaw. Yeah, same thing."

The head rolled his eyes at me. "So this seesaw—this teeter-totter—you know the story that the Old Man rides it sometimes alone at night?"

A grown—well, so to speak—man riding a seesaw at night? That would give me the chills up and down my spine if the nerve endings weren't all dead. I've seen a lot of creepy shit in this line of work—not the least creepy of which being the Old Man himself—but that just sounds downright unwholesome. "No. Why would he do that?"

The head smirked. "Patience, Jones. All in due time. Here is the story of the Old Man.

"We all know this is twenty years ago. Most deadheads live to be five. You take good care of yourself, you drink more than your share every day…maybe you live to be ten. Not the Old Man. This is his third decade on this Earth as one of our kind.

"But twenty years ago, he was an ordinary child in his mother's belly. This was 1914, the year of the war. In Europe. America would not get involved until the near the end."

I belched loudly. It wasn't strictly necessary as an autonomic response, but I could force myself to do it for dramatic flair. "America always comes in near the end. That's because no one can stand up against us for long."

Okay, I'm pretty sure I was American before I died. That seems like something only an American could say with a straight face. The head, though, had an odd look to him now, not disdainful, or even looking down on me, just…ah, shit, I already called it odd. Hate to say it twice. Or three times now. But, yeah, odd.

"Perhaps. Perhaps we'll find out if that's true soon with all that's going on in Europe these days. But I digress.

"The Old Man's mother, well, no one knows her name. For obvious reasons. But I will call her Paquita, because that was my mother's name, and it will be easy for me to remember."

"That's pretty weird. Why don't you just call her Jane?"

"Why don't you go find out this story from someone else, ah?"

"All right, all right. Unspool me your yarn, word-bird."

The head cleared his throat. Well, he made that noise. It's not like his throat was attached to anything that still needed clearing.

"So our story begins with our heroine, Paquita, coming into the family way. She fell in love with a boy, or so she told herself, and against her better judgment, they made the beast with two backs. It was a once-and-done kind of operation, but before the morning sickness even began, he ran off to France to volunteer for the Legion."

A low gasp erupted from a nearby table and a whisper that sounded like the word, *disgraceful.* I turned my neck to see two deadheads were listening, leaning close to us, even, to hear better. I was thinking of walking over there and giving them a little chin music, but one was obviously a dame in a man's suit, so I left it at that.

Huh. Something just occurred to me. The Old Man hates skirts. Chases them out of the bar every chance he gets (hence the cross-dresser.) In fact, the only woman I ever seen in the bar proper was Claudia Winston. Something stinks wrong in my nosehole about that. I'd better make a note to look into—

Oh, but the head's talking again.

"So our dear Paquita finds herself alone and without her virtue. You know, a woman might bounce back from that today, get a job with the phone company or maybe waiting tables, but twenty years ago…"

"It was a different time."

I looked up. The big gorilla was standing there, elbow on the bar, ear on his fist. Listening.

"A very different time. Before the war, you know, men didn't even smoke cigarettes. Ah, you know, speaking of which…"

He just let it trail off there. Gotta admire the head. He sure knows how to play a room. I've been living with him long enough to know better, so I didn't even let my hand fish into my pocket to make sure the half-crumpled pack of Luckies was still there. That would've been a dead giveaway I had some squares left.

The sound of a chair pushing back filled the room, and all eyes turned toward the piano player as he walked up to the bar and tickled a square between Alcibé's ivories. The head waited there patiently as the gorilla waved one of them new-fangled Zippo lighters in the general direction of Alcibé's face, until the cancer stick finally caught. I could tell by the smell it was a Pall Mall.

"Certainly, you know," the head continued, the smoke leaking from his esophagus, ensuring that he didn't have to exhale, "a fallen woman didn't stand much chance back then. If you couldn't find a husband, what would you do except starve?"

"Was she a Papist?" someone in the crowd asked.

"You know, I don't know," Alcibé replied, rolling some of the smoke around in his mouth. "But I am, so how about not another word about it, ah?"

The head was lying, or more likely exaggerating. He may have been a wafer-eater in life, but most of our kind don't have any interest in the Almighty. Something about so many of us getting up and walking makes Jesus pulling the same trick seem like not so much a miracle as a mistake.

More likely the head just said he was a mackerel snapper because he didn't want to deal with any more hecklers.

"So our poor young Paquita did what only the truly desperate ever consider: she found a doctor."

A more general sort of gasp erupted from the assemblage.

"Not in a back alley, but in a basement, not so far from here, if I'm not mistaken. And this doctor, he had a soothing manner and a kind face, but more importantly, he had all the tools of his trade, which at that time meant ether and bonesaws. And he showed her how gently he would do it—using just his hands—and there wouldn't even be a scar. She might even say goodbye to the child who wasn't meant to be.

"But, then of course, once she was ethered, out came the coat hanger, and no doubt the shot of tequila any such man must take to steel himself for such a task. And so he rooted around inside of our dear, sweet Paquita just as a plumber might clean out your sink. And he withdrew, as you might have guessed, the real hero of our story: the Old Man."

A light went out on the stage, but no one moved to replace it. It was as though the patrons were mesmerized by the head's story. His eyes went from side to side, ensuring that there were no distractions in the now deepening darkness.

"Of course he wasn't known as the Old Man then. He was just a baby. You could barely even tell he was a boy, he was so undeveloped. Flippers more than arms, and a head the size of his body…well, you've all met him. He's much now as he was then, the moment of his…well, I suppose *birth* is the wrong word."

"Like Macduff, he was untimely from his mother's womb ripp'd," a voice interjected.

That was Lazar, leaning against the bar, sipping at one of his fruit punch drinks. I hadn't noticed him slip in.

"If you like," the head replied. "The doctor waited for Paquita to come around, and when she did, he told her while she was still groggy that there had been an unforeseen accident, and that was why she would carry a scar for the rest of her life—not that he had lied to her about how simple the procedure was. And as she began to cry at the thought of being disfigured, he assured her that no one could ever know until she had already remarried, and then he brought out the baby, just as he had promised.

"Now, aside from our friend here, I have never seen a dead baby. I assume it's disturbing enough to begin with, and one that you carried in your belly for so-and-so many months, surely that's even more upsetting. But Paquita looked at her child, who never was, with instant loathing. There was no sorrow in her heart or pity, just instant hate.

"This child before her was the reason she would now carry a scar to the end of her days. This child before her had stolen her life, and much of her parents' fortune, for she had taken the money for the operation from them. She could never go back now, not after robbing them. So, just as she robbed her parents, so to had the child before her robbed her—of her whole life. She'd have to start fresh.

"She poured all of her hatred and frustration into this tiny, deformed body before her.

"'Take it away,' she said, 'I hate it.'

"And with that, the Old Man's eyes opened."

Alcibé paused for effect. The whole speakeasy was usually noisy, if not necessarily rowdy. Now, though, you could've heard a pin drop. A pin didn't drop, but a chair did squeak.

"There's no rhyme or reason to who comes back and who doesn't. No way to predict. But I do know that it's a lot more common now than it was back then. Some people say the Old Man was the first of our kind. I'm not so sure."

"I knew a guy who knew a guy who knew a Russian who turned in aught-eight," someone said.

I didn't recognize the speaker.

"Yeah, that's what they say," Alcibé agreed. "But even if the Old Man wasn't the first of our kind, he certainly didn't have the good fortune of turning near the Welcome Mat today. There's many of us here. There's a community of sorts. But the Old Man was on his own. And now, spurned by his mother, he was truly on his own.

"You see, Paquita, our heroine, gasped and ran, shouting about the accursed little demon child. And so she disappears from our narrative. For a time. But the doctor, ah, he was a man of science, and even then scientists were not prone to still believe in fairies and goblins.

"The doctor believed he had found a sideshow freak, a baby who had somehow survived the aborting process, but would die shortly thereafter. A medical curiosity, nothing more. The child could blink and waggle its flippers…" Alcibé gave an approximation, at least as close of an approximation as he could, lacking any limbs. "But that was about it.

"So the doctor, being a man of science, did what any man of science would do. Instead of disposing of the baby with whatever unsavory method he had established for such matters, he suspended the child in a jar of formaldehyde, to dissect later. Jones, can you get this, please?"

I was startled to hear my assumed name and wondered what the hell the head was talking about, but a quick glance reminded me that he had been smoking this whole time, and the ember was nearly down to his lips. He could've swallowed it like anyone else, but I suppose he was enjoying being the big man on campus and knew I wouldn't refuse him in front of so many others.

I reached out and snatched the cherry from between his lips. Before I was shot I imagine I would've been reluctant to grab a naked red ember, not to mention to stick my fingers between someone else's lips, but death has a way of not making you worry about penny-ante concerns like that anymore. I barely even felt it as I crushed the cherry between my thumb and middle finger, leaving black, concave imprints on both.

"The doctor went about his work and even forgot about the baby for a few days. But when he remembered, he came with a scalpel to begin the dissection. But as we all know by now, the baby wasn't dead—he was unliving—and the doctor was shocked to see the baby's eyes following the scalpel. After all, a regular child suspended in formaldehyde shouldn't have survived a few minutes, let alone a few days.

"But the doctor was a man of science, and though unethical in some respects, was not completely unprincipled. So he resolved to wait until the child was dead before attempting to open him up again. He theorized that perhaps he had snatched the child out of its mother's womb while it was still capable of breathing water, and so the baby was breathing the formaldehyde solution. But deprived of food and water it couldn't last more than a few more days.

"We all know how that turned out. The alcohol in the jar was all the deadhead baby needed to survive. And so every few days the doctor would come to check on it, and every few days it would stare back at him, occasionally wagging its little fin. And so, finally convinced that this was more a medical miracle than a mistake, he brought the jar out of his closet, and set it on a shelf in his operating theater, to keep an eye on it.

"While the doctor was keeping an eye on the baby, the baby was keeping an eye on the doctor right back. It listened as he spoke to patients, and it watched as he performed his operations. Little by little, the unborn child grew to understand English, and to have a sense of how the doctor was doing things." Alcibé paused and licked his chops. "I'm feeling awfully dusty with all this talking."

Without a word, the big gorilla stole away Alcibé's drained Manhattan, and replaced it with a glass of tequila. A lowball, not a shotglass, I noted. The royal treatment for sure.

"Ah, that's better," the head said, after slurping his drink through the straw with gusto. "And then the darkest time of all came for our kind: Prohibition."

A few of the men in the crowd put their hats over their hearts.

"The doctor quickly realized that he could make more money with his prescription pad than his scalpel. He made arrangements with bad men and ordered cases and cases of medicinal whiskey, far more than such a small practice could possibly have needed. But the bad men had connections, and the doctor had a license, so the whiskey began to flow.

"And as the money from the bootlegging came in, the doctor found himself taking fewer and fewer real patients. In fact, the only operation really worth his while was the same one that had produced the Old Man, who still sat in a Mason jar on the doctor's wall, observing his every move.

"And of course, when we serve two masters, we must always fail one. The doctor foolishly accepted the money of the mayor's daughter to have a child removed who would have been…let us say, a political liability. At least, the daughter thought so. She, like so many others, stole the money from her parents, and gave the doctor a false name.

"Though the procedure was a success, the mayor nonetheless found out what the doctor had done, and swore to ruin him. After all, he wasn't going to punish his own daughter. No, he focused his anger on the doctor. He had his medical license revoked. The medicinal whiskey stopped flowing in, and really that should have been the end of the story. The bad men who the doctor owed debts should have settled his account.

"But the doctor was a man of science. And though he was no expert, he knew the basics of how to brew alcohol. So he set up a still and began to brew bathtub gin and vodka from potato peels, and bourbon from corncobs and discarded perfume. It was perhaps a madness that had taken him, but he was determined to appease his partners.

"And as he did, he began to talk to the baby. Perhaps, as I said, his desperation had driven him to madness. Or perhaps he was simply going senile. But he began to explain things to the baby.

"'I got these blackberries from the bush outside the fire station, my son.'

"Or, 'I found some orange peels in the dumpster out by the Altstadt, my son.'

"And as he went on he showed the baby how the still worked and told him where to find the ingredients to turn garbage into pure profit. And so it happened that he managed to appease the bad men who had been his partners. So what happened next was perhaps unexpected."

He paused, perhaps for dramatic effect, perhaps for no reason at all. You could've cut the tension in the air with a butter knife.

"So what was it?" Lazar asked.

"A deadhead. One of our kind. Some of you will no doubt remember those days. Those dark, desperate, early days. The Welcome Mat had not yet become a haven for us. Scrounging in gutters. Desperate for just a lick of rubbing alcohol. And so many of us turning into braineaters. Jones put down a young girl this morning."

I took a sip of my Old Crow. Somehow, lost in Alcibé's tall tale, I had managed to forget about that. Now it all came rushing back, clawing at the backs of my eyeballs.

"In the early days of Prohibition, you might have had to put down ten friends a day, Jones. Not one stranger in two weeks."

There were some grumbles of assent from the crowd. A few were old-timers. I had never thought of the Mat as a particularly welcoming place to live, but it seemed better than having nowhere to go when you thought about it.

"One of our kind broke into the doctor's basement practice, having heard the rumor that he had quite the distillery. And he did. Half a dozen stills. Tubs and tubs of liquor. Empty perfume bottles and pickle jars—anything else you could fill with booze coming in by the truckload.

"There was a struggle, but I've heard that the doctor died of a heart attack. Because I can't imagine that one of our kind, even in a deranged state, would have killed someone who was producing so much precious, precious liquor."

Perhaps involuntarily, the head licked his lips.

"But whether it was intentional or not, the doctor was dead. And the deadhead leaned over and stuck his head in a bathtub full of gin, so delighted was he. And he drank and drank, and when he pulled his head back out, his brain finally functioning on all cylinders again, he began to weep.

"Not tears, of course, because we cannot cry, like a bad actress in a silent movie he bemoaned his foolishness in killing the doctor.

"'Oh, why, oh, why did I kill him! He could have done so much for us.' And so on.

"It was then that the bottled baby asserted himself. He reached up, and as he had seen the doctor do many times before, began to unscrew the lid of his jar, albeit from the inside. It was a difficult task, and it caught the attention of the deadhead, who rose and went to watch. And as he reached the jar on the shelf, the top popped off. And the baby raised his bulbous head out of the formaldehyde for the first time.

"'What are you?' the deadhead asked.

"The baby opened and closed its lips, testing its vocal cords in the air, and for the first time, he spoke.

"'I don't know what I am.'

"'Well, how long have you been there?'

"'Since 1914.'

"The deadhead whistled in appreciation, and said, 'Wow, you're old, little man.'

"And the Old Man nodded. He had already lived longer than most of our kind ever do, especially in those days, when alcohol was so hard to come by.

"The Old Man explained that he knew how to work the stills and could turn most anything into booze. He also knew the doctor's old contacts, who he saw regularly, and everything else. The doctor had sometimes called him his son, and if that was true, then the Old Man had inherited an empire from his father.

"So together the Old Man, and the deadhead who had broken in, set everything else in motion. They continued to provide to the bad men who had been the doctor's partners, but they also began to funnel alcohol into the Welcome Mat. In fact, our kind turned out to be the Old Man's most reliable customers, so much so that he relocated here, to Hallowed Grounds.

"And one might stop here and say that you know the rest of the story, and this is our little happily ever after."

Alcibé gestured expansively with his eyes at the speakeasy, such as he could.

"But there is yet one loose thread in our little passion play. You see, the Old Man had never forgotten about his mother, who I have been calling Paquita. And as he became a wealthy and prosperous bootlegger, he began to send out feelers, asking if anyone could find her. Of course, she was living under an assumed name, so it was no easy task.

"Then a few years ago, there was a break in the case, as Jones and I would say. The Old Man had been about to carve out the eyes of a breather who had crossed him, a small-time city official. But it turned out the alderman, or whatever he was, knew where Paquita had gone, and had been keeping it secret to use as an escape hatch just in case this very situation arose.

"Instead of saving him, though, the Old Man took his eyes and his tongue and…well, another part I should probably not mention in mixed company. But Paquita had been found.

"She had finally married and even had children after him, which you know is rare enough in such cases. Her new family was struggling, though. The Old Man was delighted by this news, because, being wealthy and important, if nothing else, he could move his mother and half-siblings into a nice new house, and they would never have to worry about working again.

"It's very difficult, you can imagine, to dress nicely when you are but a baby in a jar. But the Old Man brought in a doll maker to tailor him a suit and it's said even a wig. He dressed himself up as nicely as he could, which is to say he wanted to look as ordinary as he could, but with the panache and wealth to show that he was an important man. He wore a gold pocket watch and carried a cigarette holder. All the finer things.

"So decked out as he was, he decided that she would surely accept his charity. But there was still the matter of making a good first impression. To bring his mother back into his life, he decided he would appeal to her maternal instincts.

"He had never had a childhood. And she had raised others, but not him. Surely upon seeing him she would feel a rush of love. And if that did not overcome her repulsion, well, then the promise of a better life surely would.

"The deadhead who had helped him build his business took the Old Man down to the Maberry Playground, just a few blocks from here. And he set him on the low side of the…seesaw, is it called?"

I nodded.

"And the Old Man waited there, outside of his jar for the longest time he had ever spent in his life, constantly checking his fancy gold pocket watch, and brushing imaginary lint from his bespoke suit. Finally, after he had sat there for hours, and the sun had even set, a car pulled up. His partner and two other thugs had to pull a woman from the trunk. She was tied up, and if she hadn't been gagged, would have been screaming. This was his mother, Paquita.

"He was surprised she had been unwilling to come, but supposed the men had done right to bring her anyway. He gestured for them to bring her closer, and when she looked down and saw the Old Man sitting on the seesaw, she went wild and nearly broke the grip of three grown men—even bound though she was. But they got control of her and forced her to stand and face the Old Man, who was scowling by this time, confused about what had taken so long and why she still seemed so upset.

"'Mama,' he said, 'Don't you recognize me? I'm your son. You had me in nineteen hundred and fourteen.'

"Paquita stopped struggling at least long enough to stare down at the Old Man. So she did remember, after all.

"'Don't scream,' he said. 'Don't be upset. I'm here to take care of you. I'm a very wealthy man now. Wealthy and important and…respected. I know about my stepfather and my half-brother and -sisters. I can take care of all of you. None of you will ever have to work another day in your lives. What do you think about that?'

"The thugs removed the gag, but Paquita, though she didn't scream, said nothing.

"'Mama,' the Old Man said, 'I'm so pleased to see you. I've dreamt of this day. Nothing but for over ten years. And now you're here and I'm here. And I thought we could ride the seesaw together. We never got to when I was younger and…'

"He just gestured at the other end of the seesaw.

"'What do you think? Won't you come…play with me, Mama? Play with your son for just a little while?'"

A cloud of smoke passed by Alcibé's face, shrouding his features as though in a fog.

"What did she say?" Lazar asked, suddenly taking a step back as he realized he had leaned practically into kissing range of the head.

"Well, she didn't say yes. She told him he was a demon, a spawn of the devil, a ghost sent to haunt her for her past mistakes. I think he may even have tried to force her to ride the seesaw with him, but she was just struggling too hard. Finally, he told his men to get rid of her."

"Get rid of her like *get rid of her*, or get rid of her like, *get rid of her*?" asked one of the wags in the audience.

Alcibé didn't respond, though I was wondering the same thing.

"Well, you all know what happens now when a woman comes into his bar. Undisguised, anyway."

A few chuckles murmured about.

"But, you know, we are none of us so very far away from that playground. And I've heard it said that sometimes on a clear night, though the children never go down there to play, you can occasionally see a tiny figure, sitting, lonely, on the seesaw, as if waiting for someone who will never come."

We all sat, transfixed, in the dark, silent. I went to open my lips to speak, but they were so dry that they were practically glued together. I darted my tongue out to separate them from one another, but before I could utter a word, a thunderous booming cut through the air.

Had I still a beating heart, no doubt it would have frozen right then. Everyone in the room jumped, as though we were all jacks-in-the-box (jack-in-the-boxes? jacks-in-the-boxes?) with a single handle. Even the head jumped, such as he could with his stump of a neck instead of ankles, and sent himself tumbling off the bar.

The loud noise repeated. Again. And again. Our eyes all grew wider and wider. It was strange to watch a room full of deadheads become scared. So much of what you're used to in fear is human response—sweating, fainting, gasping—our bodies were cooler, but the reaction was still there.

"Oh, shit," the bartender realized. "I know what that is." He bent over and opened the trap door in the floor. He climbed down and emerged a moment later carrying a mason jar full of clear solution. Peaking his head out of the lid of the jar was the man of the hour, the buttonhooked fetus himself.

"—don't understand what's taking you so long. I've got to knock eight times before you come and get me?"

"Yes, boss. Sorry, boss."

"Put on your driving gloves. We've got business to attend to."

"Right away, boss."

The gorilla placed the Old Man's jar on the counter.

The Old Man immediately sniffed out the weird vibration in the air. "What's going on? Why are you all so quiet?" He looked from side to side, his bizarrely bulbous little head moving more like a sloth's than a chicken's. "Did somebody sneak a twist in here? No twists in my bar. You can get your booze and get out."

"Nah, no dames in here tonight, Old Man," I said.

My mistake. As part of the crowd I could blend in in my dumbfounded silence. Having spoken up, I had now made myself a spokesman for the crowd instead.

"What are you up to, Jones? What are you doing with all those napkins?"

Napkin #...Uh, I lost count.

"Napkins? Oh, you know…doodling. I'm working on a cartoon, you know, like the Katzenjammer Kids, or Pogo."

The Old Man nodded. "Working on the funny papers, huh? The hell you are. You got any money, Jones?"

I sighed. "You know I'm beat."

"Get out! All of you! Buy something or get out!"

I bent over and stuck my hand in Alcibé's topknot. "Well, joke's on you. We was just leavin' anyway."

"Hold on!" One of the Old Man's tiny, flipper-like digits shot up in the air.

I froze mid-frame, like a movie stuck on the reel.

"Alcibé. Come here."

Not sure what to do, I lifted the head, and put it next to the Old Man's jar, without taking my hand out of his greasy hair.

"I wanted to thank you for what you done for me."

"Of course, boss," the head replied.

"What the hell did you do for him?"

"Stop ruining this for me, Jones!"

No. Seriously. What the hell could a disembodied head even do that would be considered helpful?

I started to move toward the door, but as I did, I gave the *come hither* signal to the big gorilla of a bartender. He slunk up to me.

"What?"

"I don't know how true that story was or if it was true at all—" I said.

"It's true," the head interrupted.

"—but if it's true, that would mean you'd've been there. In fact, the deadhead who scared the bootlegging doctor to death…was that you?"

"Get out of here, Jones," the bartender said, tossing his dishtowel over his shoulder, and turning his back on me.

I climbed up the two flights of steps to our office having to listen to the head gibber on and on about how he had wrapped the crowd right around his finger, what a great story it all was, and everything else that he was so proud of. I tossed him in the closet to settle down, and then flopped into my chair.

A phalanx of cockroaches seemed to be working in concert to carry away the bottle of Old Crow that sat by the head of my mattress. Like a damsel in distress, the bottle was calling for help, so I rose and snatched it up, scattering the roaches, and leaving them to curse my name, if they knew it.

I went to the window and reached up to close the blinds. It was a clear night. The moon was full. The play park wasn't so far off that I couldn't see the depressing old jungle gym and everything else bathed in the moonlight. There could even have been a tiny figure sitting on the seesaw. Or it could've just been a trick of the light. I don't put much stock in shaggy dog stories.

THE END

AUTHOR'S NOTE

Thank you for reading *Braineater Jones.* Whether you liked it or not I hope you'll take a moment to leave a review on Amazon or your favorite book review site. Reviews are vitally important to me as an author both to help me market my book and to improve my writing in the future. Thank you.

GLOSSARY

alderman: A beer gut.

bean-shooter: A gun. *See also* **piece**.

beat it: To leave, usually an exhortation. *See also* **blow**, **bum's rush**, **vamoose**.

bindle: A rag tied around a stick. A hobo uses it to carry his possessions.

blat: A newspaper or a section or page of a newspaper.

blow: To leave. *See also* beat it, vamoose, bum's rush

Bohunk: A derogatory term for Eastern Europeans.

bootleg: To illegally make or move alcohol, especially during Prohibition.

brain drain: The tendency of zombies to lose their memories after being brought across for a length of time that varies by individual.

braineater: A derogatory term for all zombies, but used more specifically in the zombie community to mean a zombie sobering up or nearing the five-year mark where their minds collapse and they become mindless creatures. *Compare* **bub.**

breather: A non-zombie, a living human being.

bring across: The process by which a zombie comes back from the dead. *See also* **turn.**

bub: Thinking zombies, of the type most of the characters are, prior to brain collapse brought on by insufficient alcohol use or the passage of time. *Compare* **braineater.**

bump off: To kill.

bum's rush: To get asked to leave, typically in a rude or brusque fashion. *See also* **beat it**, **blow**, **vamoose.**

burn powder: To discharge a firearm, thus burning gunpowder.

cabbage: Money.

chizz: To chisel or swindle.

clam: A dollar. *See also* **smacker.**

clip-joint: A bar charging exorbitant prices, essentially a legal speakeasy in the post-Prohibition era.

curtains: A nasty fate, especially death, as in "It's curtains for me."

dago: A derogatory term for an Italian. See also: **garlic eater**, **ginzo**, **wop**.

dame: A woman. *See also* **skirt**, **twist**.

deadhead: Most common term for a zombie, as "zombie" was not in common usage until the 1960s, sometimes considered derogatory and less commonly used in the zombie community. *Compare* **our kind**, **unliving.**

dick: A detective, especially a P.I., but also sometimes a police detective. *See also* **flatfoot, gumshoe, private dick.**

dickbeater: Somewhat vulgar term for a hand, as in that with which one masturbates.

double dog dead: Term used mostly by Braineater Jones to refer to a zombie's destruction. *Compare* **put down.**

drugstore cowboy: A pretty boy, especially one who hangs around soda shops trying to pick up girls.

egg: A guy, especially a wealthy or well-off guy.

eye-tie: Italian, especially the language.

fence: A pawnshop or the pawnbroker, especially one that deals in stolen goods.

fer Chrissakes: "For Christ's sake," a moderate profanity.

fin: Five dollars, especially a five-dollar bill.

five and dime: A store that sells cheap goods, often with a lunch counter, sort of a precursor to modern department stores.

flatfoot: A detective or policeman. *See also* **dick, gumshoe, private dick.**

flophouse: A dingy, run-down hotel or boarding house.

gams: Legs, typically a woman's. *See also* **getaway sticks.**

garlic eater: Mildly derogatory term for an Italian. *See also* **dago**, **ginzo**, **wop**.

getaway sticks: Legs, typically a woman's. *See also* **gams**.

ginchy: Cool, groovy, sexy.

ginzo: Derogatory term for an Italian. *See also* **dago**, **garlic eater**, **wop**.

gorilla: A thug, especially a big guy. *See also* **mook**.

gumshoe: A detective, especially but not always a P.I. *See also* **dick**, **flatfoot**, **private dick**.

harp: A derogatory term for an Irish person. *See also* Mick.

hatchet man: A hit man or hired killer.

heater: A gun. *See also* **piece**.

hiney: A butt.

hot: Stolen.

jake: Cool, okay, as in "Everything's jake."

jakes: A lavatory, especially an outhouse.

jalopy: A junky old car.

jaw: As a verb, to talk, as in to move one's jaws up and down.

Jeeves: A fictional character known as the perfect valet; one who buttles well.

lid: A hat.

Mick: A derogatory term for an Irish person.

mickey: A drink that's been spiked or drugged, especially with knockout drops. An old-fashioned term for a roofie.

mook: A goon or dummy. *See also* **gorilla**.

mootah: Marijuana. *See also* **tea**.

morgue mates: Zombies killed or resurrected at the same time, sometimes considered to have fraternal or sexual relationships.

mungo: A dumpster diver or ragman.

nelly: A derogatory term for a homosexual. *See also* **queenie**.

nerts to that: To heck with that, kind of a corrupted form of "nuts to that."

nickelodeon: An old-timey device that showed movies for a nickel.

our kind, **our community**, and variations: Euphemisms used within the zombie community akin to "cosa nostra" in the mafia. Compare: **deadhead**, **unliving**.

phonus balonus: Dog Latin form of "phony baloney," that is, fake.

piece: A gun. *See also* **bean-shooter**.

plug: To shoot, as with a gun.

private dick: A P.I. *See also* **dick**, **flatfoot**, **gumshoe**.

prosty: A prostitute.

put down: More common parlance for destroying a zombie. *Compare* **double dog dead**.

put on the Ritz: To do something in a high-society style, for instance, to go out on the town well dressed.

queenie: A derogatory term for a homosexual, usually used in address, as in "Hey, queenie." *See also* **nelly**.

schnoz: A nose.

scratcher: A forger or faker; in this case, a fake doctor.

skirt: A woman. *See also*: **dame, twist**.

slug: As a verb, to punch; as a noun, a drink or a shot. *See also* **zozzle**. *Compare* **telephone slug**.

smacker or **smackeroo**: A dollar. *See also* **clam**.

speako: A speakeasy, that is, a place where alcohol is sold illegally, especially during Prohibition.

spook: a derogatory term for a black person.

squirt metal: To fire bullets out of a gun.

stewbum: An alcoholic vagrant, especially one whose homelessness is caused by or exacerbated by alcoholism.

stretch: A tall person, or, used ironically, a short person, usually used as a form of address, for example, "Hey, stretch!"

swacked: Drunk.

tea: Marijuana. *See also* **mootah**.

telephone slug or just **slug**: A metal token for use in old-fashioned pay phones. *Compare* **slug**.

tombstone: A common type of radio, usually wooden and shaped like a tombstone.

trouble boy: A gangster.

turn: The process by which a zombie comes back from the dead. *See also* **bring across**.

twist: Mildly derogatory term for a woman. *See also* **dame, skirt**.

unbirth: The process of being turned, sometimes treated as a holiday in the zombie community, as in "unbirthday."

unliving: Collective term for zombies, relatively rare in the actual zombie community. *See also* **deadhead, our kind**.

vamoose: Leave. *See also* **beat it, blow, bum's rush**.

Victrola: A brand name of phonographs often used interchangeably to mean phonograph.

wearing iron: To be armed.

wop: A derogatory term for an Italian. *See also* **dago, garlic eater, ginzo**.

zozzle: A shot or a drink of alcohol. *See also* **slug**.

ACKNOWLEDGEMENTS

I think it was Paul Simon who once said, "Art always needs somebody else's help to be any good." With that in mind, let's take a moment to thank the BJ boosters, both OG and *nouveau riche*:

I owe a debt of gratitude to the people who helped make the first edition of *Braineater* happen: first and foremost my family. Secondly, Lynn McNamee, the owner of Red Adept Publishing, and Michelle Rever and Cassie Robertson, my editors, as well as Ken Lewin and Mac Carlson, my original beta readers. As always, my thanks go out to Elizabeth Corrigan for introducing me to my first publisher, and John Waxler for introducing me to Elizabeth, as well as for his unflagging support over the years.

For the Author's Preferred Edition, thank you to Chris Enterline for the amazing cover art. I'm also grateful to Shana Festa and Devan Sagliani for originally publishing "The Old Man and the Seesaw." I'd also like to single out my audiobook narrator, Steve Rimpici, for all of his help promoting this work over the years. And an extra special thanks to you, the fans who have supported *Braineater* over the years and made this new edition viable.

Finally, all my love and thanks to my partner and the love of my life, Amy Lower.

ABOUT THE AUTHOR

Stephen Kozeniewski (pronounced "causin' ooze key") lives in Pennsylvania, the birthplace of the modern zombie. During his time as a Field Artillery officer, he served for three years in Oklahoma and one in Iraq, where, due to what he assumes was a clerical error, he was awarded the Bronze Star. He is also a classically trained linguist, which sounds more impressive than saying his bachelor's is in German.

His other novels include:

The Ghoul Archipelago

Billy and the Cloneasaurus

Every Kingdom Divided

Hunter of the Dead

The Hematophages

and

Slashvivor!